Journal of the Fantastic in the Arts
Volume 36 Number 2

I0558045

JFA

Journal of the Fantastic in the Arts
Volume 36/ Number 2

FAVIAN PRESS

Journal of the Fantastic in the Arts
—The Fantastic is the Allegory of the Actual—

Volume 36/ Number 2
Whole Number 123
Supported by the
International Association for the Fantastic in the Arts.

Editors-in-Chief	Tedd Hawks *Submissions*
	Jude Wright *Managing*
	Cat Ashton *Production*
	Miranda Miller *Production Assistant*
	Novella Brooks de Vita *Acquisitions and Reviews*
Senior Submissions and Reviews Editor	Farah Mendlesohn
Peer Review Editor	Ida Yoshinaga
Accessibility & Sensitivity Coordinator	Alexis Brooks de Vita
Regional Submissions, Accessibility, Sensitivity & Reviews Editors	Taryne Taylor Sang-Keun Yoo
Editor-at-Large	Dale Knickerbocker

COVER ART
Before the Dream

Inspired by Laura Palmer from *Twin Peaks*, the cult series created by David Lynch, this photograph explores the fragile boundary between innocence and darkness. Through reflection, it captures the moment before the dream begins - a space where beauty, mystery, and tension coexist in the surreal, cinematic atmosphere that defines Lynch's world.

Ksenia Shupenya is a photographer based in Tallinn, Estonia. Her work moves between observation and imagination, blending street sensibility with cinematic portraiture. Through her images, she explores identity, emotion, and the subtle tension between reality and dream.

Ksenia Shupenya's work can be found on
Instagram (street photography) -
https://www.instagram.com/ksenia.shupenya/
Instagram (portrait photography) -
https://www.instagram.com/black.samovar/

GENERAL INQUIRIES
Inquiries and other editorial correspondence should be directed to journal@fantastic-arts.org.

SUBMISSIONS
Like the International Conference on the Fantastic in the Arts, *JFA* welcomes papers on all aspects of the fantastic in world literatures and media, as well as interdisciplinary approaches including African/Diaspora Studies, anthropology, area studies, critical game studies, disability studies, future studies, gender studies, history, Indigenous studies, music, philosophy, political science, postcolonial studies, psychology, queer studies, religious studies, science and technology studies, and sociology. All papers are made available in English and fully refereed. The journal is indexed in the MLA Bibliography.

Submissions should contain a more in-depth discussion than a conference-length paper and demonstrate a grasp of current scholarship on the subject. The length of articles generally varies from 3,500-9,000 words and ranges from 15-35 pages.

All submissions are peer-reviewed in accordance with our peer review statement, the *Submission, Accessibility and Sensitivity Review Handbook*, and the BIPOC Anti-Racist Statement on Scholarly Reviewing Practices. If submissions are flagged at any point of the review process for the risk of promulgating potentially misrepresentative, stereotypical, ableist, or racist views, contributors will be asked to address these problems before the review process can continue.

Since the refereeing process is anonymous, the author's name should not appear anywhere on the text file itself, including the notes. No title page is needed. However, an abstract of 100-150 words must be inserted at the beginning of each submission, clearly stating what contribution the essay makes to the study of the fantastic.

Please ensure that all citations and the Works Cited entries are in current MLA style. Please do not use automatically generated notes; end notes (only) must be entered manually. A paper that doesn't meet our printing parameters can take many hours to adjust. To avoid needless changes and delays, it is best to use our guidelines from the start. For complete guidelines, please refer to the *Submission, Accessibility and Sensitivity Review Handbook* and the *JFA In-House Style Guide*. In case of conflicting instructions, defer to the *Submission, Accessibility and Sensitivity Review Handbook* and the *JFA In-House Style Guide*. Contributors are responsible for acquiring all permissions to quote and/or use illustrations that accompany their article, and for paying (or arranging to have their institutions pay) all usage fees, including copyright.

Due to the need to provide the journal in multiple formats, the journal does not currently publish images/illustrations in articles.

Scholarly articles should be directed to the *JFA*'s Acquisitions and Reviews team (under Editor-in-Chief Novella Brooks de Vita at jfa.acquisitions@fantastic-arts.org). Please send your anonymized submission to the Submissions Editor, Tedd Hawks, at journal@fantastic-arts.org and include "ATTN: JFA Article Submission" at the start of your subject line. Allow thirty days for confirmation of receipt before querying.

BOOK REVIEWS
JFA also publishes reviews of scholarly works addressing the fantastic, broadly construed. Reviews of fiction are limited to reissues of speculative works with new introductions and scholarly apparatuses, and speculative works with the potential to impact scholarship in the genre. Books and other media received are advertised on the IAFA discussion list (which can be subscribed to through the IAFA homepage at www.iafa.org), and IAFA members are encouraged to suggest titles for review.

To mail book copies for review and for queries or reviews of English-language publications, please contact the *JFA* at journal@fantastic-arts.org.

Abstracts

Steven Brehe
Is *Dracula* Anti-Semitic?

This essay questions the widely accepted critical opinion, now in circulation for thirty years, that Bram Stoker's Gothic novel *Dracula* (1897) is in some sense anti-Semitic, reflecting caricatures and stereotypes of the nineteenth century, and that Dracula's appearance and actions reflect such prejudices. The essay calls attention to Christianized religious and popular ideas about the Devil that are central to Stoker's characterization of Dracula; some of those ideas have also been used for centuries to mischaracterize Jews. These ideas explain the perceived similarities between anti-Semitic stereotypes and Stoker's independently created character, similarities that may have distorted some readers' views regarding the book and its author. This essay argues that Stoker's writings and his personal and professional associations indicate that he was not anti-Semitic and that his book does not reflect or advance anti-Semitic ideas; *Dracula* does, however, reflect lore about the Devil that may not now be widely understood.

Finley Dunn
Mapping Magic in Fantasy Novels: Magic Systems and Thematic Undercurrents in Mark Lawrence's *Book of the Ancestor*

This essay argues that magic has the potential to become a notable site for critical explorations within fantasy studies because of the ways in which magic contributes to the major themes of the text. In particular, when fantasy literature thematizes environmental concerns, it often does so through the dramatization of the environmental implications of magic use. A better understanding of how patterns of magical potential and magic's use by characters may work in fantasy will make analysis of these kinds of environmental messaging clearer. This essay proposes that magic and magic systems in fantasy operate on two core mechanics. The first is the location of the magic source. The second core mechanic is the condition of using the magic source. An aim of this essay is to suggest a heuristic approach to magic through provisional categories: intentional magic, spiritual magic, wild magic, and hybrid systems. Using textual analysis of key examples, the objective is to demonstrate that magic in fantasy can be broadly categorized through its conditions of use, as a way of approaching the questions of what magic is, how it is constructed, and what might it be doing. This essay illustrates patterns of magical potential by examining the ways in which magic constructs and supports thematic and narrative interests in Mark Lawrence's *Book of the Ancestor* series, demonstrating that magic is present not just as an instance of wonder but as a constructed element of a consistent fantasy world. As a constructed element within a consistent framework, magic can be grasped systematically and analytically. This essay recasts magic as a critical tool and presents provisional categories as a potential aid to fantastic analysis.

Amelia Kerns

Economics in Frank Herbert's *Dune* and its Use as a Storytelling Tool

This evaluation analyzes the use of in-world economics in Frank Herbert's *Dune* and its incorporation of financial principles as a storytelling tool. Herbert utilizes commodity and fiat currencies, the Law of Supply and Demand, and operations finance to create an in-depth world, give the plot depth, and enhance character motive and choice. Academic literature on *Dune* has mostly focused on economics' relationship through the purview of politics, environmental concerns, and spice's allegory to oil, drugs, or historical seasonings. In the scope of this greater dialogue, a study of *Dune*'s use of economics and finance and its corresponding impact on writing craft has yet to be fully explored. The economics presented do not exist in a vacuum, but are used in conjunction with political, religious, environmental, and social aspects of the novel. Scarcity plays a large role in both water and spice, which are then used as focal points to drive character action. In particular, the spice mining operations and their profits are of importance to the characters of *Dune* when numerical data is given. This analysis will use real-world financial models to determine these numbers' validity, including a reconstruction of partial financial statements, five-year forecasts, and net present value calculations to bring further insight into character internality and action. This essay argues that *Dune*'s inclusion of specific economics and finance adds a rich layer to the narrative with benefits to writing craft by creating a world steeped in realism and characters with tools to act that subsequently drive the plot. Through its use within the narrative, *Dune* showcases that economics is a well-poised writing tool with broader implications for use in fantastic fiction works.

Jared van Duinen
Historical Fantasy and History

This essay engages with the historical fantasy genre from the perspective of a historian. It begins by looking at how historical fantasy's close engagement with the received historical record has led some scholars to see in the genre a capacity for socio-cultural critique. It then examines the way in which historical fantasy's purposeful ambivalence regarding real and unreal, or fantastical or mythical, aspects of the past serve as a useful reminder of the ambiguity inherent in the historical record and historical sources. Analysis of Mary Gentle's *Ash: A Secret History* explicates this metahistorical aspect. The essay finishes by briefly discussing new developments in the field of history that adumbrate historical research that is more amenable to the fantastical and supernatural. This essay suggests new means by which myth and fantasy—core ingredients of historical fantasy—can be incorporated into the discipline of history, thereby introducing a new perspective of the purview of historical fantasy.

Ruchira Mandal
Faith, Dogma and Vision in *Mr. Pye*: A Quest for Synthesis

Abstracts

Published in 1953, Mervyn Peake's novel, *Mr. Pye*, is about an odd but affable evangelical who arrives at the island of Sark to convert its population to his creed of love. This tale not only reflects the author's ambivalent attitude toward Christianity but, as it becomes a discourse on art and artistic vision, examines the wholeness of human experience, as Peake perceived it. Reading *Pye* in reference to some of Peake's other works, particularly the Titus Groan novels and the novella, *Boy in Darkness*, this essay examines the theme of shared human experience via the fantastic through the lens of a Jungian reading to address the question of why Pye's evangelical mission fails, and what this failure to convert to religiosity says about the character of Pye, about twentieth-century concepts of Christianity in relation to human nature, and about the collective consciousness of mid-twentieth century colonial society. Pye is a microcosmic representation of the collective psychological fragmentation of the colonial world. This paper proposes that the failure of both Pye's mission and Thorpe's artistic visions is a result of this fragmentation; Pye's journey in this novel and beyond is an attempt to find synthesis, first in the society of Sark and then within himself, just as Thorpe repeatedly struggles to find synthesis on canvas.

Misty L. Jameson
"I'm Dead, I'm Dead, It's *Good* to Be Dead!": The Uncanny Epiphanies of Ray Bradbury's "Jack-in-the-Box" and H. P. Lovecraft's "The Outsider"

Ray Bradbury and H. P. Lovecraft are Weird writers whose works are not often studied comparatively. This essay analyzes Bradbury's "Jack-in-the-Box" as a sequel to Lovecraft's "The Outsider" and examines these stories for their similarities in plot, setting, characterization, theme, and use of the uncanny. These works have naïve protagonists whose narratives are structured around journeys and small discoveries that eventually lead to sudden, painful epiphanic moments triggered by a traumatic encounter with the abject. Using the American Gothic tradition in literature as a backdrop to understand parallels between these two

Abstracts

narratives, ultimately, this essay reveals how Lovecraft's focus on cosmic terror in the weird tale is transformed by Bradbury to an emphasis on the uncertainties and fragilities of childhood.

Contents

Contents

REVIEWS

Creative Think Piece: Frank Belknap Long Letters, Written to Michael E. Ambrose, 1976-1979

Katherine Kerestman

DESPITE THE FACT THAT H. P. LOVECRAFT would often refer to himself as the Old Man or Grandpa when writing to his numerous correspondents—and that he tended to address Frank Belknap Long as "Sonny," "grandson" or "Belknapius"—Lovecraft's deep affection for Long was that of a Best Friend Forever (BFF) or big brother. The writer's peculiar choice of endearments may be better understood when one recognizes that, with at least one of his feet firmly planted in the Eighteenth Century, Lovecraft must always have felt older than most of his peers. Long understood this eccentricity. He also understood Lovecraft.

When, subsequent to his marriage to Sonia H. Greene, Lovecraft took up residence in New York City, Lovecraft and Belknap began meeting twice or thrice a week. Regrettably, the Lovecraft marriage was foredoomed: simply put, Lovecraft was unable to endure living in an alien and threatening Gotham (alien and threatening were the same to him), particularly after Sonia, whose millinery earnings supported them both, lost her job. Lovecraft desperately missed home—genteel, old-moneyed

Providence, with all its familiar, endearing quirks and old-fashioned attitudes, as he wrote to his Aunt Lillian D. Clark:

> I am always an outsider—to all scenes and all people—but outsiders have their sentimental preferences in visual environment. I will be dogmatic only to the extent of saying that is *New England I must* [Lovecraft's italics] have—in some form or other. Providence is part of me—I *am* Providence. (Lovecraft, *Lord of a Visible World*, 198)

Lovecraft's desperate need for the old, the stable, and the familiar is most poignantly expressed in his sonnet "Background," from *Fungi from Yuggoth*:

> I never can be tied to raw, new things,
> For I first saw the light in an old town,
> Where from my window huddled roofs sloped down
> To a quaint harbour rich with visionings.
> Streets with carved doorways where the sunset beams
> Flooded old fanlights and small window-panes,
> And Georgian steeples topped with gilded vanes—
> These were the sights that shaped my childhood dreams. (Lovecraft, *Fungi from Yuggoth*, 69)

It was only the society of fellow thinkers and writers, especially Frank Belknap Long, that enabled him, emotionally, to endure living in New York. For a time. These writer friends on whom Lovecraft so desperately depended, the Kalem Club—named thus because the members' names all started with K, L, or M—along with other occasional literary visitors, provided Lovecraft with fertile minds with whom to exchange ideas. While Lovecraft was set in his ways, as are so many writers, new friendships and ongoing discussions with fellow writers in New York helped to gradually moderate his inherited social dogmatism and to prepare his mind to consider new ideas.

Following his flight from the menacing metropolis back to the sanctuary of Providence, on the verge of a breakdown, a newly-stirred Lovecraft began to travel as much as he could; and travel augmented the slow processes of psychological and philosophical maturation that had first been stimulated in New York by an enlarged social circle. Unfortunately, Lovecraft died in his forties, much too soon to fully reap the benefit of an expanding and mature vision.

Even more unfortunately, H. P. Lovecraft has been made the poster-boy of an entire generation born into a culture characterized by outdated ideas, mostly related to race. In *Midnight Rambles: H. P. Lovecraft in Gotham*, for instance, David J. Goodwin is given to frequent expressions of wonder at Lovecraft's having had so many non-Aryan friends, when he so often iterated scathing and xenophobic remarks about this group, that race, or another culture. Of Sonia H. Greene, a Jewish immigrant divorcee—with whom he surprised himself by falling in love—for instance, Lovecraft wrote:

> Mme. G. is certainly a person of the most admirable qualities, whose generous and kindly cast of mind is by no means feigned, & whose intelligence and devotion to art merit the sincerest approbation. The volatility incidental to a Continental and non-Aryan heritage should not blind the analytical observer to the solid work & genuine cultivation which underlie it. (Goodwin, 31)

—one such exception to the rule he was taught about Jewish people. Such a paradox is not in the least mystifying, however, when one considers that a person learns inductively to distrust an inherited axiom by encountering one exception to a rule at a time, repeatedly, as Lovecraft did in New York: many exceptions belie a rule. Even so, an empathetic person may still understand why Howard Lovecraft clung so feverishly to his obsolete ideas of class and race as long as he could, when she considers just how vital it was to his self-esteem to style himself an eighteenth-century Gentleman, albeit an impoverished gentleman, after prosperity had fled his home. Having lost their familial manse after the death of his grandfather, Lovecraft and his mother and aunts were reduced to renting an ever-cheaper series of lodgings, as their inheritance and their social standing diminished. This essay, however, does not concern itself with whether either H. P. Lovecraft or Frank Belknap Long was racist. Lovecraft's aesthetic and philosophical stances are mentioned here merely to provide necessary context for references to them in Belknap's letters.

*

Howard Phillips Lovecraft and Frank Belknap Long had much in common. Each had grown up a cherished son in an indulgent home, and each, deeming himself a writer, had scorned to adopt a remunerative profession; accordingly, in adulthood, each of them would suffer the miseries of penury. And yet, throughout their whole lives, both remained sociable, affable, and generous literary men. Long, for example, in his later life—he lived twice as long as Lovecraft—still liked to entertain guests, albeit with such humble fare as he could provide—"hot dogs on paper plates," according to respected Lovecraftian scholar and personal friend of the departed Long, Peter Cannon, whom I had the honor of meeting at the "Master of *Hounds* and More: Frank Belknap Long" panel at Necronomicon 2024.

There is one conspicuous dissimilarity between the two writers: while Lovecraft elected for near-starvation over surrendering his gentlemanly, or art-for-art's sake, approach to writing, Long was willing to crank out pulp stories and paperback novels as fast as he could type them—he wrote them for the pulp market in order to pay the rent. This is not to say that Long was not a very good writer. His oeuvre includes many superb tales, in his own unique and lovely style—or really styles—but he had not always the leisure to write as he pleased, nor as well as he could, with deadlines looming and creditors dunning him. Long knew the difference between good writing and hack work that paid the bills: when he had the time, he produced work that "remains memorable, distinctive, even visionary" (Joshi, 7). Unfortunately, Long's recognition, in both the long-term and the short run, has been diminished by his proximity to the luminary Lovecraft. As mentioned above, while Lovecraft dwelt in New York, the two met frequently; but, when they were apart, thousands of pages of lengthy letters traveled back and forth between Grandpa and Sonny. Their whole circle of literary friends was extraordinarily epistolary, as well. Lovecraft is thought to have penned tens of thousands of very, very long letters himself.

This essay examines a recently unearthed cache of letters written by Frank Belknap Long to Michael E. Ambrose. At the time of their writing, *Dreamer on the Nightside*, Long's affectionate memoir of his friend Howard, had just been released. *Dreamer on the Nightside* presents Lovecraft's life story as told to Long by Lovecraft. In it, Long asks his reader to consider the milieu in which Lovecraft lived when rendering judgment upon him; to that end, Long explains that, for most of Lovecraft's lifetime, a pulp magazine called *Weird Tales* was the sole venue for fantastic fiction. Mainstream publishers would not touch such stories, regardless of their literary or philosophical merit; therefore, Lovecraft's commercial and literary successes were essentially in the hands of a single man who edited a lone periodical, and who was endeavoring to select the stories he thought would increase his magazine's circulation. When Lovecraft could have remedied his dire financial situation by accepting the offer of a position as Editor of *Weird Tales*, he had to decline the opportunity, for the position would have required him to leave Providence again.

Time-travel to 1975: *Dreamer* has been published, speculative fiction is in the ascendant, Lovecraft's work is all the rage in academia, and Lovecraft has become a "cult figure" (Long, *Dreamer*, 19) in popular culture, too. *Dreamer* numbers the French and American publications which vie in their hyperboles to extoll Lovecraft's oeuvre as equal to or surpassing the literary feats of Edgar Allan Poe; and it makes the point that, while the numerous film adaptations of his stories would have "appalled" Lovecraft for their corruption of his Mythos, the sheer number of films derived from his work can leave no room for doubt about Lovecraft's cultural influence (Long, *Dreamer*, 13). In 1975, major publishers are rereleasing Lovecraft's stories in both hardcover and paperback. The intelligentsia, meanwhile, are devouring Lovecraft's correspondence:

> Most astonishing of all, perhaps, is the interest displayed in Lovecraft by various intellectual groups. HPL of course was the most fascinating of letter writers—his philosophical, aesthetic, and socio-political views are set forth on page after page in which no reading pause becomes possible. As an explorer of the unknown unique in our time, Lovecraft has aroused the admiration of many divergent philosophical circles which among themselves hold totally irreconcilable approaches to reality. (Long, *Dreamer*, 13)

Lovecraft's own mind was a pulsating reactor encompassing colliding thoughts, the implosions enabling his greatness:

HPL has also received many tributes from writers whose views are of an entirely non-surrealistic nature and who believe that only experimental laboratory science is capable of forging a key that can unlock the portals which guard the major mysteries. And this is as it should be. An author who lacks the capacity to set diametrically opposing schools into conflict can never be other than minor, for there are contradictions in every aspect of human experience with which the significant writer must struggle. Unless he has been whirled about by a few maelstroms of the inner mind, his guidance on a mountain-scaling expedition is unlikely to prove of much value, particularly in the realm of the unknown. (Long, *Dreamer*, 14)

At bottom, Lovecraft believed in a mechanistic universe:

HPL was never a narrow, rigidly unyielding positivist, but he did have a great deal of respect for [. ..] "sound science" and refused to abandon what he believed might well be the truth about the universe: that it was wholly mechanistic, some vast unknowable kind of rhythmic pulsation that had always existed and would always exist, and that this rhythm creates for us everything we perceive as reality—the whole of nature, animate and inanimate, on this planet and throughout the universe of stars. (Long, *Dreamer*, 14)

With experience, Lovecraft was required to test his social views against his cosmic position, and he was obliged to amend his initial, and once strongly held, opinions on government:

To Howard, the modern titan was Einstein (not Freud), and the Victorian counterpart, Darwin. He probably would have conceded, if pressed, that Marx was another titan, but he was never a Marxist, even though in his last few years he became converted, first to a New Deal liberalism, and finally to a kind of democratic socialism that was closely in accord with the ideology of Norman Thomas or Carl Sandburg. Since he started off as an ultra-conservative in the socio-political domain, a change of magnitude for him could scarcely have constituted a more dramatic reversal. (Long, *Dreamer*, 70)

A thinking man, Lovecraft processed new ideas as he came upon them, and he was willing to modify his own views in light of new experiences, as reason necessitated, and even at personal cost.

*

Michael E. Ambrose was, at first, to me, the enigmatic recipient of the cache of Belknap letters that I happened upon at a nefarious vendor's booth at Author Con 2024 in Williamsburg.[1] Wasting no time in gaining possession of said correspondence, I brandished my credit card![2] A few months later, at Necronomicon 2024, I strove to elucidate some of the less obvious references in the letters. Eventually, with the aid of several Lovecraftian co-conspirators—Perry Grayson, Jerry Meyer, Tim Lonegan, David E. Schultz, and also Michael Eury and Ed Catto of Two Morrows Press—who, as fate would have it, had published work by M. E. Ambrose, as well as some of my own journalism—I was able to positively I.D. the mysterious Michael E. Ambrose. As I muddled through my initial forays, I was confused by a singular coincidence: investigating *Macabre* magazine, referred to by Long in his letters to Ambrose, I came across Joseph Payne Brennan's weird fiction periodical (1957-1977) named *Macabre*. Was this a red herring? Subsequent sleuthing uncovered the curious fact that Ambrose was the much-loved and recently deceased publisher of two periodicals from Argo Press—one of which bore the name of *Macabre*, the three issues of which fanzine were published in 1972 and 1976, and another titled *Argonaut* (1977-1995). Furthermore, Ambrose had contributed some of his own stories to Joseph Payne Brennan's *Macabre* magazine. There had been two *Macabre* magazines—both of which contained fiction by Michael E Ambrose!

The plot thickens. Among his other achievements, Frank Belknap Long was a prolific staff-writer of comic books for Standard Comics, and he freelanced for other comics publishers, too.[3] In the wake of an outbreak of anti-comic book activity, which culminated in the Comic Code Authority (1954), Long's employment in comic production was adversely affected. Fawcett, the home of Captain Marvel, dropped its comic book division and laid off its staff; subsequently, its properties were purchased by Charlton Comics Group (Cooke, 64). In 2022, Two Morrows Publishing released the *Charlton Companion* by Jon D. Cooke, an homage to the Charlton Comics Group, Argo Press; Michael E. Ambrose, who was a consultant on the project, died just before it was completed (Cooke, 2). Most likely, Long and Ambrose crossed paths in comics land, as well as in fantasy magazines.

The letters, four in number dated from 17 March 1976 to 27 February 1979, are all hand-written; the cache also includes two Doubleday Books announcements of a new Long publication (*The Early Long*), one of which appears to have been enclosed in one of the letters. In these several missives, Long thanks Michael Ambrose for sending him complimentary copies of *Macabre* and *Argonaut*, reminisces about H. P. Lovecraft and describes his marriage to Sonia, discusses the critical reception of *Dreamer on the Nightside*, rails against the publishing rat-race, talks of the surviving members of the Kalem Club and other writers, and confesses to some of his own stressors. These holograph documents provide a fleeting glimpse into the mind of a harried and under-appreciated master of weird literature who endeavored to keep in touch with his friends on an impossible schedule.

Letter 1 (March 17, 1976)

The first letter, dated March 17, 1976, is written on Long's wife's stationery. With a fountain pen, Long adds the surname "Long," after "Lyda Arco" (his wife's maiden name); the rest of the printed inscription is "Artist's Representative" (Letter 1). Long pens, beneath the above line, "Frank Belknap Long, Free-wheeling Scientifantasy Writer" (Letter 1). He opens,

> Dear Mr. Ambrose:
>
> Your letter gave me great pleasure. With the exception of three letters from "inner circle" Lovecraftians, who knew HPL almost as well as I did, none of the 25 or 30 letters I've received since the publication of "The Dreamer" gave me as much pleasure and none gave me more. (Letter 1)

Long is delighted by the reviews of *Dreamer on the Nightside*, most of which are positive, with "one exception, which is distinctly in the brickbat category, but I anticipated considerable flack, since HPL was, and remains, a highly controversial figure" (Letter 1). He maintains that, when looking at Lovecraft's views, one must take into account their relation to the time in which he was living:

> I've always felt that in a biography—even in a somewhat informal memoir—a serious attempt must be made to dwell upon the period as well, since otherwise the subject will seem to exist in a vacuum [. . .] [I] willed myself to become again the boy of 18-to-22 who was once my present self. (Letter 1)

Long bemoans the drudgery of writing for a living: "I have to write at least four paperback novels a year to keep afloat economically" (Letter 1).

Doubleday Book Announcement (2 copies)

An envelope postmarked May 28, 1977 contains one of the Doubleday announcements of the publication of *The Early Long*, priced at "$7.95, 211 pgs" (Doubleday Announcement 1). This circular features blurbs from Robert Bloch, who calls Long "A Master of fantasy and horror" (Doubleday Announcement 1), and Ray Bradbury, who states, "Frank Belknap Long has lived through a major part of s-f history in the United States and helped shape the field when most of us were still in our early teens" (Doubleday Announcement 1). The notice also includes paeans from *Screen Stories*, *Scholastic Magazine*, *Whispers* magazine, *Future Retrospective*, Milton Subotsky (producer of *Tales From the Crypt*), *Xylophile*, Barry Malzberg, Prof. Joseph Neyer, Audrey L. Bilker, and S. Merlin. The return address on the envelope is

> Frank B. Long
> 421 West 21 St.
> New York, NY 10011

It is addressed to

> Mr. M. E. Ambrose
> 2408 Leon, #206-A
> Austin,
> Texas, 78705

Across the top of the second copy of the Doubleday announcement of *The Early Long*, Belknap has written, "'The Early' chalked up a sale at close to 5,000 copies within a week or so of publication and before the appearance of a single review. It seemingly stunned Doubleday as much as it did me!" (Doubleday Announcement 2). The accompanying envelope is postmarked March 21, 1976, and the announcement may have been enclosed with the March, 17, 1976 letter.

Letter 2 (June 15, 1976)

The letter of June 15, 1976 (the envelope is postmarked June 16) is written on onion-skin paper, which, for those readers who may not have lived long enough to know, was used for typing carbon copies or writing airmail letters, when thickness and weight mattered. Long opens by thanking Ambrose for a letter that cheered a "gloomy day" (Letter 2), and he bemoans the fact that he is under the "terrific pressure" of publishers' deadlines, which "can often go a long way toward making gloomy days more frequent" (Letter 2). Thanking Ambrose for his good review of *Dreamer*, Long boasts that all but three of the "20 or 22 reviews have been positive" (Letter 2). What makes Ambrose's review especially good is that it "covered all of the matters that are of importance in giving the reader a well-rounded idea of what he will find between its covers" (Letter 2), an important matter in a review, "apart from praise or blame" (Letter 2).

Long continues that there are "quite a few 1920-1930 period Lovecraftian survivors—three of them Kalem Club members, and others who either attended occasional Kalem gatherings or were in NY during that period" (Letter 2). Members of the Kalem Club included H. P. Lovecraft, Long, Reinhart Kleiner, Herman Charles Koenig, Arthur Leeds, Samuel Loveman, Henry Everett McNeil, James F. Morton, Wilfred Branch Talman, and Vrest Orton. Long writes that Loveman died within the last month, "and his passing at the age of 89 immeasurably saddened me" (Letter 2). He goes on to say,

And Wilfred Talman, Vrest Orton (He is 12 years or so my senior and still turns out books continuously for a major publisher) Alfred Galpin and Don Wandrei are all still very much extant. I have lost touch in recent years with 3 or 4 other early Lovecraftians who met and talked with him quite often. (Letter 2)

Long concludes this letter by admiring Ambrose's "stories and poems in <u>Macabre</u>" (Letter 2), thanking him for sending him a copy, and offering to "dig out" (Letter 2) some piece of his own to contribute to his magazine. And he apologizes for taking so long to answer: "I had every intention of doing so within a fortnight, but at about that time an avalanche of obligations descended upon me, and my correspondence has been piling up for weeks" (Letter 2).

Letter 3 (May 24, 1977)

Long's stress level has not abated when he writes his May 24, 1977 letter to Ambrose, the penmanship of which is significantly less steady than that of the previous letters. He adds addendums to the top and side of the first page. Across the top of the first page of the letter, which is written mostly in ink, Long writes in pencil, "That many-oared ship of unknown origin in interplanetary space has already begun to haunt my dreams"[4] (Letter 3). This sentence appears to be a quotation, but there are no quotation marks around it. A line drawn beneath it separates this sentence from the return address and salutation of the letter. Portions of the letter are written in ink and parts are in pencil. After "Dear M. E. A." in this letter, instead of the customary "Dear Mr. Ambrose," and thanking Ambrose for the copy he sent of *Argonaut*, Long apologizes once more for his tardiness in responding to his last letter, "as I've been writing under great pressure" (Letter 3).

He then discusses Albert J. Manachino, whose story, perhaps, appeared in the issue of *Argonaut* he has just received from

Michael Ambrose: "an extremely talented writer—restrained in style and approach, with a perceptive awareness of the precise point in a story when an abyss of ultimate horror should be allowed to widen" (Letter 3). Perhaps Long is responding to something Ambrose wrote in his letter about Manachino, or a letter by Manachino published in *Argonaut*, when he writes that

> in [Manachino's] letter anent HPL he is laboring, I think, under a misconception. I have never said that HPL was not racially prejudiced. Of course he was.* But this prejudice was shared by from 60% to 80% of the residents of Providence and other New England cities in the early years of the present century. There can be no gainsaying this. It was tragic, and seems in a present-day frame of reference, as I've pointed out in my preface to Michaud's reissue of The Conservative, totally unforgivable. But one has to realize that HPL was born and raised in an extremely provincial society—in a great many of its aspects. He triumphed over that and more as he grew older and ended by totally repudiating these early views. Despite all that has been said to the contrary, he was the kindest, most generous-minded individual it has ever been my privilege to know. (Letter 3)

The asterisk in the quote refers to a sentence Long has insinuated in the left margin: "*But not in his personal relationships with friends of the period. In that area he was kindliness and courtesy personified" (Letter 3). A squiggly line separates this sentence from the body of the letter.

Sonia and her marriage to H. P. Lovecraft are the next theme in this jumbled missive. No paragraph break separates all these topics on the first page. This portion in pencil:

> And Sonia was not 'reasonably well off for those times.' [Here, it sounds as if Long is responding to something said by Manachino.] She lost her high-paying millinery job right after they were married,

and there was a great deal of extreme economic hardship in the next two years. Economic factors were unquestionably chiefly responsible for the marriage failure. (Letter 3)

In *Dreamer*, Long vehemently asserts that the Lovecraft marriage failed—not because of a sex problem—but because Lovecraft could not stand New York City another minute: his mental health necessitated an immediate return to Providence. Thus, Lovecraft's friends wrote to his aunts to call him home (Long, *Dreamer*, 118-119).

On page 2—where the second paragraph of the letter begins—Long resumes his self-interrupted assessment of his exposition of Lovecraft's xenophobic views in *Dreamer*:

The portrait I've drawn of HPL in 'The Dreamer' is entirely in accord with what I said in an interview in Meade Frieson's fanzine five years ago, so I can hardly be accused of participating in a "white wash" as a recent fan reviewer has proclaimed. At that time the present fierce controversy had not arisen, and I spoke casually and freely. It did not even occur to me that I would be writing, a few years later, a book-length HPL memoir. In my letters in recent EOD mailings (To Indick, Reg Smith and others, and in a recent letter to Fantasy Crossroads) I've tried to clarify a few points I did not stress quite as much as I might have done in 'The Dreamer.' Meade also published two supplements to that first HPL huge memorial 'zine some two years later, to which I contributed letters. If Manachino could read all of this material he would, I feel, modify—[here, inserted in pencil, with a caret "even"] if only slightly—what he has set forth in his letter, for he impresses me as an unusually fair-minded guy. Of course, Sonia found HPL a little hard to live with at times. I can think of no man of letters in the entire course of English literature who would have been easy for a woman to live with. Genius always presents a problem of that nature. (Letter 3)

In *Dreamer*, Long states that one key factor which prompted H. P. Lovecraft's repudiation of his earlier opinions was his learning of the atrocities committed by Hitler (Long, *Dreamer*, 160).

Long assures Michael Ambrose that it is fine with him that Ambrose has published one of Long's letters, and that Ambrose has Long's permission to publish this one, too:

> Only on rare occasions do I object to the fullest publication of my letters, and when such an occasion arises I always caution a correspondent in advance or try to—once or twice in recent months a slight indiscretion has slipped past me in that area, but that happens to all letter-writers, and has to be taken in stride. (Letter 3)

Always remembering past kindnesses, he asks Ambrose to relay to someone named Chad, who is mentioned in Ambrose's "editorial comments" in the issue of *Argonaut*, that "I still remember the kind things he said a quarter of a century ago, about two of my stories in the old *Standard Publications*, in one of the letter columns" (Letter 3). He closes this letter by citing a favorable review of *Dreamer* by Edward Wagonknect, a "distinguished scholar" (Letter 3), who called his memoir "a vivid portrait," (Letter 3) and a review by Richard Lupoff in *Algol*.

Letter 4 (February 27, 1977)

The final letter in this packet, dated February 27, 1979 and written on the front and back of a sheet of onion skin, may be said to be scrawled. There are more scratchings out and more insertions with squiggly lines drawn around them than previously, so that it is difficult to decipher the sequence in which the various parts should be read. Two such segments occupy the top third of the first page. The main body of the letter begins a third of the way down the page. The page itself is only about sixty percent of the length it should be—the bottom has been cut off. Small ink marks reveal that something was once written at the bottom of the first page. Yet, the letter is finished and signed on the back; thus, the paper was cut before Long finished the letter on the reverse side.

Once again, pressure is the leading topic, beginning with the main body of the letter. Long cites "at least 30" (Letter 4) unanswered letters, some of them decreeing four-week deadlines for manuscripts. He paints a dismal picture:

> If you could glance into my study you would perhaps understand why letter-writing has been difficult for me—at least 30 still-to-be-answered letters on both sides of my desk, two un-completed manuscripts with story-deadline tags attached to them—"Get this in within the next four weeks or else!!" Bills in abundance—many still unpaid—fan group talk requests—Lyda's party plans, symbolized by five just-purchased bottles of Scotch—she gives at least three parties a month and I can't talk her out of it etc. etc. Never attempt to be a free-lance writer, and the husband of a socially-active wife at one and the same time, if you can possibly find some saner way of carrying on in the most high-pressure society on Earth! (Letter 4)

What Long elides in this portrait of his conjugal life is the true nature of his marriage.

During the Frank Belknap Long panel at Necronomicon 2024, Peter Cannon spoke soberly of the Longs' marriage: Lyda, he said, was verbally abusive to Frank. In *Long Memories*, his memoir of his own relationship with Long, Cannon renders many affecting, and sadly characteristic, scenes in the Long household: for instance, Lyda announcing in front of her mortified husband, "Once, when I first knew him, I was kissing him passionately and one of his teeth came out. Can you imagine, the son of a rich orthopedist [sic], and he doesn't have a tooth to call his own in his head!" (Cannon, 18)[5]

Between the Longs' marital disharmony and their poverty, Cannon and his wife, Julie, ceased their visits to the Longs at their apartment, preferring to meet Frank at other places. Cannon describes their first visit to the Long abode: he and Julie were served vodka in filthy glasses and deli take-out in deli containers; and the Longs had finished their own meal before their guests arrived and had started drinking in advance of their guests, too. Their only other guests were cockroaches. Cannon depicts Lyda as a manic afflicted with delusions and grandiose ideas, such as that President Reagan is sending her to Russia as a "cultural envoy," as well as prolonged periods of depression. Cannon and his wife cannot stand her (Cannon, 54). Nonetheless, Cannon comes to love her; and he fills the void in the Longs' family life as a sort of adopted son. Frank Belknap and Lyda Arco Long are styled gifted artists—Lyda had been a singer—who married in haste, suffered physical and mental decline, as well as poverty, metamorphosed into a cantankerous old couple whose grandiose delusions sustained them through their losses, irritated Peter Cannon, and endeared them to him.

Page two of the 1979 letter begins with a new paragraph, the topic of which is Long's triumphant return from the World Fantasy Convention in Fort Worth. Long enthuses about the change of scenery: "Texas is so BIG it makes NY seem small by contrast. I even find myself missing the Longhorns, pony express riders, and Phantom Apaches, not to mention the wagon trains" (Letter 4). "We" [Lyda and himself?] returned by bus and enjoyed the opportunity to see the Deep South on the drive. In Texas, Long received the World Fantasy Convention Lifetime Achievement Award, which

> meant a great deal to [him], particularly in view of its HPL association aspects, and the previous recipients—Bloch, Leiber, Bradbury. To be in such company still leaves me in a slight state of shock. When I saw that Borges and John Collier were among the nominees this year—well, the possibility that I might receive it

seemed remote. As you perhaps know, it involved an additional surprise—the G of H choice, along with Stephen King, at the Providence gathering in October. (Letter 4)

He closes this missive by admiring the latest issue of *Argonaut*, and especially Manachino's story, "St. George and the Mushroom." At the bottom of the page, in a wavy box in the left corner, he writes, "The Vestburgh cover was marvelous—a Time voyage in itself" (Letter 4). In the squiggly boxes at the top of the first page, Long apologizes

> for less than tidy-appearing epistles and occasional inked-out words in virtually all my letters this past few months. It's simply an indication of the tremendous pressure of recent events etc. Otherwise I'd have to postpone writing for an even longer period, for recopying ["re-" in "recopying" is inserted with a caret] is just about the most time-consuming task I can think of—at least for me. (Letter 4)

And, he says,

> A really important letter – and this is one of that nature – seems to have a way, at times, of having an extremely "dashed-off" aspect. (Letter 4)

*

Clearly, by 1979, Frank Belknap Long's best writing days were behind him. Advanced age, poor life organizational skills, poverty, diminished health, and a high-pressure spouse with psychological issues were the mire in which his literary ship foundered. From weird writer to "scientifantasy" pioneer, Long dwindled to hack writer struggling to survive. Yet, every so often, among the ashes of his former glory blazed the spark of consummate artistry and innovative vision which characterize the first writer of Twentieth-

Century science fiction. Frank Belknap Long clothed the nakedness of his human frailty in reminiscences which sustained him through the lean years, as he approached the abyss.

I have attempted to trace the provenance of these letters. The vendor from whom I purchased them said that his father had bought them from Bats over Books, a rare book dealer, but I have received no response to my inquiries regarding where they obtained the letters, such as an estate sale after Ambrose's passing. It has been a pleasure interacting with the Belknapian/Lovecraftian community as I endeavored to fully enter into the mind of Frank Belknap Long during the period when he wrote these letters to Michael E. Ambrose.

Notes

1 —as well as two issues of *Tryout* (1917 and 1919), an amateur press periodical published by Charles W. Smith of the Amateur Press Association, issues which contain several poems by H. P. Lovecraft, some of them under pseudonyms.

2 Sharing with Lovecraft some old-fashioned sensibilities, I would dearly love to say that I proffered my letter of credit.

3 Perry Grayson, of Tsathoggua Press, related in an email to this author that Long, in fact, "wrote the entire first issue of the pre-EC (and pre-comic code) horror comic book, *Adventures into the Unknown*, in 1948." (Email 24 Nov 2024)

4 David E. Schultz obligingly scanned a volume of Frank Belknap Long's poetry and did not find this line. I still hope to learn whether it is a quotation or not, and, if so, its source.

5 Perry Grayson, who is writing a biography of Frank Belknap Long, shared this anecdote:

> In a phone interview I conducted with literary agent and comic book impresario Julius Schwartz in 1995, I gained further insight into Lyda's wacky mannerisms [. . . T]he public humiliation of FBL only escalated with time. Though Julie Schwartz hung out with FBL in the 1930s, he hadn't crossed paths with him in years by the 1980s. Julie recalled that at the rather ramshackle Long residence, Lyda

propositioned him in front of her hubby and the rest of the guests: 'Want to *fuck?*' Julie was taken aback—absolutely mortified. He reminded me that he was already in his early 80s at the time. (Email 13 Feb 2025)

Works Cited

Cannon, Peter. *Long Memories and Other Writings*. New York: Hippocampus Press, 2022.

Cooke, Jon B. *The Charlton Companion*. Raleigh NC: TwoMorrows Publishing, 2022.

Goodwin, David J. *Midnight Rambles: H. P. Lovecraft in Gotham*. New York: Fordham University Press, 2024.

Joshi, S. T. Introduction. *The Centipede Press Library of Weird Fiction: Frank Belknap Long*,

edited by S. T. Joshi. Lakewood CO: Centipede Press, 2022, 7-14.

Long, Frank Belknap. *Howard Phillips Lovecraft: Dreamer on the Nightside*. 1975. Rockville MD: Wildside Press, LLC, 2016.

---Letter 1. Letterer to Michael E. Ambrose. March 17, 1976. Author's personal collection

---Letter 2. Letter to Michael E. Ambrose. June 15, 1976. Author's personal collection

---Letter 3. Letter to Michael E. Ambrose. May 24, 1977. Author's personal collection

---Letter 4. Letter to Michael E. Ambrose. February 27, 1979. Author's personal collection

Lovecraft, H. P. Letter to Lillian D. Clark. March 29, 1926. In *Lord of a Visible World: An Autobiography in Letters*, edited by S. T. Joshi and David E. Schultz. New York: Hippocampus Press, 2019.

---*Fungi from Yuggoth, An Annotated Edition*, edited by David E. Schultz, New York: Hippocampus Press, 2017.

Afro-cosmicism:
On the Craft of Seizing
Speculative Reparations

Chris Campbell, Hartwell Award Finalist

M Y NOVELLA, *IN THE PALACE OF SCIENCE*, recently
published in *Asimov's Magazine*, joins a rapidly
growing body of literature by mostly African American
writers ostensibly working within the subgenre of cosmic horror. I
use the term ostensibly because while these works sit comfortably
within the framework of Afrofuturism, their relationship with
cosmic horror is complex. Afrofuturism is a movement that
centers the significance of African and Diaspora life. Cosmic
horror, at its core, is about the absolute insignificance of humanity
and the universe's indifference to it. These modes of storytelling,
while not incompatible, are clearly in conflict. Throughout this
essay, I use Black and Blackness to refer to a sociopolitical identity
constructed for people of African descent under racial subjugation
in the United States—specifically among descendants of formerly
chattel-enslaved Africans—and to the cultural, spiritual, and
cosmological frameworks that emerged in response to that
enforced identity. In this context, Blackness in this essay names
not only a racial category imposed by U.S. White Supremacy but
also a generative site of worldmaking, meaning-making, and
survival, shaped by what Saidiya Hartman and Christina Sharpe

have theorized as the afterlife of slavery. I draw on Toni Morrison's insight in *Playing in the Dark* that being African American operates as a vital—if often unacknowledged—presence within the American literary and cultural imagination, functioning as both contrast and catalyst in the construction of Eurocentrism and Americanness. While my usage emphasizes U.S. contexts, I recognize that being of African descent also resonates as an intersectional identity across the African Diaspora, including among African and Africana peoples who choose to claim the term as part of their cultural or political self-definition. I also acknowledge that color coding people as Black by Europeans has extended to include many people with no historic roots in Africa and that there are many people both of recent African descent and not who find the term offensive as a result of its historical association with European Imperialism.

Another readily apparent conflict in the history of cosmic horror is the virulent racism of authors during the time period of the age of H.P. Lovecraft, often considered the father of the cosmic horror subgenre. Wrestling with Lovecraft's beliefs generates significant debate within speculative fiction circles. This discourse often explores Lovecraft's racism in terms of its cultural impact and the expanding role of non-European writers in cosmic horror. Generally, the discussion about deconstructing racism within cosmic horror focuses on who is doing the deconstructing and why the deconstruction of racism is essential. This essay shifts that focus to how craft as a cultural artifact promotes representation while transforming speculative fiction into a space for restorative justice. For this essay's discussion of Afro-cosmicism, I'll analyze tools employed by Victor LaValle in his award-winning novella *The Ballad of Black Tom*, Zin Rocklyn in her award-winning novella *Flowers for the Sea*, and my own *In the Palace of Science*.

LaValle wrote *The Ballad of Black Tom* as a response to one of Lovecraft's most racist stories, "The Horror at Red Hook," dedicating the piece "for H.P. Lovecraft, with all my conflicted feelings" (Lavalle frontispiece). In *Black Tom*, LaValle focuses on the central conflict between Afrofuturism and cosmic horror: "'What was indifference compared to malice? Indifference would be such a relief,' Tommy said" (LaValle 66). A deep and indescribable dread at the notion of an indifferent universe is a luxury only afforded to a person who has not experienced a life impacted by structural racism.

The prose in *Black Tom* notably sets it apart from Lovecraft's work. Lovecraft draws considerable inspiration from gothic writers, specifically Edgar Allan Poe. While the quality of Lovecraft's prose is contentious, his style is closely identified with the cosmic horror aesthetic. However, in *Black Tom*, LaValle eschews any indulgence or affectation towards a Lovecraft pastiche, favoring prose that brings a story set in the Jazz Age into the urgent and present now. This restraint allows a nuanced approach to characterizing the narrative's protagonist, Tom, enabling the reader to identify when Tom deploys diction as agency, code-switching at critical moments to adapt to different circumstances, including adopting the role of "The Clueless Negro," deploying a deeply affected accent to negotiate the dynamics of being interrogated by police officers who just robbed him (LaValle 25), and in this way depicting how subterfuge is a critical tool for survival when interacting with a complex system of racist oppression.

LaValle's unadorned prose also bridges the Harlem Renaissance with the modern Black Lives Matter era, offering a damning commentary on the United States' regress away from racial conciliation over the previous century, by framing the discourse linguistically within the present. Tom is not some relic of a bygone era; he is a vital example of an African American person experiencing United States racism in a manner that is as true in the 2020s as it was in the 1920s.

Although linguistically modern, LaValle uses the Jazz Age setting as the framework for historical metafiction that codes the cultural experience of the Harlem Renaissance within the narrative. The story begins fueled by the optimism of the Roaring Twenties and ends with a sense of disenfranchisement that uproots Tom from his hostile native soil, following the progression of many prominent figures of the Harlem Renaissance who experienced a greater sense of belonging as ex-pats somewhere else, as explored in Langston Hughes's autobiographical work *The Big Sea*. Hughes found that "a Paris where they don't care about color" is preferable to a life in "the States, where you have to live like a nigger with niggers" (Hughes 61). This sentiment reflects Tom's feelings of indifference toward liberation relative to living in a society hostile to his life and survival.

Black Tom also engages with the Harlem Renaissance in its treatment of the Great Migration and the ensuing cultural disconnect between formerly enslaved people and their descendants. During the Harlem Renaissance, the cultural anthropologist Zora Neale Hurston and the folklorist Thomas Washington Talley were part of a movement to catalog the folklore of the last generation of freed people, who were already well into their advanced years. This was a task made all the more urgent because of a widespread attitude among African Americans in the decades following emancipation that saw "[N]egro folklore like dialect, as a discursive remnant of slavery, a cultural and social embarrassment, best left behind in the mists of a deeply troubled past" (Gates xxvii). This persistence of cultural memory after the Great Migration as a tenuous link in an almost broken chain is mirrored in Tom's relationship with his father. When the reader meets Tom, he has little interest in music, a defining aspect of his parents' lives. To Tom, the guitar is a useful bit of camouflage. However, after an awakening, Tom forms a deep connection with his father by sharing music, culminating with the transmission of powerful ancestral conjure music.

Black Tom is a deeply layered work, so a full accounting of its themes and symbols is beyond the scope of this essay. However, I will draw attention to two layers I can use to explore the work's relationship with cosmic horror. The first is the representation of the unrestrained violence endemic to the United States' racial caste system. The turning point of the story of *Black Tom* is in the aftermath of a senseless shooting during which the victim represents every racially targeted U.S. citizen who was ever shot while holding something harmless. The malevolence of the act is emphasized by the casual way the gun is emptied into the man, only to be reloaded and emptied again. Unrestrained racial violence returns in the climax when a block of buildings is razed with militarized weaponry, invoking outrages such as the Tulsa Massacre, which occurred only a few years prior to the date in which the book is set, and more recent atrocities such as the MOVE bombing. These two significant acts of violence, along with many of the smaller indignities Tom experiences at the hands of police, are the true source of horror in the story, not the eldritch abomination that lies just beyond the threshold; or, to further clarify Tananarive Due's statement that "Black History is Black Horror" (*Horror Noire* 00:03:15):

the monster on the screen validates the terror that you have experienced in your life [. . .]

And in those monsters, I also found a feeling of communal suffering, a feeling of being outside of society, misunderstood by society: "Can't I just live? Can I just live without being characterized as fearsome or monstrous or criminal?" (Due 140, 136)

The other layers of symbols I draw attention to surround Tom, a trickster who travels freely, using clothing/garments as a key to allow safe passage. Tom is connected with music, and in his first iteration, he is at his most powerful after learning ancestral conjure magic. These identifying markers associate him with African American folk hero High John the Conqueror, whose sign "was a laugh, and his singing" (Hurston *High John* 2). Tom's inheritance of his father's legacy is complicated by the addition of a hidden knife, recalling that the Great Migration was a journey through a hostile land, away from the threat of racial terrorist violence in the Jim Crow South and toward the hope for an opportunity to thrive in other regions.

High John is a complicated figure with numerous interpretations. In most oral traditions recorded in the United States, he embraces cunning over violence and spiritual transcendence as revolutionary consciousness, remaining unconquered and unbroken even when chained. Regardless of his cunning and adaptability, Tom does not remain unbroken, and when he breaks, he turns to the other form of power his father left him: the knife. In this transformation, Tom resembles one of the Orishas with whom High John is identified: Eshu-Elegba (Long 6). Eshu, often culturally translated as a trickster, shares many of High John's features but has a nature that vacillates between being a relatively benign mediator of justice, "a trickster whose duplicity is moral, keeping the people, kings, and other gods off balance," to a force of capricious devastation turning neighbors and friends against each other before setting fire to their homes because "sowing dissension is my great delight" (Hoover 5; Cosentino 263). Christians and Muslims syncretize Eshu as a deity and demon who deceives and harms men (Pemberton 26).

Tom's experience gives the reader a personal account that echoes the historical context while linking African American oral tradition with deeper African roots. Doing all of this within a story that uses Lovecraft's mythos and worldbuilding with an eye to his complicated legacy allows this accomplishment and the story's themes to shine all the brighter as a masterclass in Afrofuturism.

Zin Rocklyn's *Flowers for the Sea* is inspired by *The Ballad of Black Tom* (Rocklyn, Interview). The story is set in an unknowable time and place during an endless flood. The Intradiluvian backdrop for the story makes it a spiritual successor to *Black Tom*, wrestling with and embracing the previous work's resolution. Like LaValle, Rocklyn uses the story's dedication to orient the reader: "To Courtney, for teaching me that my anger is a gift," a message bound to resonate with and comfort many Black people during the post-Obama era and the current rising tide of White nationalism. When facing betrayal, anger can be a gift because, unlike sadness, anger pushes outward against the world rather than inward against the heart. In *Flowers*, Rocklyn turns this core of anger into a tool for crafting art that captures the imagination and recontextualizes untamable anger as something that can sustain just as easily as it can destroy.

When I asked Rocklyn how she interacts with the problematic legacy of cosmic horror, the answer was simple: "I'll read something and know I can do it better" (Rocklyn, Interview). This well-earned confidence is displayed in the piece's lyrical and haunting prose, which creates an alien and dreamlike state that the novella uses to great effect as it shifts between past, present, and oracular visions of the future. Through its prose, *Flowers* enters the realm of epic poetry. Much like Lovecraft, Rocklyn's work displays her gothic influences, specifically Lord Byron, through how she weaves together anger, violence, eroticism, and liberation: "I kind of want to scare my readers and then make them horny" (Rocklyn Interview). Rocklyn is comfortable wearing the mantle of a modern-day Black Byronist, linking their work to a tradition in African American poetry inspired by Byron during the eighteen hundreds. Similar to nineteenth-century writers using Byronism to explore Black masculinity and sexuality, Rocklyn modernizes this tradition by bringing it into conversation with intersectionality–using a raw depiction of the Black female body as lusting, excreting, and existing with all the numerous imperfections that come with living to "displace the moral coordinates of conventional representations of Blackness" (Sandler 40): "I turn and see the trees plump and grow, much like the kumquat trees clear across had when I'd urinated in their soil. Fruit engorges while I watch, some ripen and fall, rotting in the next instant only to be swallowed up by the soil, after which a small sprout appears" (Rocklyn *Flowers* 87). In this passage, shortly after Iraxi, the protagonist, steps into a previously fallow garden dripping in her own slime, Rocklyn's depictions of Black femininity are acts of liberation both against internalized respectability politics and the patriarchal and racist policing of Black bodies. Rocklyn contests the classification of the libidinous Black woman as degenerate, placing the features Eurocentric society purportedly holds in disgust as the very same features that draw humans nearer to the realm of the divine.

Using the mythic space the story occupies, Rocklyn first uses the flood to take the reader through an inversion of the primeval history of the Book of Genesis, forging a new cosmology in which Iraxi, in the role of Eve, step by step unwinds the fall and returns to paradise, removing herself from the clutches of patriarchy and tools of oppression, such as shame. "I am naked when I appear above, and this time, it feels right" (Rocklyn *Flowers* 101). This poetic sensibility resonates with the profoundly intersectional thematic ecology of *Flowers*. The piece openly uses its rage to condemn patriarchy and systemic racism, illustrating within the text how these two systems of oppression feed on and support each other. The backdrop of an apocalyptic flood and passage across the endless ocean in humankind's final ark symbolically mediates and merges these twinned sources of oppression.

Right alongside their use of the flood as a means of contending with the patriarchy, Rocklyn also uses this setting to weave in themes of the Middle Passage and racist oppression. Iraxi is forced to remain below deck for extended periods, valued only as a body, not a person, and is a victim of genocide. Like LaValle, Rocklyn also uses their commentary on history to show the persistence of violence within the United States' racial caste system, with symbols that directly evoke the recent uptick of church burning with the resurgence of the White supremacist movement. This exploration of intersectionality extends to the characters within the narrative who represent the many faces of oppression. The story involves a physically dominating misogynist known as Hirat, a passive bystander called Amit, and an insidious female misogynoir named Ket, who assures Iraxi she is an ally though Ket is anything but, eventually revealing her intention to keep Iraxi alive only so long as the newborn requires her milk.

Rocklyn blends biblical patriarchy and the colonial trade in human bondage with the many-tentacled creatures that lurk beneath the waves to deliver a piece that revels in celebrating the very thing that traditional cosmic horror fears. The story celebrates the triumph of a dark-skinned semi-aquatic form of humanity granted dominion over a world transformed for their benefit, depicting the merger of man and monster as beautiful. In contrast, Lovecraft sees horror in *The Shadow over Innsmouth* at the thought of a fish people inheriting a future earth wiped clean of humankind. Rocklyn remaps a horror from Cosmicism, a world-ending apocalypse at the hands of an unstoppable and unimaginable force—with tentacles—into a transformation brimming with potential and opportunities for radical reinvention.

As the author of *In the Palace of Science,* I feel a responsibility to my future readers not to interfere with their game of meaning-making with a piece that has only recently been published. However, even with this restraint, the question of craft as a cultural artifact invites a writer of Afro-cosmicism to enter the conversation, begun by LaValle and Rocklyn, who both point toward their primary influences as they situate their work within the context of its heritage. In my analysis of *Palace,* I will foreground the three men whose legacies I used to bridge the gap and blur the divide between African American history and Afrofuturist countermemory as symbolized and carried by Eshu. The men were the inventor Lewis Latimer, the scientist and folklorist Thomas Washington Talley, and the butler Robert Roberts.

Lewis Latimer is the often-overlooked designer of the improved carbon filaments for light bulbs, dramatically increasing their luminosity and lifetime hours: practical and functional improvements absolutely necessary to the eventual mass market adoption of electric light. As a child, Latimer's family was divided after the Dred Scott decision, when his parents decided his father, a self-liberated man, should temporarily flee to Canada, never to be heard from again. While his role as an inventor was where Latimer's influence on *Palace* began, as work on the piece progressed, Latimer began to serve as a guide for numerous other aspects of the narrative, establishing the location and period as well as the central wound to drive the protagonist's choices.

Thomas Washington Talley was the first African American chemistry professor to teach at a major American university and the collector of two formative volumes of African American oral folktales. I first discovered Talley through his work as a folklorist long before I imagined *Palace* as a counter-historical narrative. I was struck by Talley's understanding of the difference between stories and tradition, a demarcation central to his critique of Joel Chandler Harris. When Mr. Harris therefore asked ante-bellum American Negroes for stories, he got their stories. He received very, very few of their traditions; and he received these in a very fragmentary way (Talley "Origin" 373).

Conversely, for Talley, craft is a cultural artifact for maintaining the transmission of these traditions, a practice that is also commonly found in Afrofuturist thought—or, as Sheree Renee Thomas explains, "[Afrofuturism] is creative alchemy. The spirit and rhythm of a culture is preserved and transformed; the past is not only contested but sacred space" (Thomas 4). Talley's work provided me with an example of how to faithfully represent an oral performance in text, offering some of the tools and mirroring the ethos behind my choice to use Talley's voice to inspire the voice of my story's narrator. The tale required the feel of an authentic oral performance by a scientist and a scholar with a keen sense of race and class consciousness and an eye toward posterity informing his performance.

Robert Roberts is the author of *The House Servant's Directory,* a detailed guide for domestic servants that covers everything from instructions for chores, cleaning, and provisioning the household to etiquette and advice for the employer-servant relationship. *House Servant's Directory* set the standard for household management for decades after it was published. Upon discovering this unique book, one of the first commercially published works by an African American, I knew it would give me a beating heart for the butler in *Palace,* the implacable Mr. Ochi.

Each of these men made noteworthy accomplishments but nonetheless faded into insignificance because they lived within a dominant culture that did not allow for their excellence to exist and be recognized. Edison's mythologizing erased Latimer's contributions, and Talley's achievements as a folklorist disappeared into the shadow of Joel Chandler Harris. Roberts, an African American domestic servant, was rendered doubly invisible to history.

H. P. Lovecraft's fears, as explored in cosmic horror, often boiled down to the possibility that someone like him would become a victim of something akin to the horrors and degradations that the global majority faced as a result of Western European imperialism. Lovecraft feared that he could be rendered as insignificant as Latimer, Talley, and Roberts were to the history books by forces beyond his control. Lovecraft looked into the cosmos and found a yawning void that was terrible to behold. The power of Afro-cosmicism comes from looking beyond this void to find new infinities teeming with possibilities. These are possibilities not just for Black futurity but also for healing and reconciliation due to the facility Afro-cosmicism has for telling stories that act as the catalyst for discussions critical to the work of reparations and restorative justice. This can be seen in the sequence of events that led to President Joe Biden's attending the centennial anniversary of the Tulsa Race Massacre as the first U.S. President to acknowledge this tragedy.

Acknowledging the past and the double atrocities first of racial terrorism and then the indignity of erasure is a vital step toward a more just and equitable future. It is important to note that former President Biden's belated official acknowledgment of the Tulsa Race Massacre was driven by the power of narrative: Afro-cosmicism, to be specific. The explicitly Afro-cosmicist TV show *Lovecraft Country* and the speculative fiction TV series with significant Afro-cosmicist elements, *Watchmen*, both featured the same terrorist attack within months of each other and brought the forcibly suppressed history of Tulsa back into the collective memory of Americans. The polarity between Afrofuturism and cosmic horror gives Afro-cosmicism a fertile substrate for cultivating stories that can both inform and entertain in a manner that lowers the barriers that impede an open and free dialogue. By reframing Lovecraft's literary legacy as a fertile space for rearticulating Blackness, Afro-cosmicism is enacting a form of speculative reparations.

While the sub-genre of Afro-cosmicism is not exactly new, tracing its roots to the work of the figurative mother of Afro-futurism, Octavia E. Butler, Afro-cosmicism has assuredly picked up steam in recent years. With writers such as N.K. Jemisin, Victor LaValle, Donyae Coles, P. Djéli Clark, Zin Rocklyn, and Cadwell Turnbull leading the charge, it is quickly becoming one of the most exciting spaces within the speculative fiction landscape. Further research could explore how Afro-cosmicism, as an important emerging sub-genre that has already garnered significant critical acclaim, commercial success, and cultural relevance, engages with various forms of Indigenous futurism and broader movements within speculative fiction and deepens understanding of this perspective's cultural impact on society.

Works Cited

Biden, Joe. "Remarks by President Biden Commemorating the 100th Anniversary of the Tulsa Race Massacre." *The White House*, 2 June 2021, https://www.whitehouse.gov/briefing-room/speeches-remarks/2021/06/02/remarks-by-president-biden-commemorating-the-100th-anniversary-of-the-tulsa-race-massacre/. Accessed 1 Dec. 2024.

Campbell, Chris. *In the Palace of Science, Asimov's Science Fiction,* May/June 2024.

---. "Afro-Cosmicism: On the Craft of Racial Consciousness within Cosmic Horror." *From Earth to the Stars,* 2 May 2024.

Clark, P. Djèlí. *Ring Shout.* Tor.com, 2020

Coles, Donyae. "Sometimes Boys Don't Know." *Nightmare Magazine,* Issue 106, July 2021, https://www.nightmare-magazine.com/fiction/sometimes-boys-don t-know/. Accessed 11 July 2025.

Cosentino, Donald. "Who Is That Fellow in the Many-Colored Cap? Transformations of Eshu in Old and New World Mythologies." *The Journal of American Folklore*, vol. 100, no. 397, 1987, pp. 261–75.

Crenshaw, Kimberlé. "Demarginalizing the Intersection of Race and Sex: A Black Feminist Critique of Antidiscrimination Doctrine, Feminist Theory and Antiracist Policies." *University of Chicago Legal Forum*, 1989, 1989, pp. 139-168.

Davoudi, Dalia. "Time-Sensitive: Teaching Afrofuturism Through the Nineteenth Century." *The Radical Teacher*, no. 122, 2022, pp. 32–41. *JSTOR*, https://www.jstor.org/stable/48694839. Accessed 31 Oct. 2024.

Due, Tananarive. "'Healing Our Histories Through the Lens of Horror': Guest of Honor Plenary Address Online at VICFA 2022, *The Global Fantastic*." *Journal of the Fantastic in the Arts*, vol. 33, no. 3., whole no.115, 3/2023, pp, 132-151.

Eshun, Kodwo. "Further Considerations on Afrofuturism." *CR: The New Centennial Review*, vol. 3, no. 2, 2003, pp. 287–302.

Fabre, Michel. *From Harlem to Paris: Black American Writers in France, 1840-1980*. University of Illinois Press, 1991.

Gates, Henry Louis, and Maria Tatar, editors. *The Annotated African American Folktales*. Liveright, W.W. Norton & Company, 2017.

Hartman, Saidiya. *Lose Your Mother: A Journey Along the Atlantic Slave Route*. Farrar, Straus and Giroux, 2007.

Hoover, Paul. "Pair of Figures for Eshu: Doubling of Consciousness in the Work of Kerry James Marshall and Nathaniel Mackey." *Lenox Avenue: A Journal of InterArts Inquiry*, vol. 5, 1999, pp. 3–20.

Horror Noire: A History of Black Horror. Directed by Xavier Burgin. Shudder, 2019.

Hughes, Langston. *The Big Sea: An Autobiography*. Knopf, 1940.

Hurston, Zora Neale. *Mules and Men*. Philadelphia: J.B. Lippincott Co., 1935.

---. "High John de Conquer." *The American Mercury*, 1943.

Jemisin, N. K. *How Long 'til Black Future Month?* Orbit, 2018.

LaValle, Victor. *The Ballad of Black Tom*. Tor Books, 2016.

Long, Carolyn Morrow. *John the Conqueror: From Root-Charm to Commercial Product*. University of North Carolina Press, 1997.

Lovecraft, H. P. "The Horror at Red Hook." YouTube: *Gates of Imagination*. 7 October 2023.

---. *The Shadow over Innsmouth.* Everett, PA: Visionary Publishing Co., 1936. 13–72, 74–125, 127–42, 144–58. https://www.hplovecraft.com/writings/fiction/soi.aspx. 20 August 2009.

Mitchell, Michele. *Righteous Propagation: African Americans and the Politics of Racial Destiny after Reconstruction.* University of North Carolina Press, 2004.

Morrison, Toni. *Playing in the Dark: Whiteness and the Literary Imagination.* Vintage Books, 1993.

Pemberton, John. "Eshu-Elegba: The Yoruba Trickster God." *African Arts*, vol. 9, no. 1, 1975, pp. 20–92.

Rocklyn, Zin. *Flowers for the Sea.* Tor Books, 2021.

---. Personal interview, March 20, 2024.

Sandler, Matt. "Black Byronism." *The Byron Journal*, vol. 45, no. 1, 2017.

Sharpe, Christina. *In the Wake: On Blackness and Being.* Duke University Press, 2016.

Talley, Thomas W. *Negro Folk Rhymes: Wise and Otherwise.* Macmillan, 1922. Reprinted with an introduction by Charles K. Wolfe, University of Tennessee Press, 1991.

Talley, Thomas W. "The Origin of Negro Traditions." *Phylon* (1940-1956), vol. 3, no. 4, 1942, pp. 371–76.

---. *Negro Folk Rhymes.* Edited by Charles K. Wolfe, University of Tennessee Press, 1991.

Thomas, Sheree Renée. "AND SO SHAPED THE WORLD." *Obsidian*, vol. 42, no. 1/2, 2016, pp. 3–10. JSTOR, http://www.jstor.org/stable/44489481. Accessed 12 Nov. 2024.

Turchiano, Danielle. "The Tulsa Race Massacre: How 'Watchmen,' 'Lovecraft Country' Raised Public Awareness for the Tragedy." *The Wrap*, 20 May 2021, https://www.thewrap.com/tulsa-massacre-watchmen-lovecraft-country/. Accessed 1 Dec. 2024.

Turnbull, Cadwell. *No Gods, No Monsters.* United Kingdom: Titan Books, 2022.

Anarres: Where Women Hold Up Half the Sky

Natalie Fourmyle, Hartwell Award Finalist

I N A 1975 INTERVIEW, Isaac Asimov states, "When you think of a future, you try to make it as plausible as possible [...] it's very difficult, really, to visualize the real future" (5:40- 7:35); by this, Asimov communicates that it is difficult to visualize a future characterized by technology beyond the existing developmental level. Similarly, across human history, mythologies may be bounded by the material realities of the cultures in which they are created. *The Epic of Gilgamesh* is characterized by and limited to the technology known to humankind during the Bronze Age. The Old Testament of the Christian Bible is limited to the technology of the Levant, and the New Testament stories reflect the technology and social systems in place during Hellenic antiquity. Moving forward in time two millennia, Asimov conceptualizes the three laws of robotics in 1950 for his book, *I, Robot*, a feat made possible by the technological advances in robotics during the early 1940s. The technology and social structures in each case predate and inform the technology of the fictional literature. As the existing technologies bound these cultures, Le Guin was bound by the social and political structures in which she lived. Following this logic, one can assess Ursula K.

Le Guin's 1974 novel, *The Dispossessed*, within the cultural and political contexts of twentieth-century socialist projects efforts, particularly those of the Chinese Communist Party led by Mao Tse-tung, toward the emancipation of women from the domestic sphere and their integration into the public sphere.

This essay assesses *The Dispossessed* in conjunction with its twentieth-century geopolitical context to argue that Le Guin draws influence from socialist thought and practices to create worlds meant to allegorize the geopolitics of the twentieth century. In this essay, I will first address the primary literature, *The Dispossessed*, and literary scholarship on the text to establish the foundation of the anarcho-communist discourse surrounding the work, thus far; this will be the historical and philosophical basis on which I form my argument. Then, I situate Le Guin in the twentieth century's geo-political history and discuss authorial intent, as well as her influence on Anarres insofar as her personal philosophies and the ideological bases of the twentieth-century major world powers are woven throughout the driving ideology of the Anarresti and the Thuvians: Odonianism[1]. Odo, or Laia Asieo Odo, the female Urrasti philosopher whose work serves as the societal groundwork for the Anarresti settlement and the Urrasti nation of Thu, is described by Le Guin as "a political philosopher, a fearless demagogue, an active revolutionary, a woman so different from" the author herself (Le Guin XVII).

The Dispossessed is a novel situated within the same universe of many interconnected worlds in which Le Guin wrote nine novels and several short stories. Two centuries before the events of the novel, there are protests on the planet Urras and this results in the immigration of Odonians—those who follow the political-philosophical teachings of Odo—to the moon, Anarres. The story follows the protagonist, Shevek, as he grows his career on Anarres as a theoretical scientist in the even-numbered chapters. In the odd-numbered chapters, Shevek is working on Urras to develop the theoretical framework to support instantaneous inter-galactic communication in a technology called the ansible, which appears in each of the other novels within the Hainish universe. Le Guin, a science fiction writer at a time when the genre was saturated by male authors writing adventure novels, stated she wanted to write about what mothers and sisters were doing at home while the men were out on these adventures. Though the story follows Shevek, special attention is given to the role of women within that society, which Le Guin executes by contrasting the attitudes towards and rights afforded to women in the two societies.

Various scholars have examined Le Guin's authorial intent when analyzing her works; literary scholar Himali Thakur borrows from Peter Kropotkin's anarcho-communism to understand Odonianism, specifically the Anarresti Odonians. Thakur focuses on the means through which Shevek, Le Guin's protagonist, can seek solitude but still return to Odonian society where "to be alone is to be dead" (Thakur 260). To do this, Thakur refers to the influence of anarchic philosophy and other scientific areas of study to place the "novel in a history of media technologies as discussed by Jussi Parikka" (260). Similar to Thakur in form, though different in scope, I intend to illuminate the novel's place within the discourse of twentieth-century socialist experiments by referring to the potential impact of the Communist Party of China on *The Dispossessed*.

Tony Burns positions Le Guin within a dialectical materialism framework in his *Political Theory, Science Fiction, And Utopian Literature* (Burns 268-74). He finishes by connecting Le Guin's insistence on her function as a storyteller rather than a prophet for the socio-political organism to a letter written by Friederich Engels on 26 Nov, 1885. Engels writes to Minna Kautsky on literature, "The writer is not obliged to offer to the reader the future historical solution of the social conflicts he depicts" (113). Le Guin does not offer her reader a future historical solution to the conflict between capitalist and non-capitalist countries, as Engel's literary philosophy permits. However, she presents to her reader an allegory of the political and scientific cold battles between twentieth-century capitalist and communist nations. With such parameters, a reader may now consider the Woman Question as addressed by Frederich Engels, Mao Tse-Tung, and Michael Parenti.

Dialectical materialist thought arose in the mid-to-late 19th century as a way of understanding societal relations and their contradictions as reflections of the material conditions in which they arise. Thus, within a dialectical materialist framework, "the position of women rests, as everything in our complex modern society rests, on an economic basis" (Aveling and Marx Aveling, np). This question stems from the historically based observations focused on the domestic sphere of women's work and women's economic roles in the larger society, as Engels writes in his *Origins of the Family, Private Property, and the State*: "the task entrusted to the women of managing the household was as much a public and socially necessary industry as the procuring of food by the men" (39), though with the advent of agricultural technology, there became an increased need for human labor power outside the home. The economically decided societal roles of women and men on Urras in the nation of A-Io parallel the development of those Engels observed. However, the material conditions on Anarres require the woman to labor alongside the man due to scarcity of resources, including labor. The use of machinery brought to Anarres from Urras allows for labor equitability where neither man nor woman is excluded from work tasks. Shevek relays to Dr. Kimoe that he is often envious of women because, although men are stronger, women work harder and longer (631).

The inextricable socialist projects of the 20th century borrowed from and built on Marxist-Engelian thought. Thus, along with the reorganization of labor, there was a considerable shift in legal rights and protections for women. Consider Chinese Communist leader Mao Tsetung's declaration that "reflects the determination by the government to raise women's status: 'women hold up half the sky'" (Li 3). This sentiment reflects Vladimir Lenin's criticism of the lack of legal equality for women within "bourgeois democrac[ies]," democracies of "pompous phrases, solemn words, lavish promises and high-sounding slogans about freedom and equality," which ultimately "cloaks the lack of freedom and the inequality of women" (186). These equalities were placed into law in Articles 122 and 137 of the Constitution of the Union of Soviet Socialist Republics, as well as in Article 6 of The Common Program of the Chinese People's Political Consultative Conference, which abolishes the semi-feudal system "which holds women in bondage" and declares that "women shall enjoy equal rights with men in political, economic, cultural, educational and social life," along with freedom in marriage for both sexes, all of which did not exist previous to the revolution (Chinese Communist Party). Though the legal equality granted to women in these socialist projects did not erase centuries of systemic oppression and cultural misogyny immediately, they were the first of many steps these new governments took to ensure equality between the sexes. Similarly, in Anarres, the biological differences between males and females cause some interpersonal prejudice, not because of looking down at the opposite sex but because of a stronger friendship bond in childhood with members of the same sex. These attitudes of the Anarresti could also be attributed to the Urrasti societies from which they emerged, along with their society's de-emphasis on the heteronormative lifestyles in which each partner has a role that stems from their sex. The Anarresti are not bound by sexually assigned roles in the same way.

Political scientist Michael Parenti points to the sharp increase in gender inequality after overthrowing Russian communism (114-

6). This inequality coincided with women "being recruited in unprecedented numbers for the booming sex industry that caters to foreign and domestic businessmen" and a sharp increase in women being murdered, primarily by boyfriends and husbands, upon the dissolution of the communist mode of government (115). Parenti's analysis of gender inequalities before the rise and after the fall of the Soviet Union in the Eastern Bloc reveals the improvement in the quality of life for women under a governing body that does not adhere to capitalist or feudal modes of production. Le Guin similarly contrasts gender equality present in Anarresti society, and presumably in Thu and among other Odonian revolutionary groups (Le Guin 848), against the gender inequality present in A-Io.

Le Guin was known as a feminist author who often spoke about women and their roles within society; during a speech in 1983, Le Guin declared she would give the speech "in the language of women." In the speech, she addresses the audience as, "my sisters and daughters, brothers and sons," similar to how the Anarresti-Odonians commonly address others, despite biological relations, as 'sister(s),' 'brother(s),' 'daughter(s),' and 'son(s).' This Odonian terminology reveals, in its comparison to the author's speech, the degree to which Le Guin's philosophies are infused into Odo's ideological framework. Through Odo, Le Guin posits an alternative to a presumed exploitative capitalist mode of production. As discussed, many twentieth-century anti-capitalist thinkers attempted to explore alternatives to the current economic system, a discourse into which Le Guin's The Dispossessed enters.

In her Mills College 1983 commencement speech, Le Guin posits women as foreigners, excluded from the "self-declared male norms of this society;" thus, she subverts this dynamic and declares men foreigners to the "language of women," in which this speech is written. Odo's teachings align with Le Guin's messaging in this speech; there is no disregard for the female sex, nor is it posited in a superior position to the male sex. In other words, on Anarres, women hold up half the sky, and men hold up the other half. Similarly, Anarres achieves a socio-political[2] equilibrium not for its overwhelming presence of feminine power but in its lack of male domination. Despite such gendered equality, the society is viewed by the Urrasti as a womanish society. The respected Urrasti scientist Atro tells Shevek Anarres is a weak society, and the failures of Anarres can be attributed to this lack of the "virile side of life" which he associates as a positive social influence of which only the male is capable (841). A society must not be womanish, according to the Ioti physicist, though Shevek and Odo would argue it should not be mannish, either. If women hold up half the sky, men hold up the other half; therefore, society should reflect both halves of the population, contributing equally to the greater good of the larger society. Le Guin takes an anti-capitalist approach, though not necessarily Marxist-Leninist, in many of her speeches and writings, without a straightforward solution to the problem she addresses, which allows her audience to sit in the uncomfortable truths realized within a capitalist society. In doing so, Le Guin allows her speech to be uninhibited because she is not promoting communism as it existed in the twentieth century. Still, instead, she promotes an anti-capitalist approach, which she refers to as being against profiteering and profiteers. Regardless of Le Guin's exact political sympathies, it is clear that she was against the capitalist mode of production and in favor of a sort of social change, from what currently seems natural to a state that is more equitable. This is in keeping with the way Le Guin described how capitalism's "power seems inescapable; so did the divine right of kings. Any human power can be resisted and changed by human beings. Resistance and change often begin in art [....] but the name of our beautiful reward isn't profit. Its name is freedom" ("Speech"). *The Dispossessed* exhibits the tensions between capitalist nation-states and anti-capitalist societies, reflecting the tensions present in the 20th century between the USA and the USSR. Two societies featured in the novel adhere to Odonian teachings: the Anarresti and the Thuvians, each faced with different material conditions that limit the capabilities of each society,

The Anarresti must adapt to life without abundant or necessary resources and practice scarcity, a practice unknown to the citizens of the abundant planet, Urras. Le Guin writes the Urrasti astronomer-priests in the Third Millennium perceived the Otherworld through a mystical lens. However, this "Eden of Anarres proved to be dry, cold, and windy, and the rest of the planet was worse" without evolved life higher than fish and flowerless plants (690). Scarcity is a natural condition of this world, unlike their mother world of Urras. Therefore, the mutual benefits from the community are all the more critical. The Anarresti are shaped not only by Odonian thought but also by the limitations placed on them by their material environment. This lawless society functions partly through "a coordinating system for all syndicates, federatives and individuals who do productive work;" rather than governing bodies, "they administer production" (677). Anarresti society is organized based on Odo's principles of mutual aid and voluntary work as posted through Divlab (the Division of Labor). The communities consist of "workshops, factories, domiciles, dormitories, learning centers, meeting halls, distributories, depots, refectories" (704); the family unit may remain whole, though each partner may choose to leave at any time, and they can leave their child to be cared for in the dormitories and learning centers. The separation of the family unit is "nothing unusual" on Anarres (901), though it affects Shevek's feelings in ways that seem unnatural to Anarresti societal standards.

The apolitical nature of Anarres is jarring to the Oiies, a wealthy Ioti family, at their dinner when Shevek tells them "what the Dust was like, what Abbenay looked like, what kind of clothes one wore, what people did when they wanted new clothes, what children did in school," the last inadvertently becoming propaganda despite Shevek's neutral intentions in informing the children of the world on their moon (733). In response to the patriarch Daemaere Oiie's question concerning what keeps the Anarresti from robbing and murdering each other, Shevek responds:

Nobody owns anything to rob. If you want things you take them from the depository. As for violence, well, I don't know, Oiie; would you murder me, ordinarily? And if you felt like it, would a law against it stop you? Coercion is the least efficient means of obtaining order. (734)

Le Guin illuminates the cultural and moral divide between Shevek and the Oiies, as well as the cultural divide between the Odonian Anarresti and the propertarian Ioti. Similarly, the Anarresti organize their society according to Odo's principles of peace and community, reflecting Le Guin's preference for peace and community over war and individualism. Le Guin discusses the exhaustion she felt from protesting the Vietnam War, only for her country to continue waging wars; this was the impetus for her decision to study peace. She started by "reading a whole mess of utopias and learning something about pacifism [...] this led [her] to nonviolent anarchist writers" for whom she felt an immediate affinity ("Introduction," Le Guin, XIV). Again, one can see here that Le Guin's personal philosophies, informed by her ethical reactions to geopolitical conflicts of the 20th century, influence the fictional philosophical thought of Odo.

Anarres is but one social group inspired by the teachings of Odo; the Urrasti state of Thu also adheres to Odo's teachings, though they have to take a more practical approach because the material conditions they are faced with differ significantly from the material conditions of the Anarresti. The Thuvians share a planet with A-Io, which causes consistent conflict between the two states within the borders of the third Urrasti state, Benbili. The Anarresti do not come into violent conflicts with the Ioti as the Thuvians do because of the spatial distance between Anarres and Urras and the Anarresti's commitment to peace. However, this does not eradicate the attempted political influence the Ioti try to have on the Anarresti. Anarres, in this respect, is neutral to both Urrasti states and vulnerable to their influences.

Though the Odonian ideology on which Anarres is formed is a fictional one, the practice of the stateless society on the resource-poor moon allows for societal and cultural practices that reflect those of the twentieth-century socialist projects that came about as a result of legal equalities afforded to the sexes, as necessitated by material conditions. The socialist revolutions of Russia and China took place in states which, previous to the revolution, practiced semi-feudalism and rampant inequality between the sexes, just as the first Anarresti settlers came from a propertied world that relies on a division of labor based on sex, similar to the division of labor Lenin notices in the bourgeois democracies of the twentieth century. Katherine Cross notes in their essay, "Naming a Star," the "tether of misogyny that connects Anarres to Urras like an umbilical cord" (1334). This is true; misogyny exists within Anarresti culture, though this is not a phenomenon that stems purely from social values but rather from social values dictated by the previous capital-driven economic system of the Urrasti at the time of settlement. These social values and economic infrastructure center misogynistic practices, which then become culturally salient and difficult to remove from a population of acculturated people. As Marx observes in his *Critique of the Gotha Programme*, "What we have to deal with here is a communist society, not as it has *developed* on its own foundations, but, on the contrary, just as it *emerges* from capitalist society; which is thus in every respect, economically, morally, and intellectually, still stamped with the birthmarks of the old society from whose womb it emerges" ("Part One" np) Similarly, the Odonian ideology and Anarresti society emerge from the capitalist society of Urras. They, thus, are still stamped with the birthmarks of the old society, including the misogynistic features of the Urrasti, though the efforts toward equality between the sexes prove to increase the options for women.

To further study this novel with the 20th-century geopolitical context in mind, I intend to engage in a comparative analysis of labor as it is done in each society, the Anarresti and the Urrasti, and existing U.S., Chinese, and Soviet societies on Earth in the twentieth century. This upcoming essay will attempt to initiate a closer study of the degree to which the gender divide dictates labor on each planet, Anarres and Uruas, the division of labor's effect on societal conceptions of the family unit, and the intense labor of child-rearing, which is capable by only one half of each population.

Notes

1. See also "The Day After the Revolution" (Le Guin 975-90).
2. Through Anarres's apoliticism, its lack of legal constraints (or coercions as Shevek refers to them), there is freedom from political constraint.

Works Cited

Asimov, Isaac. Simon Bourgin. "The Essence of Science Fiction."
  Interview with Isaac Asimov (1975). *Airboyd*, 19 Dec. 2011,
  www.youtube.com/watch?v=xUz_KkibYAs. Accessed 11 December
  2024.
Aveling, Edward and Eleanor Marx Aveling. "The Woman Question"

(1886). *Westminster Review*. transcribed by Sally Ryan, *Marxists.org*, 2000. www.marxists.org/archive/eleanor-marx/works/womanq.htm. Accessed 11 December 2024.

Burns, Tony. *Political Theory, Science Fiction, And Utopian Literature*. Lexington Books, Plymouth, 2008, pp. 268-74.

Chinese Communist Party. *The Common Program of the Chinese People's Political Consultative Conference* (1949). *Modern History Sourcebook,* Fordham University, https://origin.web.fordham.edu/halsall/mod/1949-ccp-program.asp, Accessed 11 December 2024.

Cross, Katherine. "Naming a Star: Ursula Le Guin's *The Dispossessed* and the Reimagining of Utopianism." *American Journal of Economics and Sociology*. vol. 77, no. 5 November 2018, pp. 1329-1352.

Engels, Friedrich. "from: Letter to Minna Kautsky, November 26, 1885." *Marx & Engels on Literature & Art*. edited by Lee Baxandall and Stefan Morawski, Telos P, St. Louis/Milwaukee, 1973, pp. 112-113.

---. *Origin of the Family, Private Property, and the State. Marxists.Org*, 2010, www.marxists.org/archive/marx/works/download/pdf/origin_family.pdf. Accessed 11 December, 2024.

---. *Socialism: Utopian and Scientific*. (1892). Pathfinder. 2022. pp. 49-104. Le Guin, Ursula K. "The Day Before the Revolution." *Le Guin Hainish Novels and Stories, sixth edition*. The Library of America, New York, NY, vol. 1, 2017, pp. 975-990.

---. *The Dispossessed* (1974). *Le Guin Hainish Novels and Stories, sixth edition*. The Library of America, New York, NY, vol. 1, 2017, pp. 613-919.

---. "Introduction to *Le Guin Hainish Novels and Stories, sixth edition*." *Le Guin Hainish Novels and Stories, sixth edition*. The Library of America, New York, NY, vol. 1, 2017, pp. xi-xviii.

---. "A Left-Handed Commencement Address." Commencement of Mills College Class of '83, Mills College. May 1983, Oakland, CA. Commencement Speech. www.ursulakleguin.com/lefthand-mills-college. Accessed 11 December 2024.

---. "Speech in Acceptance of the National Book Foundation Medal for

Distinguished Contribution to American Letters." National Book Awards, National Book Foundation, 19 November 2014, Cipriani Wall Street in New York City. Acceptance Speech. www.ursulakleguin.com/nbf-medal. Accessed 11 December, 2024.

Lenin, Vladimir. "On International Working Women's Day" (1919). *On the Emancipation of Women*. Progress Publishers, Moscow, pp. 80-81.

Canadian Communist League. *Study Handbook of Marxism-Leninism-Mao Tsetung Thought*. Montreal, 1978. pp. 190-192.

---. "Soviet Power and the Status of Women" (1919). *On the Emancipation of Women*. Progress Publishers, Moscow, pp. 73-76. *Study Handbook of Marxism-Leninism-Mao Tsetung Thought*. Montreal, Canadian Communist League, 1978. pp. 185-188.

Marx, Karl. "Part One." *Critique of the Gotha Programme* (1875). *Marx/Engels Selected Works*, vol. 3, p. 13-30. www.marxists.org/archive/marx/works/1875/gotha/index.htm, 1999.

Marxists Internet Archive. *Constitution (Fundamental law) of the Union of Soviet Socialist Republics*. Kremlin, Moscow, (1936). Salil Sen (2008). Works, vol. 14, Red Star Press, London, 1978. www.marxists.org/reference/archive/stalin/works/1936/12/05.htm. Accessed 11 December 2024.

Parenti, Michael. *Blackshirts and Reds: Rational Fascism and the Overthrow of Communism*. San Francisco, City Lights Books, 1997.

Thakur, Himali. "Mediated Anarchy in Ursula Le Guin's The Dispossessed." *Configurations*. vol. 32, no. 3, 2024, p. 259-278.

Magneto's Power to Survive the Holocaust: Examining the Fantastic Relationship Between Character and Setting in Greg Pak's *X-Men: Magneto Testament*

Alexander Banks, Hartwell Award Finalist

SUPERHERO COMICS AND COMIC BOOK characters often explore serious and sensitive topics. In academia, scholars are well trained to understand and respond to the important theoretical conversations around any number of these sensitive subjects. For the broader public, then, what lessons are being conveyed, re-interpreted, or perhaps even misinterpreted about these important topics when their first introductions are in superhero stories? Whether they realize it or not, fans of the *X-Men* franchise, and specifically fans of the occasional villain and antihero Magneto, will have no doubt been exposed to important aspects of not only the historical event that was the Holocaust but also to the critical conversations surrounding the representation of the Holocaust in fiction. Greg Pak and Carmine Giandomenico's comic book *X-Men: Magneto Testament* is by far the most thorough and detailed depiction of Magneto's backstory and identity as a Holocaust survivor to date. Scholars can and should use a book such as Pak and Giandomenico's to not only explore the various critical conversations around the Holocaust in comics but also to explore the parts of these important conversations that are bleeding through the stones of the academic ivory tower and out into public awareness.

Pak and Giandomenico were not the first writers to introduce *X-Men* fans to these important critical conversations. In 1981, in *Uncanny X-Men #150*, Chris Claremont revealed a deeper layer to the mutant team's long-standing arch-nemesis, Magneto. Readers discovered just how tormented the villain was by his experiences as a Holocaust survivor when they witnessed the character full of remorse upon fearing he had killed a young Jewish mutant, Kitty Pryde. Magneto, a Holocaust survivor, explained, "I swore then that I would not rest 'til I had created a world where my kind—Mutants—could live free and safe and unafraid, where such as you, little one could be happy. Instead, I have *slain* you" (Claremont, *Uncanny X-Men,* #150, 38). This brief moment had the potential to introduce readers to discussions about survivor's guilt as trauma, but also the complicated discussion around idolizing victims of genocide.

Other scholars have explored writer Chris Claremont's role in fleshing out the character's background. Scott Thompson Smith explored Claremont's development of the character from villain to sympathetic anti-hero in his article "A Likely Jew: Magneto, the Holocaust, and Comic Book History." Smith also contributed to the conversation about Magneto as a paradox: both a Nazi and a Jew. A few years later, Benjamin Morse and Benjamin Burroughs built upon this discussion with their article "Magneto was Right: The Vulgar and Genteel Shaping of a Holocaust Antihero." Their article charts a clearer path of how the character transformed over the years, from Jack Kirby and Stan Lee's original iteration, to Claremont's more nuanced portrayal, as referenced above, to Grant Morrison's darker, more genocidal turn with the character, and finally to Pak and Giandomenico's iteration in *Magneto Testament*.

Morse and Burroughs are two of only a few scholars who have engaged with this specific book in any meaningful analysis. In Smith's aforementioned article and comprehensive review of the character, he only mentions this book in a footnote to explain the history of when the character was first identified as a Holocaust survivor and then eventually confirmed to be specifically Jewish (Smith, 4 and 35).[1] *Magneto Testament* clarifies this aspect of the character's backstory.

If left unsatisfied with Morse and Burroughs's summary and brief analysis of the book, one can find a more thorough and dedicated close reading in Rachel Elizabeth Mandel's thesis "From *Maus* to Magneto: Exploring Holocaust Representation in Comic Books and Graphic Novels." In the midst of her thesis, Mandel takes a closer look at *Magneto Testament*. She concludes that Pak and Giandomenico have successfully hooked *X-Men* fans with the promise of backstory for a beloved character, but then they work hard to downplay the supernatural elements throughout, and to never specifically reference any other characters or aspects of the *X-Men* canon, all to tell the most respectful and historically accurate Holocaust narrative possible.

Much of this essay is a further development of the approach Mandel undertook as part of her thesis, and a much closer and more thorough analysis than scholars such as Smith, Morse, and Burroughs were able to provide when they treated this book as just another benchmark or era in the character's decades-long development. This essay is also a further development of how one might use this book as an educational resource. Brian Kelley wrote a Teacher's Guide for US high school students, grades 7-10 (Kelley, in *X-Men: Magneto Testament*, 139-150). This teaching guide is included at the back of the collected edition, and Kelley's guide goes hand in hand with his short overview of the book, "Rationale for Magneto Testament," in the *SANE Journal: Sequential Art Narrative in Education*. Kelley and Mandel both believe in the appeal and importance of educating the public youth with such a book. This essay takes this mission and asks, why not assess the educational merits of *Magneto Testament* beyond the high school classroom?

In *X-Men: Magneto Testament*, Pak and Giandomenico tell the story of a young man named Max Eisenhardt. The story begins in Nazi Germany in 1935 as the Third Reich is imposing increasingly oppressive restrictions. Max uses his unique superpowers and connection to metal to locate or scavenge for small bits of glinting metal to help his family survive the pre-war era. His father and uncle model different types of resistance philosophies for the young protagonist. Max is ultimately captured and taken to Auschwitz-Birkenau. In the concentration camp, he works as a Sonderkommando, and he participates in the successful mission to blow up Crematorium Four, before eventually escaping.

For this essay, two pivotal scenes stand out as exemplifying Pak and Giandomenico's ability to use both the comic book format and superhero genre to explore Max's relationship with his devastating setting, thereby revealing two slightly different approaches or entry points to important academic and critical conversations. Both scenes exemplify the relationship between Max's subtle and fictional superpowers and the oppressive and horrible real context of the Holocaust.

First, halfway through *X-Men: Magneto Testament*, Chapter Three ends with an execution scene at a mass grave in the forest. By this point, Max and his family have survived and escaped from the Warsaw ghetto. Sadly, Max, his parents, and his sister are all captured and lined up with a large crowd in front of a massive pit. From page 67 to 69, the soldiers shoot the crowd, and Max is able to miraculously stop the bullets from harming him. Up to this point, readers have no reason to believe Max would be sufficiently aware of his abilities to know what he could potentially do with them. Unfortunately, it seems that Max is unaware of the true potential of his abilities, which for this scene function only as a personal survival instinct. He falls into the pit with the other victims. A few panels later, he climbs out. Max then silently wanders around the countryside before eventually being spotted by some soldiers. The only text throughout these three pages is a quote of Max's father's from a few pages earlier. "Sometimes [...] you get a moment [...] when everything lines up. When anything is possible. When suddenly [...] you can make things happen" (Pak 64-68). The hopeful and almost heroic tone of this passage is grimly juxtaposed with the images of a mass execution.

The third and final page to examine in this scene includes six even-sized panels, in a standard two-by-three arrangement, three of which are entirely black. Reading from right to left and down, the black panels are the first, fourth, and fifth, giving the page almost a checkerboard pattern. That said, the other three panels depict very dark images, as well. The first is a wounded Max having just emerged from the grave. Then there is a panel of Max hiding behind a boulder as a wagon full of armed men rolls by. The final panel depicts a bedraggled Max, on his knees in an alleyway, and a man in a suit in the background is pointing Max out to a couple of patrolling soldiers. There is no dialogue or text of any kind on this page. One interpretation of this page could be that the three black panels represent the "holes" in Max's life, now that his father, mother, and little sister have all been killed.

This entire sequence, of not only the execution and the mass grave but also Max's surviving this horrible fate to ultimately find himself captured yet again, is a powerful and memorable sequence, made all the more powerful for how Pak and Giandomenico manipulate their panels to play with readers' perceptions of time and space. Here, the creative team has constructed a powerful sequence in which the *X-Men* comics fan can stumble into an important academic conversation. This scene, and a reader's questions about the techniques used, could introduce the hypothetical reader to comics theory.

Scott McCloud is often the first name referenced in discussions about comics theory, and fans of superhero comics interested in the medium and craft itself may have already read something such as McCloud's *Understanding Comics*. For the execution sequence at hand, McCloud's chapter "Time Frames" is particularly relevant. McCloud explains that, "The panel acts as a sort of general indicator that time or space is being divided. The durations of that time and the dimensions of that space are defined more by the contents of the panel than by the panel itself" (McCloud, *Understanding Comics*, 99). Considering the execution scene, there are two ways in which Pak and Giandomenico are using the horizontal panels stacked on top of each other, close-ups, and minimal text, all to make for two pages in which readers feel as if they are holding their breath, leading up to an entirely different style of presentation on the third page. Readers understand that the action and shooting are happening faster than they are reading these pages, but the organization of the panels and the need to turn the page all add to a slow-motion effect. Pak and Giandomenico have slowed down this scene much as Max has slowed down the bullets, or at least the bullets aimed at him. The contents and shapes of the panels do far more than any text could to convey this painfully drawn-out execution.

Moving beyond these first two pages, and returning to a closer look at the third, with the three black panels, another comics theorist bears mentioning. In his book *The System of Comics,* Thierry Groensteen suggests the entire multi-frame layout of a page should be studied as an organized system constructed to convey meaning beyond simply presenting a series of events.[2] His concepts of restrained arthrology and general arthrology can help readers to pull back their focus and study the aforementioned checkered pattern layout as a whole, and apply this new perspective to their interpretation of the story and its characters. If an *X-Men* fan comes away from *Magneto Testament* wondering how Pak and Giandomenico evoke certain emotions, they might begin some preliminary research online and they might be attracted to study McCloud's more popular *Understanding Comics*. That said, for sequences such as the one analyzed here, Groensteen provides a more appropriate set of analytic terms and concepts.

The final two chapters of the book include even more examples of creative framing and page layouts, but of course as the narrative moves into the Auschwitz-Birkenau concentration camp, there are also far more depictions of shocking violence. Many comics artists, filmmakers, poets, and novelists have attempted to reproduce or depict some sort of realistic rendering of the horrors of a concentration camp. Few, however, have had the opportunity to use the lens of a mutant drawn to metal to shift the focus away from the more graphic depictions of violence, and focus instead on the industrial and metal environment of one of these camps. In using Max's superpower to focus on these aspects of the camp, Pak and Giandomenico engage their readers with the conversation around the Holocaust as an example of the shattered industrial progress and modernity myths of the nineteenth century.

Throughout the novel and the example above, Pak and Giandomenico literally highlight some of the metal objects in Max's environment, emphasizing his connection to these materials. This technique still appears in the final two chapters, though it is really only used to draw attention to the valuable bits of gold and other metal Max finds and exchanges with other prisoners and guards to survive and navigate the politics of the camp. While important to Max's survival, these scenes in which he locates valuable, shining bits of metal are not great examples of the machinery of the industrial camp environment. While those more mechanical and industrial aspects are on full display, they are not made to shine in the same way as the other metals. The glistening effect is only included when Max's relationship with metal can help him to survive and excluded from the depictions of metallic objects that represent modern industrial violence.

Pak and Giandomenico's presentation of the industrial landscape and labor-intensive nature of the Auschwitz-Birkenau camp calls to mind the arguments of Holocaust scholar Omer Bartov on the idea of industrial killing, as explored in his book *Murder in Our Midst*. Just as the execution scene demonstrated *Magneto Testament*'s ability to introduce fans to the comics theory and work of McCloud and Groensteen, this second example provides a similar connection to genocide theory and the work of Bartov.

Within the broader context of the part of the story set in Auschwitz, the specific scene in question occurs in the middle of Chapter 4, pages 85-89. Max's old schoolteacher, Kalb, has been trying to secure a relatively safe work assignment for Max in the camp. Unfortunately, on page 85, Max discovers that he has been assigned a role in the Sonderkommando. At the bottom of the page, Max looks with wide-eyed horror through a doorway wherein he had just observed a guard tossing a basket full of small objects. Upon turning the page, readers are positioned to look into the room along with Max, to discover a massive pile of eyeglasses (Pak, 86-87). Pak and Giandomenico could have chosen a pile of any specific garment or personal object, yet they intrigue their audience with their specific choice to make this a pile full of spectacles. Glasses could be interpreted as a symbol representing a certain level of civilized sophistication and progress: not only the suggestion that medical knowledge is advanced enough to help individuals with their eyesight, but also the associations one may make between the most educated people and the wearing of glasses. For all these glasses, in this collection of superficial decoration and luxury for the wealthy and learned, to be piled in a room, with no shining highlights for Max to connect with, could mean that Pak and Giandomenico are asking their readers to consider what all of these advances in medicine and education actually mean, if they come out of the same concepts of progress and civilization that bring about the Holocaust.

First, however, readers must turn the page, and upon doing so, discover a simultaneously shocking and familiar sight. Pages 88-89 are another splash page, of a sort, with five smaller portrait-shaped panels across the top, and no concern for the spine dividing the pages. One large landscape frame covers the bottom of both pages, and every frame is entirely black, similar to the page referenced earlier, only with a far more dramatic presentation and impact in this instance. There are nine boxes of text carefully placed throughout the black frames, as Max's narration still guides readers from top-left to bottom-right of the page. The text narration concludes, "I saw my fellow workers buried alive under an avalanche of rotting corpses. I saw thousands of murdered people burning in giant outdoor pits. I have seen at least a quarter million dead human beings with my own eyes" (Pak 89). As Max recounts the horrors of working as a Sonderkommando, readers are given the privilege to look away. The horrors are only described in language for these two pages, and not depicted in graphic detail, as they are in the pages to come. From the glasses on the pages before to the final few lines of Max recounting the horrors he has seen, Pak and Giandomenico have woven together a brilliant introduction to conversations around how difficult it is to represent these horrors in a story.

In *Murder in Our Midst*, Omer Bartov explores both the horrific climax of industrial progress that was the Holocaust, and the inherent difficulties of trying to visually represent or reproduce such atrocities. Bartov writes, "Industrial killing was not the dark side of modernity [...] rather, it was and is inherent to it, a perpetual potential of precisely the same energies and ideas, technologies and ideologies, that have brought about the 'great transformation' of humanity" (Bartov, 4). In other words, Bartov argues that an atrocity such as the Holocaust was not a terrible accident or some dark and avoidable issue with so-called modernity, but rather that this type of killing was a persistent and necessary element of the industrializing, modernizing, progressing process, all along. Pak and Giandomenico often portray this industrial killing process, but more importantly for their story about a superpowered individual, they also portray Max's limited ability to resist or fight back against most of the industrial world around him.

There are no scenes of Max, in his rage, warping the metal gates of the camp.[3] There are no scenes of Max using his powers to interfere with the railroad tracks or train-cars, nor are there scenes of him using his powers to dismantle the crematoria. For these reasons, especially in scenes depicting the oppressive industrial environment, readers are left with a feeling of sympathetic hopelessness that this industrial violence is inevitable and unstoppable.

Bartov also explores the difficulties in representing historical violence, both in films and in museums. He does not discuss comics, specifically, but his critiques of various museums and, especially, his critique of the Simon Wiesenthal Center could apply to the work of Pak and Giandomenico, as Pak thanks Mark Weitzman of the Wiesenthal Center in the afterwords to both Issues 1 and 5 (Pak, 120-121). While Weitzman may not represent the institution as a whole, and he may have very little to do with Bartov's critique, the connection is worth considering, as the center is acknowledged in print, in this book made for public audiences. Fans of this book might mistakenly accept this center as the ultimate authority on all things Holocaust history. Should this happen, they would be well advised to consider Bartov's critique: "Instead of representing the phenomenon of industrial killing as a dangerous potential of modernity, the [Wiesenthal Center] exploits the tools of modernity to provide a conformist, passive perception of contemporary conditions, where emotion replaces action and image obscures reality" (Bartov, 9).

Is *Magneto Testament* an example of a place in which "emotion replaces action and image obscures reality?" The sequence in question, one splash page of the pile of glasses followed by another of empty, black panels and haunting narration, all seem to simultaneously comment on and resist such a critique, should it ever be leveled at this comic, itself. This whole sequence, with the depiction of wide-eyed horror, then the glasses taken away from the victims, and then the empty or black panels, serves to suggest an obscured reality. Here, Pak and Giandomenico admit to their inability to depict the reality of the situation. Instead, they use the glasses as a symbol of both an obscured sense of progress when worn, and an obscured and almost absurd vision of reality when removed. They then allow a span of two pages with no images that could possibly be accused of obscuring reality. Of course, following this sequence, they do go on to depict many of the horrors. In juxtaposing a version of representation absent of images with a version full of them, Pak and Giandomenico reveal their real superpowers in engaging readers in this all-important debate around what is or is not appropriate to show when representing the Holocaust.

Pak and Giandomenico have presented a rich and thorough exploration of Magneto's backstory, in which said backstory is not treated as a shocking flashback nor as a few short panels to add a grim contrast to otherwise brightly colored and exciting super-hero action. This essay is a close examination of only two sequences in which Pak and Giandomenico's skills and narrative choices pair nicely with their character's supernatural relationship to the metal in his environment. In doing this, they highlight Max's relationship to and ability to survive the horrors of the

Holocaust. For these reasons, *X-Men: Magneto Testament* serves as a great example of how the fictional, narrative, fantastic, and superhero comic book genres can engage the public with important conversations in ways that standard Holocaust studies scholarship cannot.

Notes

1. Smith discusses the history of Magneto appearances on page 4 of his article, though he does not name Pak's comic book in the article text, proper. Instead, he includes an endnote leading readers to page 35 where they can read about Pak's comic book in endnote 11.
2. Groensteen, *The System of Comics*, 2007. The summary of Groensteen's argument used in this essay only scratches the surface of this rigorously theoretical work, though the summary does capture the essence of the argument as presented in the book's introduction.
3. *X-Men*, 2000. This specific example of a young Magneto bending the metal gate of the concentration camp is referencing the opening scene of Brian Singer's film, the first live-action adaptation of the *X-Men* characters and story.

Works Cited

Baron, Lawrence. "'X-Men' as J-Men: The Jewish Subtext of a Comic Book Movie." *Shofar* vol. 22, no. 1, 2003, pp. 44-52. https://www.jstor.org/stable/42944606. Accessed 30 January 2025.

Bartov, Omer. *Murder in Our Midst: The Holocaust, Industrial Killing, and Representation.*Oxford University Press, 1996.

Budick, Emily Miller. *The Subject of Holocaust Fiction*. Indiana University Press, 2015.

Claremont, Chris. *Uncanny X-Men #150*. Marvel Publishing Inc., 1981.

Groensteen, Thierry. *The System of Comics*. Translated by Bart Beaty and Nick Nguyen.University Press of Mississippi, 2007.

Kelley, Brian. "Rationale for Magneto: Testament." *SANE Journal: Sequential Art Narrative in Education* 1, no. 1, article 7, 2010.

http://digitalcommons.unl.edu/sane/vol1/iss1/7. Accessed 30 January 2025.

Mandel, Rachel Elizabeth. "From *Maus* to Magneto: Exploring Holocaust Representation in   Comic Books and Graphic Novels." BA capstone., Syracuse University, 2015. https://core.ac.uk/download/215706083.pdf. Accessed 30 January 2025

McCloud, Scott. *Understanding Comics: The Invisible Art*. HarperPerennial, 1993.

Morse, Benjamin and Benjamin Burroughs. "Magneto was Right: The Vulgar and Genteel Shaping of a Holocaust Antihero." *Journal of Graphic Novels and Comics*, vol. 14, no. 3, 2023, pp. 426-439. https://doi.org/10.1080/21504857.2022.2138929. Accessed 30 January 2025.

Pak, Greg. *X-Men: Magneto Testament*. Marvel Publishing, Inc., 2009.

Singer, Brian. *X-Men*. Film, 20th Century Fox. 2000.

Smith, Scott Thompson. "A Likely Jew: Magneto, the Holocaust, and Comic Book History." *Studies in American Jewish Literature* vol 36, no. 1, 2017, pp. 1-39. https://doi.org/10.5325/studamerjewilite.36.1.0001. Accessed 30 January 2025

Sterling, Eric J. "The Fantastic Search for Hitler: The Fuhrer's Defense in His Own Words." In *The Fantastic in Holocaust Literature and Film: Critical Perspectives*, edited by Judith B. Kerman and John Edgar Browning. McFarland & Company, Inc., 2015.

Williamson, David G. *The Third Reich*. 5th edition. Routledge, 2018.

Parasitism, Coexistence, and Colonialism in *Animorphs*

Miranda Miller, Hartwell Award Winner

A S JOHN RIEDER EXPLORES in *Colonialism and the Emergence of Science Fiction,* the colonial gaze is the ghost that haunts the development of the science fiction genre. Alien invaders or voyages to alien planets are constantly restaging the act of colonization, with humanity playing either the colonizers or the Native peoples. This colonial ghost is apparent in the 1996–2001 *Animorphs* series. This Scholastic children's literature franchise features a parasitic colonizing species that appears to be a monolithic evil for young protagonists to battle, but author K.A. Applegate goes beyond a simple humans-versus-bad-aliens story. Applegate uses the three primary species of *Animorphs*—humans, Yeerks, and Andalites—to complicate the root colonization-as-alien-invasion narrative by showing how each species embodies a different aspect of a colonizing mindset, and how those aspects prohibit constructive communication and prevent the imagining of possible futures that allow for coexistence.

In *Animorphs*, humanity plays the role of the Native peoples resisting invasion and colonization, though the underpinnings of a colonizing mindset are still present in varying degrees in the human protagonists. Although the initial shock of discovering the crash-landed Andalite Elfangor in the first book starts to disturb the human Animorphs' ethnocentricism, navigating the reality that humanity is one of many alien cultures is an ongoing journey for the series, particularly as it relates to the final member of the Animorphs, the young Andalite Aximili-Esgarrouth-Isthill, nicknamed Ax. Even as humanity resists colonial invasion, the human Animorphs have to deal with their own internalized attitudes and preconceptions that reflect a historically colonizing mindset. As Rieder points out, the trope of the "savage as a remnant of the past" (Rieder 5) can be found in both colonizing and science fiction narratives, and *Animorphs* is no exception. The primary tool that the Animorphs use is the animal-transformation technology that the Andalites have developed. The animal-transformation technology, called morphing technology within the span of the series, allows an individual to transform, or morph, into any animal they have touched. Due to the prevalence of these terms in the *Animorphs* books, future uses of the animal-transformation technology in this essay will be referred to as morphing. As the Animorphs decide to use the Andalites' morphing technology to fight the Yeerks, Cassie, one of the Animorphs, equates the act of using animals for protection with the idea of the past. She says,

> You know, back in the old days – I mean, the real, *real* old days – the Africans, the early Europeans, the Native Americans [...] they all believed animals had spirits. And they would call on those spirits to protect them from evil [...] I guess what we're doing is sort of basic. Even though it was Andalite technology that made it possible [...] Just like thousands of years ago, we're calling on the animals to help protect us from evil. (Applegate *Invasion* 124-125)

The juxtaposition of the futuristic Andalite technology with a sense of humanity's past reflects the pervading Western European colonialist belief that cultures that engage with the idea of animal spirits are in the past—notice that Cassie doesn't mention what African or Native American peoples believe today. Though she's not intentionally disparaging animal spirit beliefs —of all the Animorphs, Cassie is the one most concerned with respect toward the animals they use—the fact that she still equates animism with the past reflects a colonizing mindset, assuming that humanity is meant to grow out of those beliefs with the passage of time.

The Yeerks operate as a colonizing force that brings the horror of colonial control down to the level of the personal. Yeerks are sentient grey slugs who are deaf, blind, and slow swimmers in their natural bodies. However, when they squeeze through a creature's ear and wrap themselves around that creature's brain, they take control of all of that creature's senses and memories, and can operate that body as easily as the creature itself. In this way, the metaphor of a colonial parasite subjugating Native peoples and draining their resources is science fictionally literalized in *Animorphs*. Earth is under attack, and human bodies are both the Native peoples forced under colonial control and the desired resource.

When Yeerks speak, it is with the assuredness of empire. When the leader of the Animorphs, Jake, is taken over by a Yeerk, the Yeerk says to him, "Your body is my home now. Mine. Body and mind, under my control. Forget resistance. It is futile. No host has ever overpowered a Yeerk. It is impossible" (Applegate *Capture* 106). When that same Yeerk dies in Jake's head after the rest of the Animorphs isolate Jake in the woods to starve the Yeerk out, Jake sees visions from the life of the dying Yeerk, and says, "The emotions were strange. Alien. I guess that's the word for them. There was no memory of love. I guess Yeerks don't do love" (Applegate *Capture* 147). In this way, the colonizing Yeerks are made completely alien and strange. They are an evil species that desires parasitic control, and they must be eliminated. But that's the story of Jake and the Yeerk called Temrash One-One-Four—it is not the story of Cassie and Aftran Nine-Four-Two.

Aftran is a Yeerk in the body of a little girl named Karen who discovers Cassie's identity as an Animorph. While lost in the woods together, Cassie tries to convince Aftran to set Karen free, and it becomes clear that Aftran does feel guilt for taking such complete and terrifying control of a child. Lassén-Seger's argument that *Animorphs* portrays childhood as a vulnerable state that must be escaped from in borrowed forms is particularly resonant in Karen's portrayal as a victim (Lassén-Seger 174). Aftran is reluctant to give up her host and her experience of senses such as sight, but in the end, Aftran says, "You ask a lot of me, Cassie the Animorph. You say we can make peace between us, just you and me and Karen. You say we can make a start. And then you ask me to give up everything, while you go on about your life, living amidst splendor and magnificence" (Applegate, *Departure* 118). Cassie makes an equal sacrifice for Aftran by permanently trapping herself in a caterpillar morph, and Aftran keeps her promise by setting Karen free; Cassie is later able to return to her human form via the loophole of the natural metamorphosis of caterpillar to butterfly. Aftran later founds the Yeerk Peace Movement, a group of Yeerks who work with their hosts to try and find a way to have peaceful Yeerk-host relationships (Applegate *Sickness* 40). Aftran and the Yeerks of the Yeerk Peace Movement thereby complicate the prevailing narrative of the Yeerks as monolithic evil conquerors.

Similarly to the humanity portrayed by the Animorphs, the Andalites may not be deliberately seeking to colonize other planets, but they do still embody a mindset of colonizer superiority above other species. The hero of the Andalite Chronicles, the young Elfangor, has preconceived perceptions of other species that he only partway deconstructs over the course of the series. While Elfangor does start out believing humans to be an inherently primitive species, he develops a growing respect and affection for the human Loren. However, for other species, he never loses a sense of Andalite superiority. For example, when his ship, the *StarSword*, sees a Skrit Na ship, the captain tests Elfangor and Arbron, two junior cadets in the Andalite military, by asking what they should do. Arbron responds, "The Skrit Na are smugglers and renegades. And they sometimes serve the Yeerks. So we board the Skrit Na ship and check for any violations" (Applegate *Elfangor's Journey* 15), and that is the answer the captain was looking for. When they are sent out to chase and board the Skrit Na ship, the Skrit Na ship begins shooting at them, and the Andalite cadets respond by damaging the Skrit Na ship's engines. When they board, they follow the standard Andalite procedure of downloading a copy of the boarded alien craft's computer files (Applegate, *Elfangor's Journey* 30), and then leave the damaged ship to float through space and figure out its own repairs (Applegate, *Elfangor's Journey* 33). This belief that the Andalites are entitled to investigate any ship in the galaxy that might be serving the Yeerks, with no sense of reparations for damage done in the investigation, portrays a colonizer's perspective. The Andalites are taught to assume that they have a right to take information from what they consider to be more primitive species for the good of the galaxy.

And yet, for most of the series, the Andalites are portrayed as the long-awaited saviors of humanity. The Animorphs endure the "sense of hopelessness and despair in the face of a nearly impossible" (Earle 221) six-person guerrilla war with the belief that they just have to last until the Andalites come with reinforcements to defeat the Yeerks for good. When Andalites arrive in *The Arrival*, it is a small 4-Andalite team on a mission to assassinate Visser Three—the Yeerk leading the Earth invasion—and a secret mission to deploy a programmable virus that is deadly to Yeerks. The only downside is the chance that the virus could mutate to be deadly to humans as well. The Animorphs manage to stop the Andalite team from releasing the virus, and realize that the Andalites really aren't coming—or if they do come, they aren't going to help humanity. This realization is proven to be correct when the full Andalite reinforcements finally arrive in *The Answer*, intending to destroy Earth in a move that will permanently weaken the Yeerk Empire. Here, Earth becomes merely a tool in the grander war of Andalite versus Yeerk, with the potential staggering loss of human life judged as an acceptable cost for victory. Earth's position as a colonized people would make it pay the highest cost in this war of two opposing colonial powers. To avoid this fate, the Animorphs and their allies manage to defeat the Yeerk command on their own at high personal cost, and they convince the Andalite fleet to stand down.

One of the major issues the characters debate is the issue of access to technology, specifically access to Andalite technology. As Rieder points out, access to technology is one of the main ways of showing the contrast between the colonized who are seen by their colonizers as remnants of the past and the colonizers with their superior technology (Rieder 32). Technology is unevenly distributed, and those who have it are considered by the colonizing culture to be further advanced in a concept of linear time than those who don't have the same technologies. Historically, technological development was a driving force for European imperialist projects and helped lead to "myths of racial and national supremacy" (Csicsery-Ronay 233). As with many science fiction franchises, the Andalites have a non-interference policy with species who haven't attained a certain level of scientific and technological capability, but their reason for enforcing non-interference is not out of a desire to allow natural societal development, but shame. Seerow's Kindness is the great Andalite shame—when an Andalite gave a species faster-than-light technology to allow them to travel the stars. This species was the

Yeerks, and they used it to begin conquering the galaxy. Part of the reason the Andalites fight the Yeerks with such passion is out of the Andalites' sense of guilt for what they have caused, and they swear never to replicate this error. The very act of giving the human Animorphs morphing capabilities was tantamount to Andalite treason, and this potentially treasonous act causes a lot of tension between Ax and his people when he takes the blame for it.

The Andalite determination to keep other species in their own precolonial past and deny them access to Andalite technology is a sort of reverse missionary fantasy. Rather than believing an introduction of alien technology would fulfill the needs of colonized Native peoples, the Andalite command believes that refusing to introduce Andalite-created alien technology would fulfill the needs of Native peoples (Rieder 31). Either way, the belief still comes from a colonialist perspective of the colonizers knowing what is best for a more supposedly primitive species, and the arc of the narrative, as a whole, shows that no species is capable of making correct choices for another species.

Animorphs demonstrates that communication requires productive contact zones. Each narrator of the *Animorphs* series begins with a mindset that is deeply ingrained in their own experience, and that experience makes it challenging to consider other people's—and species's—perspectives accurately. Much of the difficulty in considering other species's perspectives lies in the monolithic othering of those species: in the opinion of humans and Andalites, the Yeerks are monsters. To Yeerks, other species hate them for the biological fact that they are parasites. To Andalites, humans are a primitive species being conquered by a different primitive species that was given too much power. Seeing the world as single-minded others does not allow for accurate or productive communication, and communication is the necessary step to establishing a galaxy that all species can live within.

The third book of the *Andalite Chronicles*, a prequel to the main series, gives an apt metaphor for the Yeerk-human-Andalite struggle that pervades the main series. In *An Alien Dies*, the Andalite Elfangor, human Loren, and Yeerk Visser Thirty-two— who will later be promoted to Visser Three—in an Andalite host, all place their hands on the Time Matrix, a device able to transport beings through time and space. With all three of their influences, they create a horrifying pocket reality that is a jumbled amalgamation of Yeerk, Andalite, and human homeworlds. As Elfangor says, "I think that in order to direct the Time Matrix you need to form a mental image of where and when you want to go. We couldn't do that because all three of us were fighting for control. We each – you, me, Visser Thirty-two – had ideas of where to go. You wanted your home. I wanted mine. I guess he wanted his. Nobody's vision was complete" (Applegate *An Alien Dies* 53). The refusal to listen to each other, much less cooperate, leads to the creation of a terrifying space that collapses under the weight of its own conflict. This moment serves as a microcosm of the galaxy, and the future doesn't look good. As Kodwo Eshun argues, "science fiction is neither forward-looking nor utopian": meaning that, rather than envisioning the future, science fiction reflects a "becoming present" (Eshun 460). The present reality of the Animorphs' galaxy in the *Andalite Chronicles* is that the galaxy's species are unable to envision a possible future because they're so busy fighting each other for present control. And narratively, this inability to imagine a future comes true: in the future, when the Animorphs are granted the morphing technology, nothing has fundamentally changed between Andalites, humans, and Yeerks, and they pick up the stalemated fight right where Elfangor, Loren, and Visser Thirty-two left off.

The first step in establishing productive communication lies in the creation of contact zones, as defined by Mary Louise Pratt. Contact zones are "social spaces where cultures meet, clash, and grapple with each other, often in contexts of highly asymmetrical relations of power, such as colonialism, slavery, or their aftermaths as they are lived out in many parts of the world today" (Pratt 34). *The Alien* deals with the culture clash through Ax's eyes as he adjusts to living in hiding on Earth. Ax attempts to follow the colonizing Andalite policy of studying and learning about humans while not allowing humans to learn about Andalites (Applegate *Alien* 16), but that policy very quickly causes distrust and resentment in the Animorphs who can sense that Ax is keeping valuable information from them. Still, the humans model the communication they want to see from Ax by deliberately introducing him to human spaces such as the mall and their families. The humans create those social spaces where Ax can talk with them as a friend as well as an Andalite researcher, and the strength of that created community is what builds enough trust for Ax to share with them the necessary context of the history of the Yeerks, Andalites, and Seerow's Kindness.

In order for communication to begin, the various species have to enter each other's native environments and planets in a collective act of morphing rather than infestation. The Animorphs' morphing and the Yeerks' parasitic infestation are both methods for traversing a native environment, with different ethical repercussions. The Yeerks can pass through native environments as a semi-native species by taking over a member of that species. The Animorphs can also pass through native environments as a native species, but the morphing technology allows them to create their own DNA-copy of an animal, rather than subjugating an actual member of that species to their will. The complication, however, is that the DNA copies still come prepackaged with animal instincts that the Animorphs have to fight to control each time they morph. An Animorph's first moments in an animal form are usually portrayed as a pushing down of those instincts. Cassie is the Animorph most uncomfortable with morphing more intelligent species, such as dolphins, as the line between instincts and consciousness appears to get thinner. She attempts to navigate this discomfort by both playing with the dolphins to show them what she is doing (Applegate *Message* 150), and by rationalizing that she's morphing dolphins to save them. As Ostry points out, this is "a moment Donna Haraway would like, of human and animal interacting in the same 'contact zone'" (Ostry 418).

A counterpoint to the Animorphs' discomfort with their animal instincts is that the instincts provide a behavioral guide that allows them to pass through various environments without causing unnecessary harm to native species. While the Animorphs have fought rival wolves and confused flocks of birds, as a whole they behave in line with their animal instincts while still pursuing their mission of the day. When the Animorphs are monkeys, they swing through the trees. When they are bats, they fly with the colony. While actual bats might be confused as to why those five bats chose to crawl through a random crevice in their roosting cave, they don't come to actual harm because of the Animorphs. On the other hand, the Yeerks who are obedient to the Yeerk Empire also have a behavioral guide in the form of their host's memories, but only follow the hosts' guides if they are most efficient. If it is more efficient to corner a human in an alleyway and threaten them with a space gun, then that's the policy that Visser Three enforces.

Morphing allows for more coexistence and cooperation between native species and morph-capable individuals, while a Yeerk infestation entails absolute control by the Yeerk over the parasitized native species. Of course, there are exceptions to this in the Yeerk Peace Movement, and there is evidence in the text that the Yeerks could potentially evolve to have mutually fulfilling symbiotic relationships with biologically engineered partner species (Applegate *Attack* 52), but that's not a current solution for Yeerks who desire to have both full bodily autonomy and a body with the ability to enjoy sight and sound and taste. Morphing, however, is a technology that could grant Yeerks that body and that autonomy, without taking away another sentient creature's free will.

But this juncture is where the Andalites' colonizing mindset causes significant damage. As a result of the disastrous repercussions of giving the Yeerks faster-than-light technology in Seerow's Kindness, the Andalites have sworn to never share any type of technology with another species again. The Andalites have made this choice for all other species, and refuse to even think of granting morphing technology to the Yeerks. The inability to communicate and create community with those whom the Andalites colonize has solidified the fact that the Andalites will be unable to make good choices for other species, and it is Cassie, whose empathy has been tested and hard-kept throughout the series, who sees that granting morphing technology to the Yeerks is a possible solution. Ostry observes, "A peaceful end to the conflict is possible[.] [...] Cassie hints at a nonviolent solution, one of compromise and negotiation, a way for the Yeerks to have independent bodies, removing the impetus for war[.] [...] This is a posthuman solution, decentering the human and acknowledging the needs of other species" (Ostry 426). Unfortunately, the Andalite command is not willing to entertain this solution, and the Animorphs have to deal a crushing defeat to the Yeerk Empire resulting in the death of seventeen thousand defenseless Yeerks and significant loss of other sentient life (Applegate *Beginning* 16). It is only after the Animorphs can guarantee that the Yeerks are defeated that they can negotiate with Andalite command as equals, and gain possession of morphing technology to grant the captured Yeerks a permanent alternative form. The solution came, but at great loss of life and under more limitations than if communication had been open from the very start.

While the authors of "Always a War Story" read the arc of *Animorphs* as "a lesson of unresolved tension and loss" (Gracia and Mirra np) that critiques social ills without a sign of a "hopeful speculative future" (Gracia and Mirra np), I argue that there is still hope for the children who read *Animorphs*, if not in the story, then in applying the stories to the real world. K.A. Applegate, who grew up with the Vietnam War as the backdrop for her childhood, wrote what she knew in *Animorphs*. In her letter to the fans after the series' conclusion, Applegate said, "Animorphs was always a war story. Wars don't end happily" ("K.A. Applegate's Response" np). If science fiction is a reflection of the present, then Applegate was writing her present. This war story is children's Time Matrix—a place with no conceivable future. There are no perfectly good aliens or irredeemably bad aliens, and a colonizing mindset only takes away others' choices. But the Time Matrix can be escaped, and technology can be used to allow less harmful navigation of various environments. Colonizing mindsets are present in *Animorphs*, and child readers can learn what consequences those mindsets bring, but children can also learn the steps toward intentional understanding in smaller moments with Cassie and Aftran: the first step towards allowing mutual choice and respect lies in contact zones that foster communication and coexistence.

Works Cited

Applegate, K.A. *An Alien Dies*. The Andalite Chronicles, vol. 3, Scholastic, 1997.

---. *Elfangor's Journey*. The Andalite Chronicles, vol. 1, Scholastic, 1997.

---. "K.A. Applegate's Response to Criticism of Final Animorphs Book." *Hirac Delest: An Animorphs Archive.* https://hiracdelest.com/database/articles/kaa_response_54.htm. Accessed 1 Feb. 2025.

---. *The Alien*. Animorphs, vol. 8, Scholastic, 1997.

---. *The Answer*. Animorphs, vol. 53, Scholastic, 2001.

---. *The Arrival*. Animorphs, vol. 38, Scholastic, 2000.

---. *The Attack*. Animorphs, vol. 26, Scholastic, 1999.

---. *The Beginning*. Animorphs, vol. 54, Scholastic, 2001.

---. *The Capture*. Animorphs, vol. 6, Scholastic, 1997.

---. *The Decision*. Animorphs, vol. 18, Scholastic, 1998.

---. *The Departure*. Animorphs, vol. 19, Scholastic, 1998.

---. *The Invasion*. Animorphs, vol. 1, Scholastic, 1996.

---. *The Message*. Animorphs, vol. 4, Scholastic, 1996.

---. *The Sickness*. Animorphs, vol. 29, Scholastic, 1999.

Earle, Jason, et al. "Chapter 10: 'You Have to Save the Planet,' He Said: Reading the Animorphs." *Counterpoints*, vol. 158, 2004, pp. 205–26. *JSTOR*, http://www.jstor.org/stable/42977356. Accessed 1 Nov. 2024.

Eshun, Kodwo. "Further Considerations on Afrofuturism." *Science Fiction Criticism: An Anthology of Essential Writings*, edited by Rob Latham. Bloomsbury Publishing Plc, 2017. *ProQuest Ebook Central*, https://ebookcentral.proquest.com/lib/fau/detail.action?docID=6210966. Accessed 1 Jan. 2025.

Gracia, Antero and Mirra, Nicole. "Always a War Story: Speculative Pedagogies and Breaking the Narrative of Multicultural Education Possibilities." *Speculative Pedagogies: Designing Equitable Educational Futures*. Teachers College Press, 2023

Istvan Csicsery-Ronay, Jr. "Science Fiction and Empire." *Science Fiction Studies*, vol. 30, no. 2, 2003, pp. 231–45. *JSTOR*, http://www.jstor.org/stable/4241171. Accessed 27 Jan. 2025.

Lassén-Seger. "Child-power? Adventures into the animal kingdom – the Animorphs series." *Children's Literature as Communication*, p 159-176. John Benjamins Publishing Company, 2002.

Ostry, Elaine. ""Billions of Lives Weighed Against the Ethics of Six 'Kids ...'": The Moral Universe of the Animorphs." *Children's Literature Association Quarterly*, vol. 48 no. 4, 2023, p. 412-434. *Project MUSE*, https://dx.doi.org/10.1353/chq.2023.a930099. Accessed 1 Feb. 2025.

Pratt, Mary Louise. "Arts of the Contact Zone." *Profession*, 1991, pp. 33–40. *JSTOR*, http://www.jstor.org/stable/25595469. Accessed 1 Nov. 2024.

Rieder, John. *Colonialism and the Emergence of Science Fiction.*
Middletown, Connecticut. Wesleyan University Press, 2008.

Is *Dracula* Anti-Semitic?

Steven Brehe

I S *DRACULA* ANTI-SEMITIC? This question was raised by Jack Halberstam, writing that, in the novel *Dracula* (1897), "[t]he vampire merges Jewishness and monstrosity" (Halberstam 14). Bram Stoker's character, Halberstam writes, "embodies and exhibits all the stereotyping of nineteenth-century anti-Semitism": Dracula's "peculiar physique, his parasitical desires, his aversion to the cross and to all the trappings of Christianity, his blood-sucking attacks, and his avaricious relation to money, resembled stereotypical anti-Semitic nineteenth-century representations of the Jew" (Halberstam 14, 86).[1] Halberstam's conclusion has often been repeated, as in *Anti-Semitism: A Historical Encyclopedia* and in *The Cambridge Companion to* Dracula. Nadia Valman writes that "Dracula can be read [. . .] as a monstrous composite of a number of fin-de-siecle discourses, including antisemitism" (Valman 188), while Anthony Bale puts the matter more strongly: Halberstam "has influentially identified [. . .] Bram Stoker as a likely anti-Semite" (Bale 106). David Glover writes that, of the "attempts to give the Count a Jewish profile and to argue that anti-Semitism is integral" to horror fiction, Halberstam makes "the fullest and most convincing case" (Glover 91). Clive Leatherdale, in his critical edition, finds "the spectre of anti-Semitism in *Dracula*" (Leatherdale 268, n. 57). Among scholars, then, one of the most popular and influential Gothic novels, is now regarded as a book of hatred: "a strain of anti-Semitism [. . .] runs through the book" (Stoker *Dracula* Luckhurst's edition 390, n. 324; see also 370-371, n. 40).[2]

But is this assessment true? This is the reasonable but long-delayed question that this essay addresses. Considering Stoker's text, Halberstam set portions of the novel in the context of anti-Semitic caricature and stereotype; in that context, in such a comparison, those portions may indeed appear anti-Semitic. But if one considers those portions in other relevant contexts, one finds reason to doubt. The idea that *Dracula* is anti-Semitic is based partly on questionable readings of several passages in the novel, passages that require re-examination.

It has been argued that a passage in Chapter 26 of *Dracula* is overtly anti-Semitic. Jonathan Harker and Van Helsing seek out an official at the port in Galatz, Romania:

> We found Hildesheim in his office, a Hebrew of rather the Adelphi type, with a nose like a sheep, and a fez. His arguments were pointed with specie—we doing the punctuation—and with a little bargaining he told us what he knew. This turned out to be simple but important. He had received a letter from Mr. de Ville of London, telling him to receive, if possible before sunrise, so as to avoid customs, a box which would arrive at Galatz in the *Czarina Catherine*. This he was to give in charge to a certain Petrof Skinsky, who dealt with Slovaks who traded down the river to the port. (Stoker *Dracula* ch. 26, 319)

"A Hebrew of rather the Adelphi type": Harker finds that Immanuel Hildesheim resembles characterizations typical at the Adelphi Theatre of London; the phrase is significant because Stoker worked for decades in London's theatrical world. The

Adelphi was "infamous for cheap, 'blood-and-thunder' melodrama" (Steinmeyer 52), relying on crowd-pleasing formulas and stock characters:

> Though spectacle was not lacking, stirring sentiment proved their stock in trade, and unlike the Drury Lane performer, the Adelphi actor was given his head to rouse the men by his athleticism and enchant the women by his looks. (Rowell 142–143)

A critic for the *Athenæum* magazine once panned one of Stoker's books by suggesting that its "stilted phrases were better 'adapted for the Adelphi stage'" (quoted in Steinmeyer 52). Harker's remark about Hildesheim acknowledges that the Adelphi characterization does not reflect the reality of an entire people, but is a theatrical shorthand, a readily recognized stereotype of the sort common at the Adelphi—as I might say that I met a Southerner who resembled the Hollywood version of the rural Anglo-American working class. The remark may be unflattering to the individual, but it implicitly recognizes that the stereotype misrepresents the group. This recognition of a theatrical stereotype is nothing like the thinking of actual anti-Semites.

It has been argued that the Hildesheim passage (his words "pointed with specie") represents the stereotypical assumption of avarice as a characteristic of Jews, but Hildesheim is one of many minor characters in *Dracula* who accept money for information. In Chapter 11, a London reporter pays the zookeeper for his story about the escaped wolf (Stoker *Dracula* 135). In Chapter 17, Harker pays laborers at the Whitby train station and at King's Cross to learn about Dracula's boxes of earth and pays movers to tell him about the delivery to Carfax (Stoker *Dracula* 213–214). In Chapter 20, he pays the mover Smollet for information about his deliveries and then buys information from a deputy in Potter's Court, from "a surly gatekeeper and a surlier foreman," and from another mover (Stoker *Dracula* 244–245). Later, a real estate agent refuses to answer Harker's questions or compromise his client's privacy: "The affairs of their clients," the agent sniffs, "are absolutely safe in the hands of Mitchell, Sons & Candy." So, Harker suggests that cooperation may bring the agency lucrative business with Lord Godalming; Mitchell, Sons & Candy soon tell all they know (Stoker *Dracula* ch. 20, 247, 253). Quincy Morris and Van Helsing pay a functionary at Doolittle's Wharf to guide them to dock laborers, and pay the laborers to tell about the departure of the *Czarina Catharine* (Stoker *Dracula* ch. 24, 291). In *Dracula,* buying and selling information is common among Gentiles.

A few pages before the Hildesheim passage, Harker, now in Budapest, writes, "We think that we shall not have much trouble with officials or the seamen. Thank God! this is the country where bribery can do anything and we are well supplied with money" (Stoker *Dracula* ch. 25, 306). Although he has recently paid ten or more Englishmen for information, Harker speaks of bribery as a practice distinct to Eastern Europe. Here, surely, Stoker is ironic about the ways stereotypes distort perceptions of others—and of self—and he makes the point again immediately after the Hildesheim passage. After Hildesheim sends Harker to Petrof Skinsky, Harker learns that Skinsky has been murdered, "and that the throat had been torn open as if by some wild animal." Harker reports, "Those we had been speaking with ran off to see the horror, the women crying out, 'This is the work of a Slovak!'" (Stoker *Dracula* ch. 26, 319–320). But readers know that no Slovak is guilty. What does the women's outcry accomplish but to remind readers how stereotype and ethnic hostility mislead?

If Stoker intends Harker's description of Hildesheim to be anti-Semitic, why does he include the words "of rather the Adelphi type"? If Stoker intends readers to find Hildesheim avaricious because he sells information—specifically, the name of the person who picked up a crate recently arrived at the port—why does he make Hildesheim the last of a series of characters who do the same? How avaricious is Hildesheim compared with Mitchell, Sons & Candy? The sea captain Donelson, the German-Jewish Hildesheim in his fez, the Slav Petrov Skinsky: these characters, appearing in that order, serve as narrative signposts that Harker and his companions pass, marking their way eastward more dramatically than place names such as Galatz, Fundu, or Veresti. Further, when Hildesheim gives Harker Skinsky's name, the moment serves another narrative purpose: the reader anticipates that Harker and his companions are about to catch up with Dracula, until Skinsky's murder indicates that Dracula has again eluded them.

In *Dracula*, Stoker makes other references to actual people who are Jewish, and not merely literary characters: Mina Harker cites (to Van Helsing's approval) the ideas of Hungarian Zionist and social critic Max Nordau and Italian criminologist Cesare Lombroso, both Jewish (Stoker *Dracula* ch. 25, 313). She uses their ideas to prove that Dracula is a criminal type (as if that required proof). She refers indirectly to Nordau's best-known work, *Degeneration* (1892), wherein he declared anti-Semitism a symptom of personal and cultural decline:

> German hysteria manifests itself in anti-Semitism, that most dangerous form of the persecution-mania, in which the person believing himself persecuted becomes a savage persecutor, capable of all crimes (the *persécuté persécuteur* of the French mental therapeutics). (Nordau 209)

Stoker, through Van Helsing, also refers to the Jewish academic Arminius Vámbéry, whom I discuss below.

In Chapter 17, Harker tracks down one of the laborers who delivered boxes to Carfax. The laborer, after accepting money, recalls his impressions:

> 'That 'ere 'ouse, guv'nor, is the rummiest I ever was in. Blyme! But it ain't been touched sence a hundred years. There was dust that thick in the place that you might have slep' on it without 'urtin' of yer bones; an' the place was that neglected that yer might 'ave smelled ole Jerusalem in it. But the ole chapel—that took the cike, that did!' (Stoker *Dracula* ch. 17, 214)

It has been argued that the reference here to "ole Jerusalem" is an anti-Semitic remark, a version of the old slander about racial odor, the "fetor judaicus" (Halberstam 96; cf. Trachtenberg 47–49). But the full context clarifies: it is the odor of a long-enclosed space that the laborer recalls from the deserted building, and certainly not the odor of Dracula, who had not yet inhabited the place when the laborers arrived. Victorian readers would have recognized Jerusalem as the holiest city of Judaism and Christianity, the most sacred destination of Christian pilgrims, and, because of religious observance and education, the oldest city many European people knew. Probably no Victorian reader associated Jerusalem with bad smells.

It has been argued that Stoker's description of Dracula resembles in several features the grotesque physical stereotype promoted by anti-Semites. These features reveal, David Skal writes, "the tacit anti-Semitism in Dracula's physical appearance" (Skal 373). But consider one of Stoker's descriptions of Dracula in Chapter 2:

> His face was a strong—a very strong—aquiline, with high bridge of the thin nose and peculiarly arched nostrils; with lofty domed forehead, and hair growing scantily round the temples, but profusely elsewhere. His eyebrows were very massive, almost meeting over the

nose, and with bushy hair that seemed to curl in its own profusion. The mouth, so far as I could see it under the heavy moustache, was fixed and rather cruel-looking, with peculiarly sharp white teeth; these protruded over the lips, whose remarkable ruddiness showed astonishing vitality in a man of his years. For the rest, his ears were pale and at the tops extremely pointed; the chin was broad and strong, and the cheeks firm though thin. The general effect was one of extraordinary pallor. (Stoker *Dracula* ch.2, 27)

These features are suggestive of a predatory animal: the teeth, the hands like claws, the nose aquiline, like an eagle's beak. In Chapter 21, the physician John Seward compares Dracula to "a wild beast" (Stoker, *Dracula* ch. 21, 261) and later describes him as "panther-like," "unhuman," "lion-like," and snarling (Stoker *Dracula* ch. 23, 281). If Dracula resembles any anti-Semitic stereotype, it is because both his image and the stereotype contain bestial features. Each representation, vampire and stereotype, has been created independently to resemble a well-known figure of myth and scripture.

Devils are represented with the features of animals in many paintings and illuminations from medieval and early modern art: Giorgi reproduces works representing devils as dragons (Giorgi 156-162) or as bizarre beasts (Giorgi 28-32, 75-76, 92; cf. Graf, 42, 108, 116, 151). The Hellmouth, the gateway to Hell, is customarily represented as the jaws of an immense predator, as in the twelfth-century illumination reproduced by Giorgi (33; see also Graf, 173-175). These monstrous images emerge from the belief that devils, as rebels against God, may no longer exist in the image of God, the human-divine form, nor may they take permanently the forms of animals, which are also works of the Creator. And so, devils are customarily represented in European literature and the visual arts in fantastic and absurd forms, as semi-human predators with tails, horns, sharp teeth and claws, pointed ears, hawkish beaks, cloven hooves, bat wings, and other predators' features. According to Strickland, who offers many examples (Strickland 61–65, 77–78), such images are "the most striking and consistent feature of demons in medieval art [. . .] To fashion a devil," she writes, "medieval artists combined features of all God's creatures into a hideous hodgepodge" (Strickland 61).

According to Sara Lipton, a commonplace feature is a hooked nose, turned upwards or down: "Long or large, downward-curved, snout-like or beak-like noses, especially when combined with brutish expressions and shaggy beards, had long served as visual indictor of bestiality, brutality, irrationality, and evil," Lipton writes (Lipton *Dark Mirror* 107-108; cf. Strickland 122). Lipton offers examples from the late twelfth century, an image of a devil in a stained-glass window and a manuscript capital portraying brutish Syrians battling the Maccabees. On the significance of noses in medieval Christian art, Strickland finds that "to the Christian moralists, crooked noses signify those who cannot take the correct path to God" (Strickland 77):[3]

> That this same feature is also observable in images of non-Jewish negative figures, such as executioners and torturers of saints [. . .] is another reason not to see an exaggerated, hooked nose solely as a mark of Jewishness. Noses provided artists with one of many points of contrast in their efforts to physically differentiate the good figures from the evil ones. In any case, it is the demonic identification that remains consistent in both form and meaning in negative images of Jews and other negative figures. (Strickland 77–78)

Those who, in the eyes of the Church, did the Devil's work were made to resemble the Devil (Lipton 107-108). Both Dracula and anti-Semitic stereotypes have been shaped independently to resemble demons.

Stoker deliberately emphasizes Dracula's association with the Devil, most emphatically in the very name *Dracula* (Stoker *Drafts* 25–26), with its etymological connection with the Romanian word "drac": "devil," derived from Latin "draco," "dragon." Charles Darling Buck records similar verbal associations between "devil" and "dragon" in other Indo-European languages (Buck 22.34). Stoker pointedly begins his novel on the feast day of St. George, the saint and dragon-slayer, and he causes Dracula to be repelled, like the Devil, by sacred objects such as crucifixes (Russell, *Satan* 175; *Lucifer* 51).

During the European Enlightenment and after, belief in Hell and devils faded, and images of devils became less monstrous and more acceptable in secular contexts. The range of bestial features were reduced to those several that remain familiar now – the horns, hooves, and tail; the glowing eyes, sharp teeth, aquiline nose, and pointed ears; sometimes a moustache and goatee – and often, only a few of these. An early example appears in *The Temptations of Saint Francis of Assisi*, c. 1610, a painting by Giovanni Mauro della Rovere and reproduced in Giorgi (Giorgio 132). In this more human form, the Devil becomes a familiar figure in nineteenth- and early twentieth-century advertisements. Jeffrey Burton Russell reproduces an image from 1856, used on the packaging for a toy (Russell *Mephistopheles* 203). A similar image appears in an advertising lithograph for *Fil au Démon* sewing thread, circa 1885 (Graf 246). Stage magicians of the era made frequent use of the Devil in their advertising to represent their performances as mysterious and other-worldly, as in the 1894 theatrical poster "Kellar and His Servants" and the 1900 poster "Kellar's Wonders." Well into the twentieth century, stage magicians used similar advertisements, and in most of these the resemblance to Dracula is obvious: the glowing eyes, pointed ears, aquiline nose, and sharp teeth. The graphic artists and publishing houses that produced these images drew from a commonly held notion of devils that Stoker also employed when he described Dracula.

In his *Personal Reminiscences of Henry Irving*, published in 1906, a year after Irving's death, Stoker recalled his years working with Irving, and his observations as Irving prepared for performance. Here, Stoker describes Irving preparing for *The Merchant of Venice*, which Irving first performed in 1879:

> Though I have seen it done a hundred times I could never really understand how the lips thickened, with the red of the lower lip curling out and over after the manner of the typical Hebraic countenance; how the bridge of the nose under his painting—for he used no physical building-up—rose into the Jewish aquiline; and, most wonderful of all, how the eyes became veiled and glassy with introspection—eyes which at times could and did flash like lurid fire. (Stoker *Reminiscences* vol. 1, 139–40)

This description of Irving's Shylock makeup has moved some readers to renew the argument that Stoker's description of Dracula is anti-Semitic: pointing to these details, M. L. Malchow writes, quite accurately, "Eyes that flash, red lips, and aquiline nose are characteristics Stoker gave Count Dracula" (Malchow 155–56). But Stoker's description of Shylock as played by Henry Irving resembles Dracula because Dracula was a part that Stoker hoped would someday be played by Henry Irving. With his description of Dracula, Stoker is, in a sense, writing for an audience of one, the actor himself, offering a character that Irving might readily create with makeups he had used in other roles, including Mephistopheles in a version of Goethe's *Faust*. Frederick Donaghey, reviewing in 1929 a stage adaptation of *Dracula*, recalls Stoker telling him that he wrote *Dracula* to provide a play for Irving: "The Governor [Irving] as Dracula would be the Governor in a composite of so many of the parts in which he has been liked,"

Stoker told Donaghey of the *Chicago Tribune*, "Matthias in 'The Bells,' Shylock, Mephistopheles, Peter the Great [. . .] and ever so many others [. . .][.] But he just laughs at me!"[4] (Donaghey 37).

This can be confirmed by turning to descriptions of characters Irving played using similar makeups. Here, Stoker describes Irving in an early performance of *Vanderdecken*, W. G. Wills's 1878 adaptation of the *Flying Dutchman* story:

> It was marvelous that any living man should show such eyes. They really seemed to shine like cinders of glowing red from out the marble face [. . .][.] [Here Stoker quotes from a review he wrote at the time.] 'In his face is the ghastly pallor of the phantom Captain and in his eyes shines the wild glamour of the lost in his every tone and action there is the stamp of death [. . . .] The chief actor is not quick but dead.' (Stoker *Reminiscences* vol. 1, 56)

And here Stoker describes Irving as Don Quixote (1895): "His own physique tall and lean, his fine high-bred features heightened by the resources of art to an exaggerated aquiline, all helped to the efficacy of the illusion" (Stoker *Reminiscences* vol. 1, 256-257). The tall, lean physique, the pallor, red lips, red eyes, and aquiline nose all appear in Stoker's descriptions of Dracula.[5]

In his *Reminiscences*, Stoker also describes Irving's role as host at scores of grand dinners. Stoker lists many of the guests, twelve pages of names in no discernible order (Stoker *Reminiscences* vol. 1, 315-326), compiled from his handwritten notes made in the moment, among them prominent people, Gentile and Jew. To illustrate: the hundreds of British guests across the years included the Prince of Wales (later Edward VII), Prime Minister William Gladstone, Lord and Lady Randolph Churchill (Winston Churchill's parents), artists John Tenniel and Edward Burne-Jones, historian and physician Bruce Seton, explorer and translator Richard Burton, playwrights James M.

Barrie, W. S. Gilbert, and George Bernard Shaw, composer Arthur Sullivan, poet laureate Alfred, Lord Tennyson, and authors Arthur Conan Doyle, Thomas Hardy, and Oscar Wilde.[6]

Irving's Jewish guests, as recorded by Stoker, included Zionist Israel Zangwill, banker Alfred de Rothschild, businessmen Alfred Beit, Arthur Frankau, and Barney Barnato, publisher William Heinemann, concert pianists Ilona Eibenschutz and George Henschel, linguist and spy Arminius Vámbéry, actors Leopold Teller and Sarah Bernhardt, managers of the New York Metropolitan Opera Maurice Grau and Heinrich Conreid, a "Prof. Brodsky" who is perhaps Adolph Brodsky the concert violinist and teacher, and theatrical producers David Belasco and Charles and Daniel Frohman.

In the *Reminiscences*, Stoker recalls his impressions of some of these guests. He gives a short chapter to legendary actor Sarah Bernhardt (1844–1923), who for four decades was an international celebrity and an international target of anti-Semitic caricature and slander. Stoker's accounts of her are consistently glowing: "She was always charming and fresh and natural. Every good and fine instinct of her nature seemed to be at the full when she was amongst artistic comrades whom she liked and admired. She inspired everyone else and seemed to shed a sort of intellectual sunshine around her" (Stoker *Reminiscences* vol. 1, 166).

An objection could be raised that Stoker's praise of Bernhardt may have been hypocritical, a pretense designed to gain favor and financial advantage from some hypothetical future theatrical association with her even though there never was such a project. Stoker, however, was on good terms with Jewish figures a good deal less eminent than Bernhardt, people who could never have rewarded him for his friendship. In the *Reminiscences*, for example, he reports having dinner in 1881 with a party that included Leopold Teller, a Jewish Hungarian and, he writes, "a fine actor." Later that year he dined again with Teller and others:

"Another delightful gathering about that time [. . .] a supper given by [John Lawrence] Toole. Amongst the guests were Irving [. . . and] Leopold Teller [. . . . E]very one wanted to hear what everyone else said. So the conversational torch went round the table − like the sun, or the wine" (Stoker *Reminiscences* vol. 1, 153). Teller was a respected actor but never a wealthy man or a star like Bernhardt, and he was in England only a short while before returning to the Continent. When Stoker published these words in 1906, Teller had, years before, retired from the stage to teach ("Teller").

Stoker gives a short chapter (Stoker *Reminiscences* vol. 1, 371-372) to the remarkable Arminius Vámbéry, traveler, spy for the Empire, and professor of languages at the Royal University of Budapest: "He is a wonderful linguist, writes twelve languages, speaks freely sixteen, and knows over twenty." And again: "He soared above all the speakers, making one of the finest speeches I have ever heard"; "he shone out as a star!" The two met in 1890, about the time Stoker was beginning *Dracula*, and possibly Vámbéry gave Stoker useful information, perhaps about eastern European customs or beliefs, for he found his way into the novel, when Van Helsing twice refers to valuable information provided by "my friend Arminius, of Buda-Pesth University" (ch. 18, 225; ch. 23, 278). Vámbéry writes in his memoirs, published in English (1904), that he suffered anti-Semitic slurs even from his university colleagues, who questioned his competence (Vámbéry vol. 2, 263). Stoker's praise in the *Reminiscences*, published two years later, could be, in part, an effort to defend him, but could not have been a ploy to gain favors from him, for Vámbéry, as an academic in Hungary, was in no position to offer any.

Stoker has been accused of anti-Semitism because of his alleged friendship with the explorer and translator Sir Richard Burton (1821–1890), who wrote an anti-Semitic work that was never published.[7] Stoker includes a short chapter about Burton in his *Reminiscences*, and, in what he records, there is little evidence of a close friendship; instead, Stoker writes about a controversial and accomplished man who was a fascinating topic for readers even years after his death. Here, Stoker describes Burton as he laughs: "Burton's face seemed to lengthen when he laughed; the upper lip rising instinctively and showing the right canine tooth" (Stoker *Reminiscences* vol. 1, 355). This canine-baring feature of Burton's Stoker chooses to attribute to Dracula in Chapter 2: "The Count smiled, and as his lips ran back over his gums, the long, sharp, canine teeth showed out strangely" (24). In this feature of baring his canine teeth when he smiles, Dracula resembles not an anti-Semitic stereotype, but an actual anti-Semite.

In the same chapter of *Reminiscences*, Stoker recounts two "delightful meetings" with Burton and his wife in 1886, and he repeats a story Burton had denied for years:

> There were passages in his life which set many people against him. I remember when a lad hearing of how at a London dinner-party he told of his journey to Mecca [. . .][.] He had to pass as a Muhammedan [. . .] and suspicion at such a time and place would be instant death. In a moment of forgetfulness, or rather inattention, he made some small breach of rule. He saw that a lad had noticed him and was quietly stealing away [. . . . C]oming after the lad in such a way as not to arouse his suspicion [he] suddenly stuck his knife into his heart. When at the dinner he told this, some got up from the table and left the room. It was never forgotten. (Stoker *Reminiscences* vol. 1, 358–359)

Despite Burton's many denials across intervening years, Stoker, as he tells it, asked Burton about the story:

> He said it was quite true, and that it had never troubled him from that day to the moment he was speaking [. . .][.] As he spoke the

upper lip rose and his canine tooth showed its full length like the gleam of a dagger. (Stoker *Reminiscences* vol. 1, 359)

This is not a friendly observation on Stoker's part.[8]

Association cannot prove guilt—or innocence—but association can reveal character. If Stoker's friendships may be considered to reveal more about his opinions on anti-Semitism or tolerance, instead of Burton one might consider Stoker's admiration for, and long working relationship with, Henry Irving, whose portrayal of Shylock in *The Merchant of Venice* was hailed as one of his great achievements. A critic for the *Chicago Tribune* wrote,

> Praise has already been accorded Irving's Shylock, because it is a type of the medieval Jew, interpreted, not according to the traditions of a bigoted age, but in the light of the liberality of the nineteenth century. This creation is, perhaps, the best proof of the assertion that Henry Irving has embodied in his art the spirit of his age, and therein lies his greatness. (qtd. by Hatton 333)[9]

Irving's first important theatrical success was a role he chose for himself, in Leopold Lewis's *The Bells*, premiered in 1871 and performed hundreds of times. Irving played an innkeeper, crushed by debt, who murders an innocent Jewish traveler for his money after the traveler's last words to the innkeeper, as he leaves the inn, are "God bless you" (Mayer 73). Later, during the murder, the innkeeper urges himself on and rationalizes the crime by repeating anti-Semitic expressions to himself. Years after, increasingly anxious and haunted by guilt, represented in the play by the auditory hallucination of the traveler's sleigh bells, the murderer collapses and dies on the day of his daughter's wedding. The murder takes place on Christmas morning; the young man marrying the daughter, and asking upsetting questions about the crime, is a police officer named Christian. The play is an implicit critique of Christian anti-Semitism.

One may consider Stoker's long friendship with Hall Caine (1853-1931), whose popular novel *The Scapegoat* (1891) sympathetically examined the lives of persecuted Jews in Morocco. According to Vivien Allen, when Caine's publisher asked for a one-volume edition of the novel, it was Stoker who negotiated favorable terms for Caine. After *The Scapegoat* was published, Hermann Adler, Chief Rabbi of the British Empire and chairman of the Russo-Jewish Committee, asked Caine to travel to Poland and Russia to report on the massacres of Jews there (Allen 214– 21).[10] Until Stoker's death in 1912, Caine was a close friend: Stoker dedicated *Dracula* to him, and in 1901 Caine dedicated a story collection to Stoker, asserting the value of their long friendship and praising "his simplicity, his unselfishness and his honour" (qtd. in Kenyon 125–126). To believe that Stoker, deliberately or unaware, employed an offensive Jewish stereotype in *Dracula* requires one to believe that Caine was unable to see potential anti-Semitism in Stoker or unwilling to object to it.

The belief that *Dracula* is anti-Semitic has found a place in reference works, scholarly articles, and critical editions. But opinions of the book are thereby much distorted: if *Dracula* is widely considered an anti-Semitic work, for that reason, perhaps, some may have chosen not to read it, and educators may have chosen not to teach it; ignorance of the work sows further misunderstanding rather than contextual analysis. Moreover, as a text for critically examining intolerance, *Dracula*, which has been accused of communicating intolerance, can instead be used to teach critical discernment.

Stoker seems to have left no explicit statement of his opinions on tolerance or anti-Semitism, or on almost any personal matter; his biographer Belford found that he "frustrated intimate probing; his reticence was monumental" (Belford xi). As he describes his life and work with Irving, however, one sees a cosmopolitan, interesting and demanding life, and, apparently, a life of tolerance for ethnic and religious differences. One might expect Stoker, raised in the Church of Ireland, to be by his era and upbringing anti-Catholic, but in a journal entry from about 1877 he criticizes his mother's anti-Catholicism (146). And in *Dracula*, Jonathan Harker, receiving a crucifix from an old woman, remarks that, "as an English Churchman, I have been taught to regard such things as in some measure idolatrous." But later Harker remembers her gift with gratitude (Stoker *Dracula* ch. 1, 15; ch. 3, 36-37). Still later, in Chapters 8 and 9, Harker is a patient in the Hospital of Saints Mary and Joseph in Budapest; his fiancé Mina corresponds gratefully with a nun there about his health. The captain of the *Demeter* is Catholic; so is Abraham Van Helsing. These details reveal in Stoker greater religious tolerance than existed among many Irish Protestants of his time.

Stoker's apparent tolerance of religious diversity and sexual difference is demonstrated by his long friendship with Walt Whitman. When many considered parts of *Leaves of Grass* obscene, Stoker argued for the beauty and importance of the poetry, though he later tried to persuade Whitman to remove the more controversial passages from new editions. Whitman refused (Stoker *Reminiscences* vol. 2, 94–97, 106-107). Stoker nevertheless visited Whitman during Irving's tours of America, and they remained friends until the poet's death. "I found him all that I had ever dreamed of," wrote Stoker. He was "large-minded, broad-viewed, tolerant to the last degree; incarnate sympathy; understanding with an insight that seemed more than human" (Stoker *Reminiscences* vol. 2, 92–111).[11] As at other points in his life, Stoker's relationship with Whitman, who seems to have been an agnostic religious individualist, shows that Stoker was neither intolerant of religious diversity nor a man of rigid adherence to Protestant Christian moral beliefs.

For Stoker, Dracula resembles the Devil. For anti-Semites, Jews resemble the Devil. And so, Dracula resembles, in some ways, the anti-Semitic stereotype current when and where Stoker wrote. However, this essay has demonstrated that nothing about the atmosphere in which Stoker wrote makes Stoker resemble avowed anti-Semites. That the accusations against Stoker and his book have been so long accepted is a measure of how far lore about the Devil has receded from collective current memory. Nineteenth-century readers, whatever their religious opinions, would more likely have recognized Stoker's allusions and perhaps read them more readily as metaphor. Unless better evidence is brought forward, Bram Stoker should not be considered an anti-Semite, nor should *Dracula* be accused of being a book reflecting or advancing anti-Semitism.

Notes

[1] Jack Halberstam first published the article in *Victorian Studies*; it has been reprinted in Halberstam's book *Skin Shows* (from which I cite), in Ledger and McCracken's collection, 248–266, and in the 2021 Norton Critical Edition of *Dracula*. For the convenience of readers consulting other editions of *Dracula*, in citing the Norton edition I give both chapter and page.

[2] Other scholars accept these conclusions, including Skal (in the first and second Norton Critical Editions of *Dracula*, Auerbach and Skal, eds., 373; Browning and Skal, eds., 411), Beal (127), and Malchow (153–61).

[3] Alfred David, surveying physiognomic texts and interpretations, explains that, across history, the meaning of facial features has changed with writers' purposes and their eras' cultural assumptions, with no fixed association with any ethnic group or character.

[4] Wynne cites letters in which Stoker discussed a possible dramatization of the book for Irving. She points out that Stoker's first public read-through of a rough stage version (in 1897) was performed when Irving's

career was at a low point (Wynne "*Dracula* on Stage" 165, 169, 176; cf. Irving 600, 607).

5 On Stoker's use of the aquiline nose in his other fiction, to describe other (non-Jewish) characters, Skal writes "[Stoker's] sinister characters repeatedly take the form of human raptors [. . . .] It is sometimes hard to determine whether Stoker was invoking a persistent archetype or just indulging in lazy writing" (Skal *Something* 436).

6 Shaw, Wilde, and the Prince of Wales do not appear in Stoker's list, but Belford finds that they attended some of the dinners (Belford 127, 153, 308).

7 Burton's work summarized, with no supporting evidence, alleged ritual murders from the Middle Ages to the nineteenth century. When the book appeared as *The Jew, the Gypsy, and El Islam,* the publishers omitted this portion (Brodie 265-66; 363, n. 7; Rice 536).

8 Lovell, in her biography of Burton, believes Burton invented the story of the murder because "the rapt attention and discomfort of his listeners provided him with amusement" (Lovell 186). Nothing in the biographies of Burton by Lovell, Brodie, or Rice suggests that Stoker and Burton were more than acquaintances, though they seem to have been mutually cordial.

9 Hatton quotes similar praise for Irving's sympathetic portrayal from a Cincinnati newspaper (Hatton 358–9). According to Belford (288), Eliza Aria, a Jewish journalist (and later Irving's lover), once thanked Irving in public, "in the name of all Jews, for his interpretation of Shylock." But Belford does not provide a source.

10 After a cholera epidemic halted Caine's travels in Russia, he went to Germany, where the anti-Semitism he witnessed appalled him. Returning to England, he spoke about his experiences to the Jewish Workmen's Club in London (Allen 214–21, Kenyon 168-69).

11 On Whitman's attitudes toward the Jewish community in Camden, NJ, see his 1842 articles for the *New York Aurora* on his visit to the Crosby Street synagogue. Horace Traubel, his long-time friend and literary executor, was Jewish.

Works Cited

Allen, Vivien. *Hall Caine: Portrait of a Victorian Romancer*. Sheffield Academic Press, 1997.

Bale, Anthony. "Dracula's Blood." *The Cambridge Companion to Dracula*, edited by Roger Luckhurst, Cambridge University Press, 2018. 104–113.

Beal, Timothy K. *Religion and Its Monsters*. Oxfordshire: Routledge, 2002.

Belford, Barbara. *Bram Stoker: A Biography of the Author of Dracula*. New York: Knopf, 1996.

Brodie, Fawn M. *The Devil Drives: A Life of Sir Richard Burton*. New York: Norton, 1967.

Buck, Carl Darling. *A Dictionary of Selected Synonyms in the Principal Indo-European Languages*. 1949. University of Chicago Press, 1988.

Caine, Hall. *The Scapegoat*. New York: Appleton, 1899. *Project Gutenberg*, https://www.gutenberg.org/files/1303/1303-0.txt. Accessed December 20, 2022.

David, Alfred. "An Iconography of Noses: Directions in the History of a Physical Stereotype." *Mapping the Cosmos*, edited by Jane Chance and R. O. Wells, Jr., Rice University Press, 1985, pp. 76-97.

Donaghey, Frederick. "Dracula." *Chicago Daily Tribune*, April 3, 1929, p. 37. *Chicago Tribune Archive,* https://chicagotribune.newspapers.com/ image/354922544/?terms=Dracula&match=1. Accessed December 28, 2022.

Giorgi, Rosa, ed. *Angels and Demons in Art*. Translated by Rosanna M. Giammanco Frongia, Los Angeles: J. Paul Getty Museum, 2005.

Glover, David. "*Dracula* in the Age of Mass Migration." *The Cambridge Companion to Dracula*. Edited by Roger Luckhurst, Cambridge University Press, 2018, pp. 85–94.

Goethe, Johann Wolfgang von. *Faust: A Tragedy*. Translated by Walter Arndt, edited by Cyrus Hamlin, Norton Critical Edition, 2nd ed. New York: Norton, 2001.

Graf, Arturo. *Art of the Devil*. New York: Parkstone, 2009.

Halberstam, Jack. *Skin Shows: Gothic Horror and the Technology of Monsters*. Durham, NC: Duke University Press, 1995.

---. "Technologies of Monstrosity: Bram Stoker's *Dracula*." *Victorian Studies*, vol. 36, no. 3, Spring 1993, pp. 333-352. *Gale Literature Resource Center,* eds.a.ebscohost.com/eds/pdfviewer/pdfviewer?vid= 5&sid=e11b5209-8bed-48e5-8f82-85fd1600d7da%40sdc-v-sessmgr01. Accessed August 2, 2021.

Hatton, Joseph. *Henry Irving's Impressions of America*. London: Low, Marston, Searle, & Rivington, 1884. https://babel.hathitrust.org/cgi/pt?id=loc.ark:/ 13960/t77s83j27 &view= 1up&seq=5&skin=2021 *Hathi Trust Digital Library*. Accessed Sept 1, 2024.

Irving, Lawrence. *Henry Irving*. London: Macmillan, 1952.

Kenyon, Fred C. *Hall Caine: The Man and the Novelist*. 1901. New York: Haskell House, 1974.

Ledger, Sally, and Scott McCracken, editors. *Cultural Politics at the Fin de Siècle*. Cambridge University Press, 1995.

Lipton, Sara. *Dark Mirror: The Medieval Origins of Anti-Jewish Iconography*. New York: Henry Holt, 2014.

Lovell, Mary S. *A Rage to Live: A Biography of Richard and Isabel Burton. New York: Norton, 1998.*

Malchow, H. L. *Gothic Images of Race in Nineteenth-Century Britain*. Stanford University Press, 1996.

Mayer, David, ed. *Henry Irving and* The Bells. Manchester UP, 1980.

Nordau, Max. *Degeneration*. 1895. 2nd ed. Lincoln: University of Nebraska Press, 1993.

Pacher, Michael. *Saint Augustine and the Devil. Circa* 1473. *Wikimedia Commons,* https://commons.wikimedia.org/wiki/File:Michael_Pacher_004.jpg Accessed June 5, 2022.

Rice, Edward. *Captain Sir Richard Francis Burton: A Biography*. New York: Harper, 1991.

Rowell, George. *Theatre in the Age of Irving*. Lanham: Rowman and Littlefield, 1981.

Russell, Jeffrey Burton. *Lucifer: The Devil in the Middle Ages*. Cornell University Press, 1984.

---. *Mephistopheles: The Devil in the Modern World*. Cornell University Press, 1986.

---. *Satan: The Early Christian Tradition*. Cornell University Press, 1981.

Skal, David. "'His Hour upon the Stage': Theatrical Adaptations of *Dracula*." Stoker. *Dracula*. Norton Critical Edition, 1st ed., pp. 371–381.

---. *Something in the Blood: The Untold Story of Bram Stoker, the Man Who Wrote* Dracula. New York: Liveright, 2016.

Steinmeyer, Jim. *Who Was Dracula? Bram Stoker's Trail of Blood*. London: Penguin, 2013.

Stoker, Bram. *Dracula*. Edited by Nina Auerbach and David J. Skal, Norton Critical Edition, 1st ed., New York, 1997.

---. *Dracula*. Edited by John Edgar Browning and David J. Skal, Norton Critical Edition, 2nd ed., New York: Norton, 2021.

---. *Dracula*. Edited by Roger Luckhurst, Oxford World's Classics. Oxford University Press, 2011.

---. *Dracula Unearthed*, 2nd ed. Edited by Clive Leatherdale. Essex: Desert Island Books, 2006.

---. *The Lost Journal of Bram Stoker: The Dublin Years*. Edited by Elizabeth Miller and Dacre Stoker. London: Robson, 2012.

---. *Personal Reminiscences of Henry Irving*. Heinemann, 1906. 2 vols. *Internet Archive*, https://archive.org/details/personalreminisc01stokiala/page/n9/mode/2up. Accessed October 8, 2021.

Strickland, Debra H. *Saracens, Demons & Jews: Making Monsters in Medieval Art*. Princeton University Press, 2003.

Strobridge Lithographing Co. *Kellar and His Servants*. Cincinnati, OH: 1894. *Wikimedia Commons*, https://commons.wikimedia.org/wiki/File:Flickr_-_%E2%80%A6trialsanderrors_-_Kellar_and_his_servants,_magician_poster,_ca._1894.jpg. Accessed July 18, 2022.

---. *Kellar's Wonders*. Cincinnati, OH:1900. *Wikimedia Commons*, https://commons.wikimedia.org/wiki/File:Kellar%27s_wonders_LCCN2014637424.tif. Accessed July 18, 2022.

"Teller, Leopold." *The Jewish Encyclopedia*, edited by Isadore Singer and Frederick T. Haneman. New York: Funk & Wagnalls, 1906. *The Jewish Encyclopedia*, https://jewishencyclopedia.com/articles/14297-teller-leopold. Accessed May 28, 2025.

Trachtenberg, Joshua. *The Devil and the Jews: The Medieval Conception of the Jew and its Relation to Modern Antisemitism*, 2nd ed. Philadelphia: Jewish Publication Society, 2002.

Valman, Nadia. "Dracula." *Anti-Semitism: A Historical Encyclopedia of Prejudice and Persecution*, edited by Richard S. Levy et al, vol. 1, ABC-CLIO, 2005, pp. 188–89.

Vámbéry, Arminius. *The Story of My Struggles: The Memoirs of Arminius Vámbéry*. Vol. 2, London: Fisher Unwin, 1904. *Internet Archive*, https://archive.org/details/storyofmystruggl02vm/mode/2up. Accessed December 1, 2022.

Whitman, Walt. "Doings at the Synagogue." *New York Aurora*, 29 March, 1842. *The Walt Whitman Archive*, https://whitmanarchive.org/published/ periodical/journalism/tei/per.00419.html. Accessed January 10, 2023.

---. "A Peep at the Israelites." *New York Aurora*, 28 March 1842. *The Walt Whitman Archive*, https://whitmanarchive.org/published/periodical/journalism/tei/per.00418.html. Accessed January 10, 2023.

Wynne, Catherine. *Bram Stoker, Dracula, and the Victorian Gothic Stage*. London: Palgrave Macmillan, 2013.

---. "*Dracula* on Stage." *The Cambridge Companion to Dracula*, edited by Roger Luckhurst, Cambridge University Press, 2018. 165–178.

Mapping Magic in Fantasy Novels: Magic Systems and Thematic Undercurrents in Mark Lawrence's *Book of the Ancestor*

Finley Dunn

MAGIC IS A COMMON AND IMPORTANT feature of fantasy fiction. Magic is also an area of fantasy studies that has received little critical scholarship and consequently lacks accepted methods of interrogation. Existing critical studies of magic in fantasy are few, and their discussions tend to be scattered or very specific. Existing discussions, both critical and non-critical, provide insights, but there is no theoretical consensus on how contemporary representations of magic might be categorized into broad types for analysis. Therefore, there is also no existing understanding of what an analysis of magic might be able to offer to the field. Current critical studies of magic may discuss only specific fantasy texts or series (Filonenko 27; Poradecki 113; Ravikumar et al. 265; Rosu 381) or be focused on magic as it appears in fantasy gaming, as in Dungeons and Dragons™ or computer-based role-playing games (RPGs) (Bezio 134; Howard ch. 2; Stern 257; Tresca n.p; Vander Ploeg and Phillips 142). Some authors have published their own thoughts about how to categorize magic through their author websites, such as Brandon Sanderson's First Law, which separates magic into three categories: hard, soft, and middle (Sanderson,

"Sanderson's First Law"). Sanderson aims for hard fantasy in which magic operates based on strict rules that govern who gets to access magical potential and how, akin to speculative technologies in hard science fiction. At the other end of the spectrum, N. K. Jemisin's blog post "but, but, but – WHY does magic have to make sense?" insists that magic is dreamlike and mythological, and therefore, in her writing, has a symbolic implication, rather than rigid rules. Though all these contributions are helpful to get a sense of the field, they offer few analytical tools for discussing the contribution that magic makes to contemporary fantasy, more generally.

One of the aims of this essay is to argue for magic's critical relevance by demonstrating how the type of magic system in texts can contribute to analyzable implications in the fantasy world. By magic system, what I mean is not necessarily the hard fantasy idea of rules working to generate specific effects, such as might govern a tabletop role-playing game or computer game. Instead, the term magic system refers to the coherent patterning that happens within the narrative consistency of an imagined universe that creates an impression of what magic is and does in that world.

The series I have chosen to examine in this essay is Mark Lawrence's *Book of the Ancestor*, singularly known as *Red Sister*, *Grey Sister*, and *Holy Sister*. I have done this because it is a complex series that exemplifies a construction of magic commonly found in contemporary fantasy literature. It also contains imagery that draws attention to the state of the fantasy world through an ecological centrepiece. The centrepiece exists as a fundamental part of the worldbuilding and receives continued emphasis throughout the narrative. In *Book of the Ancestor* the centerpiece is the pending environmental destruction caused by the ice wall that is encroaching upon the territories of the Corridor, which are a "green belt" around the equator of the world (Lawrence *Red Sister* ch. 12). A more critically well-known author that has environmentally significant imagery in common with Lawrence is George R. R. Martin. Both of these authors use the imagery of pending ecological disasters as environmentally significant centerpieces. Although Martin has more critical recognition than Lawrence, his series is currently unfinished, and this makes drawing conclusions about it an uncertain endeavor. The substance and sustainability of Martin's engagement with the environment is under critical discussion (DiPaolo 235; Laukkanen 456; Martins 203) and there is not space to examine this entire debate here. Nonetheless, the analysis of magic developed in this essay may help to approach the question that arises in relation to Martin, regarding the difference between pro-ecological engagement versus using an environmental disaster as a convenient background against which to stage a narrative about what power struggles look like when some actors have magical powers. According to journals such as *Clarkesworld* (Hodges n.p), Lawrence is a comparable author who has a completed series that can demonstrate how an analysis of the magic type reveals and supports the major themes of a text. In the case of *Book of the Ancestor*, these themes are the political struggles generated by an impending environmental disaster, in a narrative that focuses on power relations more than ecological activism. Magic is central to the power struggles, but its relation to the environment is not unlike that of a technology to nature, which means that the series is not necessarily a sustained engagement with the ecological themes that it gestures toward.

This demonstration leads into the other aim of this essay, which is to suggest a heuristic approach to magic through provisional categories. These provisional categories are intentional magic, spiritual magic, wild magic, and hybrid systems. Though a full discussion of these categories is beyond the scope of this essay, I will return to them at the end of the discussion of *Book of the Ancestor*. Using textual analysis of key examples, the objective is to demonstrate how magic in fantasy can be broadly categorized through its conditions of use, as a way of approaching the questions of what magic is, how it is constructed, and what it might be doing for the world and themes of a particular novel or series such as *Book of the Ancestor*.

It has been noted above that critical discussions of magic are limited. It is therefore reasonable to point out that magic also has no agreed upon definition. According to Brian Attebery in *Strategies of Fantasy*, fantasy requires a "sharper break with reality" (Attebery 15) than some other forms of speculative fiction. By all appearances, magic is one of fantasy's elements that initiates this break. This is because it breaks the laws of consensus definitions of reality and grants access to instances of metaphysical or supernatural power. Meanwhile, Clute, in his *Encyclopedia of Fantasy*, gives an overview of numerous different types of magic as found in fantasy, which makes its own argument for why magic is not easily defined by what it does. Although Clute acknowledges that "magic, when present, can do almost anything" (Clute "Magic" 615), he does note that it is likely to "obey certain rules according to its nature" (Clute "Magic" 615).

Orson Scott Card discusses the idea of writers of fantasy creating a "useful magic system" as early as 1990, in *How to write science fiction and fantasy* (Card 48). Under the heading "The Rules of Magic," Card advises that authors should be clear about the rules of magic, and its limitations, to mitigate the impression noted by Clute that magic without these has the potential to do anything (Card 48).

The earliest roots of the concept of a magic system, and the idea that the performance of magic by characters should be obvious, effective and with clear limitations within the narrative, are likely to be located in the fantasies that followed the creation of tabletop role-playing games in the 1960s. Although the inspiration for early tabletop games came from the worlds of fantasy literature, such as Tolkien's Middle Earth, in order for players to vicariously experience arcane power by playing a character that has access to magic, the operation of magic had to have limitations. Clearly defined rules for magic use became part of the translation from fiction to fictional, interactive game, where various abilities need to be balanced to provide the optimum experience (Vander Ploeg and Phillips 142-147). In order to facilitate these balances of power, magic, as a result, becomes more systematized in its expression. This interchange between mediums also, potentially, signals a shift into a tendency for magic to be accessible to the protagonist, rather than a secondary companion character, which also would make its representation in fantasy literature more palpable than it might be in earlier examples of the genre.

Developments in the tropology of fantasy surrounding magic, such as the idea of magic as a system with specific rules, the idea that magical incidents should be obvious when they occur, and the likelihood that the protagonists have access to magic, are facets that make magic more apparent to readers. The heightened visibility of magic in contemporary popular fantasy primes it for exercises in analysis. All critical discussions must start somewhere and, for the purposes of this essay, the most approachable and applicable definition of magic comes from Jeff Howard in *Game Magic: a designer's guide to magic in theory and practice*. Howard posits:

> Magic entails contact with forces and entities beyond the physical (the literal meaning of metaphysics) [. . .] Magic allows humans to pull aside the veil between the ordinary world and another world beyond. Magic then offers the promise of putting these otherworldly forces to use in everyday life. (Howard *Game Magic* 9)

It seems reasonable to observe from my preliminary surveys into this field, and building from Clute and Howard's descriptions, that magic is an extraordinary force in a fantasy world and that it involves a mobilization of and intervention into the structures, substances, and causal powers of the world, all of which comprise what is often termed nature, in its broadest sense (Clarke 6).

In relation to literature, Howard's other world beyond could be more broadly described as a higher order of nature. This higher order, in a fantasy universe, exists as an extraordinary and excessive tier of causal law. This is the domain of magic, while magic itself would be the metaphysical presence and/or entity that belongs to this extraordinary tier.

In order to simplify Clute's observations into a statement, it could be posited that what magic *does* is to provide the power to act, to create, and to cause a response from the world, which contravenes the laws of everyday reality as they are known. It might then be suggested that if magic is defined as the metaphysical force or entity that mobilizes and intervenes into everyday nature, then the magic system is what determines the features of the magic that is present and sets the foundation for its use.

However, just as there is currently no agreed-upon definition of magic, there is also no agreed-upon framework for the analysis of magic in fantasy literature. This essay proposes that magic and magic systems in fantasy operate on two core mechanics. The first is the location of the magic source. This mechanic stands for the observation that magical power, at its most basic, seems to exist within one of two opposite types of location. It can exist externally as a form of sentient presence, or it can exist as a form of internal or external natural potential. The second core mechanic is the condition of using the magic source. This condition exists on a continuum, with acceptance and mastery being the two major options that the wielding of magic power might require of the practitioner. If there is no condition of either acceptance or mastery, the magic of that universe would most likely fit into the category of purely random, uncontrollable, or chaotic magic, and therefore exist outside of the continuum. These core mechanics play an integral role in the construction of magic in fantasy novels and are likely to have implications for the themes that are engaged with because they dictate the terms on which a magic-user gains access to magical power.

It is important to recognize the contribution that magic makes to fantasy narratives—not just in the sense of the wonder it adds to a secondary world, but the work it does in communicating the themes of the text. If "the question of what to include, how much to include, can only be answered with regard to what, precisely, we mean to create" (Turchi n.p), then the magic system has an important part to play in unpacking the world that is created from its inclusion. This applies not only to what magic system is included in the narrative, but how that magic is characterized and framed by the text, including in what spheres of influence it gives the practitioner access to.

Mark Lawrence's *Book of the Ancestor* trilogy is a series which tells the story of Nona, a girl with ancient magical bloodlines who is recruited into ranks of the nuns of the Sweet Mercy Convent, a religious and political organization that trains nuns according to the talents of their bloodline for battle, stealth, and political manipulation. At the periphery of Nona's experiences in and out of Sweet Mercy, there is a threat that looms in each book of the trilogy. This is the threat of the ice wall enclosing upon the territories of the Corridor, which are a "green belt" around the equator of the world, and the rumored falling of the moon and dying of the sun, which keep the green belt from icing over like the rest of the world (Lawrence *Red Sister* ch. 12).

The narrative interplay between the politics of Nona's empire and the looming external threat of the ice wall seems to promise readers that a solution to this environmental threat is something that the series may reach at its conclusion. However, an analysis of the magic system at play suggests that the text's priorities are the interior tensions created by this outside threat. Through analysis of the magic present within the series, it becomes clear that the focus of the text is primarily on internal political intrigue and clashes of power, with magic that is defined by its usefulness to characters as a tool and a weapon to be honed and then deployed at will. The text's potential to comment on the environmental crisis that forms its backdrop is not supported or reinforced by the type of magic system, which is one of intentional magic.

Intentional magic is the provisional category that accounts for the most common form of magic found in fantasy novels. At its most basic, intentional magic requires nothing more than the ability and desire to do magic. Its ideal poles of reference are a location of potential and a condition of mastery. A location of potential typically means that the magic is sourced from the magic user directly, from a wellspring of power, inherited bloodline, or natural talent that gives them access to magical power. A condition of mastery means that in order to access power, the magic user must have a developed (or masterful) form of intent, will or desire to perform magic. Commonly in fantasy literature, in examples of intentional magic, a magic user will be trained in how to master/control their magic power, through the achievement of spell-casting competence, mastery over an occult symbology, familiarity with an arcane knowledge, or the like.

Magic, in *Book of the Ancestor*, is inherited. Consequently, the magic in *Book of the Ancestor* locates magical potential in any person with the genetic inheritance of magic. Magical abilities are specific to the genetic bloodline the practitioner comes from. There are four different bloodlines in the *Book of the Ancestor* series, through which various magic abilities are granted. Gerants are large and strong of body, leading to impressive physical strength and endurance. Hunska are swift and, by virtue of that swiftness, can effectively slow down time around themselves to move beyond the limits of normal perception. Quantals can see and take energy from the path, an energy spring which runs through all living things, and use it to fuel themselves physically or channel it into other matter. They can also use thread work to manipulate matter and materials as a subtler power. Marjals possess more elementally aligned powers such as rock work, ice work, shadow manipulation, and empathy (Lawrence *Grey Sister* "Story So Far"). Of these bloodlines, Nona possesses the traits of three of them: hunska, marjal and quantal. The fact that Nona spends three books learning how to properly master these powers, but requires no training to access them, also necessarily means that the condition of the magic in this series is one of mastery.

Nona is selected by the Abbess of Sweet Mercy because her rare collection of bloodlines seems promising, something which saves her from execution. The political entanglements that Nona is involved in across the series stem equally from this moment. The moment her potential for magical power is recognized by the Abbess, and she is taken away to be trained, begins a rumor that she is part of a prophetic duo who will save the world (Lawrence, *Red Sister* ch. 16). This same moment, when she is not executed for the murder of a powerful family's son, begins a feud that spreads across all three novels and embroils Nona in the politics of her empire from the very beginning of *Red Sister* (Lawrence ch. 2, ch. 16). Throughout the series, it is the narrative of Nona as an agent of intrigue that the magic supports. This is signposted at the very start through the use of an intentional magic system, which grounds the magic in the materiality of Nona's being, her perspective and her body, through her special genetics. How the protagonist uses magic, what effects it has, and what sort of access it gives its wielder to the wider world are thematically salient points of interrogation because magic is an element that serves to reinforce the internal logic and coherence of the world and narrative in which it appears.

According to Mark J.P. Wolf, "*consistency*" in worldbuilding requires "a careful integration of details and attention to the way everything is connected together" (Wolf 43, emphasis original). Narratively, by granting power to the protagonist, part of magic's intervention into the life of the protagonist is that it provides access to material and metaphysical spheres that were out of reach previously, and provides opportunities in the wider world that weren't there before. Functionally, the magic should align with the text's narrative and thematic intentions and allow "the author to send messages about narrative sequence, about character, and about [...] the boundary between the fictional and the real" (Attebery 55). In video game RPGs such as *Baldur's Gate III*, there is a mechanic known as effect, status, or condition stacking. This is when battle or spell effects, like "blinded," "charmed," and "maimed" for example, stack on top of one another to affect a character, so that this character could be affected by all three conditions at once (*Baldur's Gate Wiki*: "Conditions"), or by one condition multiple times. As Wolf and Attebery imply in their observations, magic can function as a level of "metonymy and metaphor" (Attebery 55), where the construction of a fantasy world and its narrative repeat the same thematic focus throughout different elements to create layers of meaning. These layers of meaning function in a similar way to status conditions in fantasy gaming, in that they stack to create more significant effects.

The beginning of *Book of the Ancestor* highlights Nona's status as a friendless child slated for execution, and the change in her status when she is taken away to Sweet Mercy for training because of her magical potential. In this case, the world that magic has made accessible to Nona is not the actual, physical world that surrounds her where the environmental threat lies, but a world of opportunity within Sweet Mercy. The magic is connected to Nona's personal advancement in the social and political world she is exposed to through her training at Sweet Mercy, and so this element has additional internal meaning layered onto it, or thematic stack. Thematic stack accrues across the novels. As the magic, the narrative, and the themes of political intrigue and power continue to align together, these elements reinforce each other and draw focus to the personal, institutional, and imperial machinations Nona takes part in, thwarts, and is surrounded by. The location, conditions, and thematic qualities of the magic are focused inward and on the personal stakes of the protagonist, such as defeating her enemies and stopping them from using the moon as a weapon (Lawrence, *Red Sister* ch. 41, *Holy Sister* ch. 25). For these reasons, and because magic is used primarily as an instrument for action, as a tool and a weapon, it becomes characterized by its utility to Nona. An example of this utility is Nona's access to the path, a source of power that turns Nona's "flesh to gold, her mind to crystal" and can armor and strengthen her in a fight (Lawrence *Grey Sister* ch. 29, ch. 41). The path is described as a "boundary between what lives and what does not. It runs through all things and around them" (Lawrence ch. 8). However, the path is primarily a way to access energy. The path is "about power" (Lawrence ch. 28), and the boundaries it allows Nona to contravene are ones associated with endurance, strength and force. Marjals and quantals have the most environmentally aligned magic, drawing on "the power of place" (Lawrence *Red Sister*, ch. 20). Marjals form their magic from Abeth's material nature, learning "the deepest secrets of their world [...] down to the bedrock and beyond" (Lawrence ch. 11). However, the only characters that perform elemental magic in this series are Yisht and Zole, both using rockwork. In both cases, rockwork is used as a means to an end, a way for Yisht to tunnel secretly into Sweet Mercy (Lawrence ch. 41), and a way for Zole to hide from the Noi Guin in their earthen fortress (Lawrence *Grey Sister*, ch. 33, ch.

47). In neither of these cases does the reader get an understanding of rockwork from Yisht or Zole's point of view, so there is no evidence that performing such magic provides any additional connection to the earth that is being manipulated.

When taking the magic into account as an additional layer of narrative and thematic production, the threat of the ice wall, although it looms large, becomes limited to a significant, evocative element. Even though it is central to the makeup of the world, it is only depicted in the peripheral of the narrative. The encroachment of the ice is a consistently highlighted narrative element in character observations, but little more:

> Time and again she found herself thinking of the moon that some distant ancestor of hers had set to hang above the world, and about how one thin and breakable mirror seemed to be all that stood between everyone she might ever know and the ice advancing from north and south. (Lawrence *Red Sister* ch. 12)

The magic, founded as it is in Nona's special genetics and her willpower to enact it, has no way to additionally highlight anything that is outside of Nona's immediate experiences or interests. This includes her use of the path, despite its nominal connection to the environment, the depiction of which, across the series, is never substantiated as actively connected to anything but pure energy, maintaining magic's focus on Nona's individual and interior power and prowess. Applied differently, the benefits of thematic stack, where narrative, theme and magic construction are aligned, mean that a similar magic system could be used to build environmental themes in a different story or even in *Book of the Ancestor*, but this is not what Nona's access to and use of magic communicates here.

This essay has previously suggested that the magic in the *Book of the Ancestor* could be termed intentional magic, because it is a magic that requires personal aptitude to perform, training to master, and no will or intent other than the practitioner's to use. Further, based on its utility, it could be additionally classified as intentional, instrumental magic. Intentional, instrumental magic is calculated, formula-based, and success-orientated. For magic to have an orientation to success means that magic is treated as a tool to be deployed, with strict methods for successful execution. Materials and internal magical potential are resources to be used in the process of creating or performing successful magic. Magic's placement within the domain of nature, both causal and material, means it always possesses the potential to raise the environment as an object of analysis. However, intentional systems such as the one in *Book of the Ancestor*, which belong to this subfield of magic that is underpinned by an instrumental attitude in the magic's construction and execution, are unlikely to engage with this potential.

The conceptual basis for thinking about this subfield comes from Adorno and Horkheimer's insight into instrumental reason, where "[w]hat human beings seek to learn from nature is how to use it to dominate wholly both it and human beings" (Adorno and Horkheimer 2). Adorno and Horkheimer's insight is connected to complex philosophical discussions that need not be delved into here. Nonetheless, this insight is particularly useful for clarifying why this subfield has limited engagements with environmental allegories, even though it is the most well-understood form of intentional magic. It is limiting because the use of things as instruments for successful manipulation is implicitly permitted by the narrative positioning of magic as it is expressed in this subfield. A direct consequence is that nature can only be treated as a raw material for successful exploitation or manipulation within this subtype. This instrumentalist construction pairs well with the condition of mastery found in intentional magic systems and the tropology of magic use requiring specific training but relegates magical power, and, therefore, nature and the environment, to resources to be used in service of the magic user's advancement. This instrumental use of magic—and Abeth, as the source of magic—means that this series has structural difficulties with creating meaningful connections to the world.

The layers of additional meaning and consistency that magic can accord to a theme are applied to align with different narrative and thematic elements, which gives the interior view of Nona's experiences the most benefits of thematic stack. Abeth and its ice wall are, as Patrick D. Murphy calls it in *Voicing Another Nature*, merely the "site for human endeavors" (Murphy 59), with the struggle over the ice wall framed in terms of resources, political borders and territories: "The ice is closing. There's not enough room or food. Someone has to die. Lots of someones [...] the point is that it not be *us* who dies!" (Lawrence *Holy Sister* ch. 29). This idea that the environmental threat is narratively only an external threat creating internal pressure is supported by environmental disconnection from magic and, through that, the environment's lack of meaningful connection to the protagonist. Disconnection exacerbates the internal problems Nona, Sweet Mercy and the empire are facing and provides striking imagery.

Similarly, the ability to control the moon is posited as a power-based tool, a potential weapon to use against others, as well as the only means of preserving the Corridor. When Nona is given control of the moon by Zole, it is the social and political landscape of the empire that she aims to maintain. It is not possible to melt the ice; only to buy time to find another solution to the problem (Lawrence *Holy Sister* ch. 29, ch. 30). The internal problems remain the narrative focus and are supported by a magic system that adds additional layers of emphasis on top of them. And even though the environmental threat does not get a resolution, Nona does get a personal resolution that acknowledges the social and political power her access to magic has given her the opportunity to accrue. By the end of the series, she has ascended from an unpopular and dangerous initiate to a Holy Sister with the respect of her convent. Her enemies are destroyed and she has forged a lifelong partnership with fellow initiate of notable noble descent, Arabella Jostis. Such a change in her status from friendless, soon-to-be-executed child to powerful Holy Sister is in line with the thematic stacking that magic has helped place on these elements of the story. The interpretation of this series that an analysis of its magic lends itself to is that of a fantasy that is focused on the elevation and triumph of its protagonist through personal physical, mental, and social battles, which then accrue physical, mental, and social power.

Another example of this subfield of instrumental magic would be Robert Jordan's *The Wheel of Time*. In the first book of the series, *The Eye of the World*, the source of magic is external and takes the form of a reservoir of power called the True Source. In accessing this source, magic users are able to channel the One Power to enact feats of magic. The magic is intentional magic because it has a location of external potential that relies on the magic user having an active role in channeling it: "He drew on the True Source deeply, and still more deeply, like a man dying of thirst. Quickly he had drawn more of the One Power than he could channel unaided" (Jordan "Prologue"). The magic also possesses a condition of mastery because it is enacted by willpower at its most basic level: "With all his heart and desperation he silently shouted at Bela to run like the wind, silently tried to will his strength into her. Run! His skin prickled, and his bones felt as if they were freezing, ready to split open. The Light help her, run! And Bela ran" (Jordan ch. 11: "The Road to Taren Ferry"). However, the brief glimpse into the magic of the series provided in *The Eye of the World* displays a success-orientated instrumental system, where the application of intent by the magic user creates the desired magical outcome and the environment is relegated to a mere backdrop to human affairs. This point is aptly demonstrated by the mage Moiraine when she tells the promising but untrained young woman Egwene, "Things do not have the Power, child. Even an angreal [magical artifact] is only a tool. This is just a pretty blue stone. But it can give off light" (Jordan ch. 12: "Across the Taren"). In a world where things do not have magical power, only people do, and people's use of that power requires magic to be passively channeled from an endless river of natural potential and applied to the world through force of will. The implication is that people are going to be the focus in the narrative, because they're the ones who get to access and use magic. Here, the pretty blue stone exemplifies the relationship between the environment and instrumental magic use, where magic exists as a tool to be used for successful manipulation of raw material by humans.

One final example of instrumental magic that is calculated, formula-based, and success-orientated, nominally connected to the environment for the purpose of accessing magical energy (like Nona's use of the path), and exists as a tool akin to a form of technology is the magic in Brandon Sanderson's *Elantris*.

It has been suggested that intentional, instrumental magic may occur more commonly in stories that are orientated towards the material world, rather than the metaphysical, and have a focus on the social, political, and personal gain of the magic practitioner. Although not empirically proven, this is at least the case for *Book of the Ancestor*. It may be that this subfield is particularly common in fantasy because it benefits from an inherited legacy of the systematic magic systems and tropology developed in the popular fantasy of the 80s and 90s. These constructions are familiar to contemporary audiences and the instrumental perspective echoes perspectives found within western culture. Additionally, even when the source of potential is external, as it is in *The Eye of the World*, the ability to harness magic remains within the personal aptitude of the magic user. When combined with a success-orientated, instrumental approach, this can endow magic with a sense of individualism in its expression.

An example of intentional magic that is not instrumental in its approach would be the protagonist Agnieszka's magic in Naomi Novik's novel *Uprooted*. This magic is process-orientated and improvised, creating a sense of cooperation in the expression of her magic. The spells she is most proficient at often make use of material nature, such as lemons and pine needles, as spell elements; and she thinks of spell components as picking her way through a forest and gleaning for berries and mushrooms (Novik ch. 6). This highlights Agnieszka's approach towards magic as something that works with an understanding of her raw materials and environment and is instinctual, rather than an approach solely based in the manipulation of materials in the pursuit of a successful result, as demonstrated in this exchange with the Dragon who is training her:

> He wanted exact syllables and repetitions, he wanted to know how close I had been to his arm, he wanted the number of rosemary twigs and the number of peels. I did my best to tell him, but I felt even as I did so that it was all wrong, and finally I blurted out, as he wrote angrily on his sheets, 'But none of that matters at all. [...] It's just —a way to go. There isn't only one way to go.' I waved at his notes. 'You're trying to find a road where there isn't one. It's like—it's gleaning in the woods,' I said abruptly. 'You have to pick your way through the thickets and the trees, and it's different every time.' (Novik ch. 6)

In comparison, Nona from *Book of the Ancestor* uses her access to the path to make herself more powerful, without any reference to the path's connection to the world around her, because her magic is both sourced from within herself and entirely geared towards the successful execution of her desire to perform calculated acts of magic—merely a tool to be deployed in her arsenal of skills.

Why make this distinction, with care to name the types of magic and establish criteria to define them? Doing so makes it easier to notice as a potential formulation in fantasy literature and then investigate it further. Clute's discussion of magic is very specific. It covers examples of true names; coloured magic in white, black, grey, and green spells; shape-shifting; music; and more, as distinct types of magic (Clute 615-618). While potentially helpful for an analysis of an individual story's magic, Clute's discussion takes too much into account to be broadly applicable. Still, if there is no way to categorize magic, "no system [...] no sense of what magic can achieve" (Mendlesohn 63-64), then, as Farah Mendlesohn attests, how magic works and its contributions to a fantasy world seem arbitrary. The discussion above shows that the presence of magic can be very meaningful. However, not all magic looks like the magic in the *Book of the Ancestor*, and not all magic can be classed as intentional magic. Therefore, this essay proposes the additional magic system categories of spiritual magic, wild magic, and hybrid magic. These provisional categories are proposed based on the core mechanics mentioned above. The source of magic can be located in a separate sentience, or in a character's innate potential. The condition of magic's use can be one of acceptance or mastery; or there may be no condition at all. Spiritual magic and intentional magic contrast each other, while wild magic accounts for the deliberate presence of a chaotic or uncontrollable element within the magic. Hybrid magic allows for cross-over between different types, or the presence of multiple types, within the same world.

In *Rhetorics of Fantasy*, Mendlesohn affirms Clute's assertion that immersive fantasies are not about the discovery of a world, but the loss of it. Such fantasies "rarely tell of building, because building is a venture into the unknown. Instead they start with what is and watch it crumble" (Mendlesohn 113). The *Book of the Ancestor* exemplifies this rhetorical strategy. The ice is closing and the tension mounts as everyone tries to save what they can. The magic in the *Book of the Ancestor* has an individualism and instrumentalism in its construction that reflects that. It doesn't build into anything beyond Nona. It is intentional magic, so it is based on Nona's potential and her mastery of magic, and the depiction of magic is restricted to her use of it as a tool to further her own aims.

In contrast, spiritual magic is suggested as having a location of sentience and a condition of donation-and-acceptance. Spiritual magic is donated from a sentient magic source with obligations that must be fulfilled. This agreement with a magic source allows the source to share some of the protagonist's viewpoint and impose restrictions on the magic user, though the magic user maintains most of the power of action in the relationship. Spiritual magic systems may thematically stack more commonly with stories that are orientated towards the metaphysical and the breaking of barriers between the self and the other, the self and the divine, and the self and nature. This is because the sentience of the magic source exists as an exterior, metaphysical factor that dictates the use of magic for the practitioner and directly influences them, creating space for the magic to highlight narrative elements that are, likewise, exterior to the practitioner.

An example of this type of magic occurs in Robin Hobb's *Soldier Son* trilogy. *Soldier Son* centers on the story of Nevare Burvelle, a young man from a prominent family who is expelled from his military school and sent to the frontier of his empire, where he is confronted by the environmental destruction his empire is enacting on the Specks, the forest people who live there. He learns over the course of the trilogy that he has his own Speck-self, due to a magical encounter in his youth, and that the Speck magic is using Nevare against the empire to save its land and its people. The sentence of the magic is demonstrated a number of times: through Nevare's greater awareness of the wellbeing of the environment when using Speck magic, because it is connected to the being that is known as 'Forest' (Hobb *Renegade's Magic* ch. 3); conversations that reiterate that the magic has a will of its own (Hobb, *Forest Mage* ch. 1, ch.17); and the admission that Forest "might as well be a god with all the power Forest has" (Hobb *Renegade's Magic* ch. 28). Unlike Nona's interior view of magic in *Book of the Ancestor*, Nevare's perspective is influenced by his connection to the sentient source of magic. Therefore, just as he has power over it, it has power over him: "In my dreams of her, she often cautioned me that the magic now owned me. 'It will use you as it sees fit' (Hobb *Forest Mage* ch. 1). However, Nevare can use the magic power that Forest has donated in ways that it is not intended to be used, such as when he uses his magic to encourage plants and trees to overgrow the road the Gernians are trying to build into the Speck's land. This is ineffectual, as all his work will be "undone by the rising sun as the plants wither and fade. What a waste!" (Hobb *Renegade's Magic* ch. 4). He can also negotiate and alter the chosen course of the magic for his own purposes:

> I felt the magic, felt its anger that I had torn it from its chosen course and set it into mine. I knew, in a way that defied explanation, that my path would work. It would be more convoluted, but it would serve just as well. Even the magic accepted that, but it accepted it coldly, with an angry promise of vengeance to come. (Hobb *Renegade's Magic* ch. 26)

These elements prove that although the magic possesses sentience, Nevare is not wholly subordinate to its power or purposes. Meanwhile, the condition of donation-and-acceptance and the magic's thematic stack within the narrative are demonstrated most clearly in the moment where Nevare and Soldier's Boy, his Speck-self, merge into one being:

> I had no sense of becoming one with Soldier's Boy. I felt no encounter with some 'other self' hidden in my flesh. Instead, I was besieged by a decade of memories and thoughts. They were mine, they were his, but they had belonged to both of us, and I had always been aware of my twin lives and experiences. I had always been me, never Soldier's Boy, never Nevare, always me.
> [...] I was home. I was complete and all I had been meant to be. I was the perfect vessel for the magic and ready now to take up my task. (Hobb *Renegade's Magic* ch. 26)

Prior to this, neither Nevare or Soldier's Boy had been able to successfully fulfil the magic's purpose because it requires this moment of acceptance and the integration of his two selves before its full power becomes accessible to them (Hobb *Renegade's Magic* ch. 26). The magic, through its location of sentience and condition of donation-and-acceptance, facilitates the change in Nevare's understanding of his environment and the othered culture of the Specks. It enables him to experience the world from the point of view of the Other through Soldier's Boy and a spiritual connection to the magic's source, Forest. By the end of the trilogy, these experiences have opened his eyes to his own culture's acquisitiveness and an understanding of the environment beyond the richness of its resources:

> Now I saw it with the eyes of a forest mage. Here life balanced as it had for hundreds, perhaps thousands of years. Sunlight and water were all that was required for the trees to grow. The trees made the food that fed whatever moving creatures might venture through this territory, and became the food that replenished the soil when their leaves fell to rot back into earth. This working system was as refined

and precise as any piece of clockwork ever engineered by man. (Hobb *Renegade's Magic* ch. 3)

Another particularly well-known example of spiritual magic is Brandon Sanderson's *Stormlight Archive*, but Hobb's work has been chosen here because it lends itself to brevity.

Different from both intentional magic and spiritual magic is wild magic. Wild magic is magic that exists without explanation or cause. It is chaotic, unstable, or unpredictable, producing unknown, unintended, or menacing effects when used. This volatility of wild magic means that it cannot be fully harnessed by practitioners, and, because of this, it interferes with the protagonist's power of action in a way that the other categories of magic discussed so far do not. Intentional magic and spiritual magic elevate human powers of action, though spiritual magic possesses a condition of donation-and-acceptance that means that magic can dictate to the practitioner how it gets used. Wild magic, in contrast, interjects as a force that humbles the protagonist through the elevation of a magically enriched environment. It does this through its conditions of use, which are directed towards neither mastery nor acceptance, but present as no condition of use at all or as a condition of risk. Wild magic with no condition of use accounts for forms of magic where the agency of humans to harness magic is the most limited and magic can just happen. Without intervention, wild magic with no condition possesses the ability to exist and cause magical outcomes completely on its own. A condition of risk is present when humans have some agency to harness magic, but only at an unknown or unpredictable cost and/or danger to themselves.

An example of this type of magic is Gail Z. Martin's *The Ascendent Kingdoms Saga*. In this series, an exiled lord Blaine Macfadden returns home after a war has destroyed much of the kingdom in a magical backlash (Martin *Ice Forged* ch 7). Blaine and his compatriots fight to restore order to a land split into parts by ambitious warlords and ravaged by unrestrained magic, which must be ritually bound in order to be usable by humans again. Wild magic storms rage across the countryside, destroying everything in their path, once the tame magic that controlled the weather before is undone: when the wild magic's reaction to a protagonist's magical artifact causes an avalanche, a rescuer explains, "'What you experienced was a storm, of sorts. Magic has come untethered from the places of power and from those who wield it. It's like an untamed horse, full of potential and dangerous to everything around it unless properly harnessed'" (Martin *Ice Forged* ch. 19). The cataclysmic magic event takes the magic system from one of intentional magic, based in a location of external potential and a condition of mastery, to a no-condition system. Magic is no longer available to humans but is available to the environment through the presence of wild storms that cause magical anomalies. These storms cannot be stopped or harnessed and have the power to turn humans and animals inside out if they get caught out in one (Martin *Ice Forged* ch. 29, *Reign of Ash* ch. 13). Attempts to wield the wild magic that the storms are generated from, once the magic is ritually re-bound and moves from no condition to a condition of risk, also tend to go wrong and kill the practitioner through unexpected surges of magical power and the activation of damaged magical artifacts (Martin *War of Shadows* ch. 1, ch. 3).

An example that takes the implications of a wild magic system to the extreme is Terry Pratchett's *Tiffany Aching* series, where magic is built into people and the landscape (Pratchett *I Shall Wear Midnight* ch. 1), but witches practice almost no magic at all because it is dangerous and, therefore, impractical when other skills will do (Pratchett *A Hat Full of Sky* ch. 6, ch. 7). Another notable example of wild magic is Mercedes Lackey and James Mallory's *The Obsidian Mountain* trilogy. Susanna Clarke's

Jonathan Strange and Mr Norrell is an example of wild magic in a more traditional format, featuring unpredictable and overwhelming encounters with faerie magic. For this discussion, Gail Z. Martin's *The Ascendent Kingdoms Saga* has been chosen as the example because of its stark demonstration of a no-condition-to-condition-of-risk system.

The final provisional category encompasses hybrid systems. Hybrid systems account for additional complexities. This category includes magic systems that possess the traits of more than one magic system or are not easily identifiable because there is more than one magic system present in the fantasy world, and these systems fulfil different functions. Many fantasy texts will fall into this grey area of hybrid systems and will also possess complexities beyond the categories provisionally suggested here. What these suggested categories do provide are specific poles of reference broader than what has been offered by Clute, while offering flexibility for further refinement, because magic is one of the most common elements of a fantasy world and there are no theories for how magic might be analyzed for its various contributions to different fantasy texts. For Nona, in the *Book of the Ancestor*, the type of magic she has access to allows her greater mobility in a hierarchically structured society with divisive political factions. Magic gives her access to status that allows her to operate outside of the normal restrictions for her class and gender within this world, and equips her with the allies necessary to forestall the impending destruction of her world. Examining the *Book of the Ancestor* retrospectively and through the lens of magic demonstrates the threads of narrative and thematic layering that can be traced and pulled apart to see what rhetorics, cosmologies, relationships, and other social and cultural systems are supported and reinforced by the structure of the world through its expression of magic, and what is not.

This essay has analyzed how the magic of Mark Lawrence's *Book of the Ancestor* series supports and reinforces narrative and thematic layering, with an overview of the magic classifications, which center on the identification of the magic system elements of location and condition of use. In undertaking this analysis, this essay contributes to the field of fantasy studies by making a case for recasting magic as a critical tool, and by presenting provisional categories as a potential aid to this endeavor. As yet, there has not been enough work done in this area to support a critical discussion of what magic says about its narrative world and how the type of magic present can support thematic meaning. It is clear that analysis of magic in fantasy can add salient new dimensions to existing and emerging discussions in this field.

Works Cited

Attebery, Brian. *Strategies of Fantasy*. Indiana University Press, 1992.

Bezio, Kristin. "Maker's Breath: Religion, Magic, and the 'Godless' World of Bioware's Dragon Age II (2011)." *Heidelberg Journal of Religions on the Internet*, vol. 5, 2014, pp. 134–61.

Card, Orson Scott. *The Writer's Digest Guide to Science Fiction & Fantasy*. Writer's Digest Books, 2010.

Clarke, Timothy. *The Cambridge Introduction to Literature and the Environment*. Cambridge University Press, 2011.

Clarke, Susanna. *Jonathan Strange and Mr Norrell*. Bloomsbury, 2005.

"Conditions." *Baldur's Gate Wiki*, 20 Feb. 2024, https://bg3.wiki/wiki/Conditions. Accessed 23 February 2024

DiPaolo, Marc. *Fire and Snow: Climate Fiction from The Inklings to Game of Thrones*. State University of New York Press, 2018.

Filonenko, Oleksandra. "Magic, Witchcraft and Faerie: Evolution of magical ideas in Ursula K. Le Guin's Earthsea Cycle." *Mythlore*, vol. 39, no. 2, 2021, pp. 27–48.

Frye, Northrop. *Anatomy of Criticism: Four Essays*. 1957. Ebook, Princeton University Press, 2000.

Hobb, Robin. *Forest Mage*. Ebook, HarperVoyager, 2007.

---. *Renegade's Magic*. Ebook, HarperVoyager, 2007.

---. *Shaman's Crossing*. Ebook, HarperVoyager, 2006.

Hodges, Peter. "The Art of Brutal Prose: An Interview with Mark Lawrence." *Clarkesworld Magazine*, no. 74, November 2012, https://clarkesworldmagazine.com/lawrence_interview/. Accessed 26 February 2024.

Horkheimer, Max, and Theodor W. Adorno. *Dialectic of Enlightenment*. Stanford University Press, 2002.

Howard, Jeff. *Game magic: a designer's guide to magic systems in theory and practice*. CRC Press, 2014.

Jemisin, N. K. "But, but, but – WHY does magic have to make sense?" *nkjemison.com*, 15 June. 2012, https://nkjemisin.com/2012/06/but-but-but-why-does-magic-have-to-make-sense. Accessed 17 March 2022.

Jordan, Robert. *The Eye of the World*. Ebook, Hachette Digital, 2009.

Lackey, Mercedes, and James Mallory. *The Outstretched Shadow*. Ebook, Tor, 2003.

---. *To Light a Candle*. Ebook, Tor, 2004.

---. *When Darkness Falls*. Ebook, Tor, 2006.

Laukkanen, Markus. "Literalizing Hyperobjects: On (Mis) Representing Global Warming in Song of Ice and Fire and *Game of Thrones*." *Fantasy and Myth in the Anthropocene: Imagining Futures and Dreaming Hope in Literature and Media*, edited by Marek Oziewicz, Brian Attebery & Tereza Dêdinová, Bloomsbury Academic, 2022, pp. 456–76.

Lawrence, Mark. *Grey Sister*. Ebook, HarperCollins*Publishers*, 2018.

---. *Holy Sister*. Ebook, HarperCollins*Publishers*, 2019.

---. *Red Sister*. Ebook, HarperCollins*Publishers*, 2017.

---. "Magic." *The Encyclopedia of Fantasy*, edited by John Clute and John Grant, St. Martin's Press, 1997, pp. 615-18.

Martin, Gail Z. *Ice Forged*. Ebook, Hachette Digital, 2013.

---. *Reign of Ash*. Ebook, Hachette Digital, 2014.

---. *Shadow and Flame*. Ebook, Hachette Digital, 2015.

---. *War of Shadows*. Ebook, Hachette Digital, 2016.

Martin, George R. R. *A Clash of Kings*. Voyager, 1998.

---. *A Dance with Dragons*. Voyager, 2011.

---. *A Feast for Crows*. Voyager, 2005.

---. *A Game of Thrones*. Voyager, 1996.

---. *A Storm of Swords*. Voyager, 2000.

Martins, Vincent. "'Winter is coming': From Climate Threat to Political Collapse." *Caliban: French Journal of English Studies*, vol. 63, 2020, pp. 203–15.

Mendlesohn, Farah. *Rhetorics of Fantasy*. Ebook, Wesleyan University Press, 2008.

Murphy, Patrick D. "Voicing Another Nature." *Dialogue of voices: Feminist literary theory and Bakhtin*, edited by Karen Hohne & Helen Wussow, University of Minnesota Press, 1994, pp. 59–82.

Novik, Noami. *Uprooted*. Del Ray, 2015.

Pratchett, Terry. *A Hat Full of Sky*. RHCP Digital, 2014.

---. *I Shall Wear Midnight*. RHCP Digital, 2014.

Poradecki, Mateusz. "The limits of magic: A study in breaking through barriers in fantasy fiction." *Lodz University Press*, vol. 57, no. 2, 2020, pp. 113–28.

Ravikumar N, Shanmugan N & Chandrasekar R. "A Comparative Study of Magical Divulging and Modern Schema in C.S Lewis' *The Chronicles of Narnia* and J.R.R Tolkien's *The Lord of the Rings*." *Language in India*, vol. 18, no. 12, 2018, pp. 265–73.

Rosu, A. "Magic/Science in Patrick Rothfuss." *Journal of the Fantastic in the Arts*, vol. 31, no. 3, 2020, pp. 381–403.

Sanderson, Brandon. "Sanderson's First Law." *Brandonsanderson.com*, 20 February. 2007, https://www.brandonsanderson.com/sandersons-first-law/. Accessed 17 March 2022.

---. *Elantris*. Gollancz. 2016.

---. *Oathbringer*. Tor, 2017.

---. *Rhythm of War*. Tor, 2020.

---. *The Way of Kings*. Tor, 2010.

---. *Wind and Truth*. Tor, 2024.

---. *Words of Radiance*. Tor, 2014.

Stern, Eddo. "A Touch of Medieval: narrative, magic and computer technology in massively multiplayer computer role-playing games." *Proceedings of the Computer Games and Digital Cultures Conference June 6-8, Tampere, Finland*, edited by Frans Mayra, Tampere University Press, 2002.

Turchi, Peter. *Maps of the Imagination: The Writer as Cartographer*. Trinity University Press, 2004.

Tresca, Michael J. *The Evolution of Fantasy Role-Playing Games*. Ebook, Jefferson, North Carolina and London, McFarland & Company, Inc. Publishers, 2011.

Vander Ploeg, Scott, and Kenneth Phillips. "Playing with Power: The Science of Magic in Interactive Fantasy." *Journal of the Fantastic in the Arts*, vol. 9, no. 2, 1998, pp. 142–56.

Wolf, Mark J.P. *Building Imaginary Worlds: The Theory and History of Subcreation*. Routledge, 2012.

Economics in Frank Herbert's *Dune* and its Use as a Storytelling Tool

Amelia Kerns

FRANK HERBERT'S 1965 *DUNE* contains economic and financial detail for its in-world components of alternate conditions, magical spice, high-speed space travel, and governance. In many cases, it provides specific numerical figures. In relation to these economics, academic literature on *Dune* has mostly focused on economics' relationship through the purview of politics, environmental concerns, and spice's allegory to oil, drugs, or historical seasonings. In the scope of this greater dialogue, a study of *Dune*'s use of economics and finance and the corresponding impact of economics on writing craft has yet to be fully explored. This essay argues that *Dune*'s inclusion of specific economics and finance adds a rich layer to the narrative, benefitting the writing by creating a world steeped in realism, and giving characters tools that subsequently drive the plot.

Economics and finance are two sides of the same coin, with the first being an observation of how wealth and goods are consumed, distributed, or otherwise managed within society, and the latter the study and active management of large money and investments. In this essay, the word economics will be used in reference to both fields, though occasionally the word finance will be used for specific applications of financial statements and time value of money considerations. But prior to engaging with *Dune*'s economics directly, it would be useful to first pose the question: why focus on economics at all?

This is a question of two layers. The first, broader question, is why consider economics in science fiction? The second, more specific question, is why analyze economics in *Dune*? While this essay primarily concerns itself with the second inquiry and what benefits might be derived from such an inclusion, the first is invariably linked to the second. Therefore, it is useful to address the first inquiry and engage existing modes of thinking. One proposed reason, and a topic of recent essays, is the external value economic speculations could potentially bring to the real world. A common theme between economic speculations and the real world is that much of modern day financial capitalistic economics is reliant on possible value to be derived from fictional imaginings of the future (Fisher, Vint, Davies, Chang). As Sherryl Vint notes, currency, stocks, and societal confidence in future profits in relation to current market worth are all inherently tied to belief (Vint, "Promissory Futures" 11-12). Using such correlations as a base, Fisher, Vint, Davies, and Chang argue that economic fictions may have transferability to the real world. Mark Fisher suggests that science fictions "can be machines for designing the future" (12), and William Davies states, "[t]o write science fictions about the economy is to insist on the possibility that imagination can intrude into economic life" (Davies 29-30). This essay acknowledges that *Dune*, with its resuscitated antiquated semi-feudalistic economic system, may act more as a warning more than as one of the bright new futures these analysts had in mind.

This consideration leads to a similar discussion about the proposed benefits of economics in science fiction: its use as a literary critique of real economic systems. Mathias Nilges writes from this perspective. Nilges argues that speculation is at the heart of current finance-focused economy, and this then prompts stories within the science fiction community in the form of literary critiques (Nilges 38, 42-44, 48-49). The author further argues that "[w]e can understand speculative fiction as a mode of critique, therefore, that probes the limits and immanent contradictions of speculative finance, thereby creating the conditions for its transcendence" (Nilges 38). Nilges emphasizes evaluating limitations rather than trying to imagine something new, and is careful to clarify that not every work is an evaluation of limitations (Nilges 41, 57). Does *Dune* qualify as an evaluation of limitations? Joshua Pearson explores the parallels he draws between Paul Atreides's rise to power with "exceptional consciousness" and the financialized subjectivity of power management seen in markets in the twenty-first century (Pearson 155, 158).

Economics' interweaving with society and, of particular interest to science fiction, science and technology is a concept this essay believes has merit and will explore in relation to writing craft. Frank Herbert, the series' author, subscribes to this philosophy of interconnectedness, saying in an interview about *Dune*:

> I am writing about the political ecology, the—ah religious ecology, the social ecology, and the physical ecology of our world. And I think you do not separate any one part of this [sic] from the others. [...] I'm writing about the economic ecology, the the—politics of all these things that influence our lives. (Herbert *Waldentapes*)

Interrelatedness is observable in the relationship between the Enlightenment and the Industrial Revolution's explosive leaps in technological gains, which, as others such as Peter Weingart and Luz María Hernández Nieto have noted, led to the creation of the science fiction genre (Weingart and Nieto 37-39, 41-42). Joel Mokyr explores the impact of culture in events that led up to and created the Industrial Revolution in Europe. Mokyr starts by defining culture as a "set of beliefs, values, and preferences, capable of affecting behavior, that are socially (not genetically) transmitted and that are shared by some subset of society" (Mokyr 8). He goes on to specify religious, social, political, and economic ecologies as aspects of culture (Mokyr 34) that drive an explosive change in society, technology, and economy (Mokyr 3-4, 339-340). "Nations and their economies grow in large part because they increase their collective knowledge about nature and their environment [physical ecology]," he writes, "and because they are able to direct this knowledge toward productive ends [economic ecology]" (Mokyr 339). Mokyr clarifies that sustained growth cannot happen without influencing cultural thought with a large enough impact on social ecology to lead to change within key institutions (Mokyr 3, 59, 68-69, 61). Cultural entrepreneurs can only flourish when powerful religious or governmental institutions, political and religious ecologies, are conducive to these changes (64). Science, economics, and politics have become even more intertwined. As Weingart and Nieto point out, weapons of mass destruction irrevocably tie science to politics (Weingart and Nieto 44-48). What does this mean for economics in science fiction? Science is linked to social, political, religious, and economic considerations. Economics as a writing tool works best in a symbiotic relationship. For this essay, realism refers to logically conceivable environments, and plot driven by conditions that might be reasonably expected from characters or nature. The opposite might be a more whimsical story whose characters take on mythical qualities, whose settings are fanciful or mysterious, and whose plots include the unexpected.

In science fiction, this has been particularly debated as it relates to science. For example, Robert Heinlein, an early influential voice, defined science fiction as a "realistic speculation about possible [mostly] future events, based solidly on adequate knowledge of the real world, past and present, and on a thorough understanding of the nature and significance of the scientific method" (Heinlein 17). Such definitions have largely fallen out of favor. Vint poses the question, "what are we to make of the scientific 'realism' of a film such as *Alien*, which focuses on science's embedded relationships with capitalism and the military rather than on the physics of space travel?" (Vint "Culture" 307). For Vint, the answer is found in the "culture of science" (Vint "Culture" 305), which helps "us remember that science does not exist in a vacuum but is produced by, and in turn shapes, a contingent, malleable, complex social world" (Vint "Culture" 315).

For economics, those in favor of realism are quick to point out its importance to a reader's suspension of disbelief and the avoidance of plot holes. Ha-Joon Chang hints at this when he writes, "SF [science fiction] writers could do with a more solid understanding of economics" (Chang 41), going on to give an example: "brilliant though it may be in many ways, Ward Moore's *Bring the Jubilee* failed to totally convince me, because its alternative future starts from the utterly [economically] implausible premise that the South won the American Civil War" (Chang 41). Conversely, there are those who might point out that detailed or realistic elements would be out of place in dreamlike worlds such as *Alice's Adventures in Wonderland*, where very little makes sense (from time to size to endless tea parties). Though not a science fiction book, it does provide a good example of a story where more detailed or realistic economic inclusions are irrelevant, and perhaps even detrimental, to the story's attempt to cultivate a mysterious, unusual, and unexpected narrative. Thus, it can be inferred that the benefits of realism in economics depend on the type of story being told. Tonally serious science fiction stories will find many benefits in incorporating realism, while more whimsical stories may find scientific realism counterproductive. *Dune* takes great pains in its pursuit of realism in human machinations. For example, while some characters may take on larger-than-life qualities (namely, Paul Atreides), the narrative ensures such events are explained by individual steps rather than portraying him as a mythical messiah. The economics also reflect the narrative's quest to reflect realism within carefully noted business logistic concerns and stated numerical figures for revenues and costs. In observing economics then, this essay assumes that economic portrayals, especially as they pertain to the real-world models they incorporate, matter.

But should these elements be accurate or merely believable? Giving specific numerical figures may lend a sense of realism, even if the numbers are inaccurate. Some may claim that such considerations, especially as they pertain to the small numerical figures of spice mining operations in *Dune*, are immaterial to the greater story. For example, does it matter if a character says something vague, such as "our business is going to suffer," or, as Hawat states in *Dune*, "our profit margin will be reduced to a very narrow six or seven per cent" (Herbert 144)? In the portion of this analysis dedicated to spice operations, this essay argues that *Dune* uses accuracy, as opposed to believability, to lend a greater depth of understanding to character internality, motivations, and subsequent actions.

In the next sections, I demonstrate that *Dune*'s coinciding use of economics with social, religious, political, and environmental factors adds a rich layer of depth to the narrative as a well-positioned writing tool in terms of writing craft's elements of setting, character, and plot. Financial methodologies will focus on plot-relevant components, namely monetary usage on the planet Arrakis and the spice trade. Models will include an examination of how the Law of Supply and Demand defines the role of scarce resources within *Dune* and how financial statement reconstruction, five-year forecasting, and net present value calculations can be used to bring clarity to character decisions.

Lastly, a brief review will cover how these elements drive the plot to its conclusion.

Currencies of Worldbuilding: Solari and Water on Arrakis

Dune uses monetary considerations in setting and, more specifically, worldbuilding. "Worldbuilding" refers to the components of setting involved with creating a new fictional world—something apart and different from Earth. Fiat and commodity currencies are used to add depth to the setting and strengthen *Dune*'s larger narrative through a framework of competing character interests in a relationship in which the environment shapes the people, and the people shape the environment.

Fiat money has no intrinsic value of its own, but instead derives its value from a government promising the currency has worth, and—so long as the society uses the fiat as money—it does. Fiat currency is beneficial in that it gives governing bodies greater control of money interest rates, liquidity, and velocity, but it carries risk of governmental overprinting or a general societal loss of faith in value. This currency type can be seen in *Dune*'s imperial unit of solari, which has "its purchasing power set at quatricentennial negotiations between the Guild, the Landsraad, and the Emperor" (Herbert 858).

Commodity money has intrinsic value as an object on its own, regardless of whether it is traded as money. Commodity currency is beneficial in that it has worth outside of currency purposes, and governmental institutions cannot overinflate the economy, but it bears risks of fluctuations in natural supply or costs in transportation and storage. On Planet Arrakis, the harsh desert climate and extreme scarcity of moisture causes water to become highly valued (Herbert 85). The Law of Supply and Demand defines the relationship between scarcity, demand, and price: the price of an object will rise if demand is high and availability is low, and vice versa. But when something is valued highly, such as water on Arrakis where there is "only so much water to support human life" (Herbert 100), and has characteristics such as portability, uniformity, and divisibility that are needed for functionality as money, that commodity can become money itself. "On Arrakis, water was money" and "a major mark of wealth" (Herbert 504, 85).

Dune employs two economic tools as they relate to the nature of these currency types: water's physical scarcity and fiat's traceability. Scarcity, especially in its use of commodity currencies, creates a focal point that all vested parties must consider in their relations to each other. In this regard, water and spice can be seen to mirror each other, but more discussion of spice will take place later in this essay. This scarcity aids in the creation of unique business practices, customs, and religious beliefs that greatly enrich the depth of the world in *Dune* and allows for political maneuvering. For example, water, due to its immediate scarcity, is of primary concern to those on Arrakis. In the cities, a unique industry of water shippers and peddlers generate enough wealth to create water magnates (Herbert 210, 220). *Dune* uses this to stir tensions between various political and economic parties. This can first be seen in the populace's response to the arrival of House Atreides when they have "water riots when it was learned how many people the Duke was adding to the population" that "stopped only when the people learned" of the installation of "new windtraps and condensers to take care of the load" (Herbert 101). Tensions are further visible in the dissatisfaction among those in the established water industry when House Atreides voices intentions to change the climate of Arrakis so that "[o]ne day, water will not be a precious commodity" and water shippers should "diversify [...] holdings" (Herbert 211).

Water is also used to create the unique practices, customs, and religious norms of the Fremen who live "at the desert's edge" (Herbert 6). Since Fremen are separated by large swaths of barren land, reducing water loss takes paramount importance. To combat this, Fremen wear special "still-suits" to prevent loss of more than a "thimbleful of moisture a day" (Herbert 178). Special customs spring from water's scarcity: "water belongs to the tribe [...] except in combat" and "flesh belongs to the person" (Herbert 503). When a person dies, their water is recovered and weighed (Herbert 502-503). Other customs can be seen in the sacred significance placed on the act of crying for the deceased, which is referred to as giving "moisture to the dead" (Herbert 509, 765). Further, Fremen give water a sense of mystic admiration: "Here there was a substance more precious than all others—it was life itself and entwined all around with symbolism and ritual" (Herbert 509). From a writing craft standpoint, *Dune* uses the scarcity of water to build unique customs and business practices revolving around this scarcity. In these examples, the environment shapes the people and their tensions, driving them to create such inventions as still-suits or religious practices set in conserving water. But the people and their religious, political, and personal passions also shape the environment. As pointed out by Mokyr, "Religious beliefs and metaphysical attitudes condition a society's willingness to investigate the secrets of nature, alter its physical environment irreversibly, and 'play God'" (Mokyr 7).

The Fremen's religious beliefs hold water in reverence as they await the "Lisan al-Gaib" or the "Voice from the Outer World" (Herbert 158), a promised messiah who will change Arrakis to bring "[w]ater from the sky" (Herbert 762). In essence, the Fremen are hoping for money to fall from the sky, creating a utopia wherein the planet is green and rich and there is a great abundance of wealth. Two figures rise to political power among the Fremen using the promise of a future wealthy, terraformed Arrakis: Pardot Kynes and by extension his son, Liet Kynes; and Paul Atreides. While they each rule at separate times, both Kynes and Atreides use this underlying promise of future wealth to secure their place. The Kyneses promise a terraformed planet rich in water within 350 years (Herbert 802). Paul Atreides joins the Fremen after Liet Kynes is dead, and thus has an opportunity to fill the vacuum of such a promise of wealth. Instead of waiting hundreds of years, he offers them a new proposal: help him rise to power within the greater inter-stellar Imperium, and he will bring "flowing water here open to the sky and green oases rich with good things" (Herbert 792). In the Fremen's rush to follow Atreides and bring water to Arrakis, they do not seem to take into consideration that Paul Atreides will essentially collapse their current currency system. Leto Atreides promised to do as much in the cities, as well, which the water shippers minded a great deal. Such considerations seem not to bother the Fremen, as Paul Atreides would supposedly bring an even greater paradise.

As it relates to Paul Atreides's rise to the throne, fiat currency plays a smaller—though crucial—role in its noted absence among the Fremen: keeping their population size a secret. The Fremen bribe the Guild with spice to keep weather satellites, which monitor the terrain and thus would reveal their activities, from being installed (Herbert 311). In a similar vein, the Fremen's use of an off-the-grid currency source likely aids in keeping their true numbers hidden from institutionalized tracking. The Guild has a monopoly on international banking (Herbert 208, 382, 842), though what influence this has in smaller communities on planets is unclear. Though it can be assumed that the Guild has at least some indicator of the wealth of various political factions within the Imperium, the Guild states, "Very little's known of the deep desert" (Herbert 218, 233). The environment and the people shape each other. As a writing tool, scarcity of water is used as a commodity currency and a driving plot point that creates a single focus for various parties to align interests or vie for power. Commodity currency also has a unique potential for ties to religious and cultural customs due to its physical and often essential nature, which paper or digital currency would struggle to reproduce. *Dune* uses commodity currency's less institutionally manipulatable and traceable nature to create a blind spot for the higher administrative powers that use fiat currency. Water's use as a currency obviously does not scale beyond Arrakis. While this section has predominately focused on worldbuilding and related plot uses, the next section will focus on Arrakis spice operations and its relation to character.

Opportunity Costs and Character: Profits of Arrakis's Spice Trade

Economics is particularly well suited as a craft tool for writing character due to its close ties to human desire and emotional well-being, and as an observable indicator of character intent. Most notably, economics proves an excellent tool in the hands of the characters themselves, giving them a means to interact with their environment in meaningful ways and to subsequently drive the plot. Additionally, *Dune*'s use of accurate, as opposed to believable, figures provide a deeper insight into these characters. Given that the Arrakis spice trade and its associated profits are key drivers of character-focused economics within the plot, they provide an excellent study of these benefits. "Character" refers to a being—human or otherwise—that interacts within the world of the narrative. In genre fictions of Western Europe and its linguistic and literary former colonies, a well-written character should have motive, agency, and make decisions within the plot that make sense given that character's personality and circumstances. They should be imperfect, flawed, and see the world painted by their worldview. This analysis uses this assumption in its review of character. The Emperor, House Harkonnen, and House Atreides use the spice trade as tools to manipulate each other. In each of these circumstances, character intent is clear in an observable way to the reader, thus lending greater insight into each character, whether through implied or direct interaction. The close relationship between politics, economy, and social ecologies can be observed. This analysis reviews these schemes to demonstrate this concept.

First, it is necessary to establish spice's key role in the Imperium. Spice is key to the Combine Honnete Ober Advancer Mercantiles (CHOAM) Company, which has a monopoly on all Imperium trade, including "logs, donkeys, horses, cows, lumber, dung, sharks, whale fur—the most prosaic and the most exotic" (Herbert 68). Ownership of CHOAM is broken into directorships, and these are "the real evidence of political power in the Imperium" (Herbert 32). CHOAM is reliant on the Guild to ferry goods between planets, and the Guild's navigators "use the spice drug of Arrakis to produce the limited prescience necessary for guiding spaceships through the void" (Herbert 828), meaning that transport for all goods throughout the Imperium is dependent on a single substance: spice. The Guild "must have the spice to exist" (Herbert 783).

In a move that sets events into motion, an insecure Emperor rests uneasy eyes on House Atreides, a royal-blooded dukedom seated on planet Caladan that often acts as an unofficial spokesbody for other Houses and possesses a well-trained army (Herbert 106). Since the Emperor cannot move against the well-loved House Atreides himself without drawing scorn, he lures House Harkonnen to aid him with the promise of a CHOAM directorship as a reward (Herbert 31-32). House Harkonnen proves agreeable to the bribe not only for the power and wealth, but also because of an "old feud" between the Harkonnen and Atreides bloodlines (Herbert 103). With this agreement in place, the Emperor attempts to use House Harkonnen's spice operation as the trap to bring House Atreides to ruin. In an order disguised as an honor, the Emperor offers House Atreides CHOAM directorship and high-status spice mines. As previously arranged with the Emperor, House Harkonnen surrenders Arrakis with the intent to repossess it (Herbert 67). In this example, the Emperor has two things necessary to drive the plot forward: incentive and means. First, House Atreides's growing political influence and wealth create an incentive for him to act, and then he is able to use economics as a tool to act subtly. In this sense, economics gives the character a direct tool to interact with, and shape, environment. Given *Dune*'s use of realism, these logical and rational character choices lend a great sense of depth. From a craft standpoint, realism lends many benefits in that the characters have motive and agency.

However, economics does not exist in a vacuum but in a world full of complex layers consisting of the social, political, and physical. As Herbert says in his interview, "You don't separate mind and body and understand the human being, and therefore you don't separate any of these elements and understand what's going on in our world" (Herbert, *Waldentapes*). Mokyr notes that great economic growth during the Industrial Revolution was brought about by "the belief that power and government are there not to serve the rich and powerful but society at large" (Mokyr 341). In the next two examples of characters wielding economics, the Emperor and House Harkonnen's self-serving choices cost other factions, most notably the Atreides, in a series of events that cause great economic, political, and social turmoil to the detriment of the Imperium: a period of contraction instead of growth.

House Harkonnen leaves House Atreides with faulty mining equipment, hoping that the reduced spice production will lead to supply constraints.. This resulting shortage of spice will cause prices in existing spice markets to rise because demand will remain the same while supply dwindles. CHOAM profits would plummet as they would not have a supply of spice to sell. Additionally, since spice is necessary for space travel, and all trade, including that of the Great Houses, runs through CHOAM and the Guild, an increase in transportation costs will also increase cost of business, causing losses for CHOAM and some Great Houses. However, those that have a stockpile of spice will make great gains (Herbert, 68). As Paul Atreides states, "They mean spice production to fail and you to be blamed," to which Leto Atreides responds, "Think how [allies would] react if I were responsible for a serious reduction in their income.[...] They'd look the other way no matter what was done to me" (Herbert 68). Duke Leto goes on to ascertain that the Emperor is behind the plot by identifying who would profit by House Atreides's failure to produce spice (Herbert 69). This example shows that the Emperor and House Harkonnen have little concern for smaller factions that might suffer from a spice shortage as they price-gouge, demonstrating a very targeted use of market manipulation as a political tool to alienate House Atreides from their allied social factions.

The consequences of these actions can best be seen in House Atreides' response. This section will focus on two aspects of House Atreides's relationship with spice operations: emotions and use of economics as a tool. Before focusing on either, however, this analysis will pause to look at the financial risks and benefits to House Atreides in spice operations by producing financial income statements and then examining these figures with net present value analysis. I will also demonstrate that accurate—as opposed to believable—economics provides greater insight into House Atreides's circumstances. Effort will be made to preserve Herbert's presumed original intent, though some assumptions will be required to create a complete analysis. These assumptions will be covered briefly within the analysis, with a full list provided in the appendix.

Spice "cannot be manufactured, it must be mined on Arrakis" (Herbert 68). As "Arrakis is a one-crop planet" (Herbert 443), spice operations are the sole economic output, representing the overall health of the planet's industry. Since the events of *Dune* take place as one Great House takes over spice mining operations from another, this takeover involves large-scale logistics of removing previous personnel from Arrakis and installing new staff. Each House implements vastly different business strategies with varying accessibility to production assets for their operations, creating the need to reconstruct both financial statements. From *Dune*, the following data can be extracted: House Atreides acquires Arrakis spice mines from House Harkonnen, who had previously run operations for eighty years after being granted a contract by CHOAM (5). After Hawat—advisor to House Atreides—evaluates the facilities, he says, "We'll be lucky to get half the equipment into operation and luckier yet if a fourth of it's still working six months from now" (Herbert 139). Hawat further reports:

> Under the Harkonnens, maintenance and salaries were held to fourteen per cent [of revenue]. We'll be lucky to make it at thirty per cent at first. With investment and growth factors accounted for, including the CHOAM percentage and military costs, our profit margin will be reduced to a very narrow six or seven per cent until we can replace worn-out equipment. We then should be able to boost it up to twelve or fifteen per cent where it belongs. (Herbert 144)

Lastly, Hawat states that "the Harkonnens took ten billion solaris [in revenue] out of here [Arrakis] every three hundred and thirty Standard days" (Herbert 138), and the Atreides "output [for] the first two seasons should be down a third from the Harkonnen average" (Herbert 145).

Table: Harkonnen Operations

	in millions
	Year One
Revenue	10,000
Cost of Goods Sold (COGS)	5,725
Salaries & Maintenance	1,400
CHOAM Lease on Prod. Facilities	1,500
Depreciation on Prod. Equipment	1,163
All Other, incl. Oper. Fuel & Utilities	1,662
Gross Profit	**4,275**
Selling, General, & Admin (SG&A), incl. Non-Production CHOAM Lease, Military Costs, and Non-Operations Depr.	2,925
Operating Income	**1,350**
Operating Profit Margin	13.50%

With this data, it is possible to reconstruct a partial income statement to the operating profit margin line, which excludes interest and taxes. See the reconstructed chart representing 330 days, herein referred to as a year, of Arrakis spice production under the Harkonnens. Revenue and operating profit margin are populated with Hawat's given figures of 10 billion solaris and 13.5%. To determine operating income, I used algebra alongside the operating profit margin formula, so that Operating Profit Margin = Operating Income / Revenue x 100, resulting in an operating income of 1.35 billion solaris. Costs can be further deduced with the operating income formula, so that Operating Income = Revenue − (Cost of Goods Sold + Operating Expenses), resulting in total costs at 8.65 billion solaris. Assumptions in allocating this 8.65 billion in costs between CHOAM payments, depreciation expense, and indirect costs is required as further detail is not provided in-text. Briefly, CHOAM payments will be treated as a percentage lease—a lease paid primarily based on income. It can be reasonably assumed the mining contract issued to the Harkonnens by CHOAM eighty years prior included such a clause. While it is sensible at first glance to assume that CHOAM payments are dividends, this is incorrect given Hawat's mention of CHOAM payments within the context of profit margin, in which dividends are not accounted for. In this analysis, 15% of revenue is used. While this is a sizable percentage, it is reasonable given that spice profits hold political weight—enough for the Emperor to express concern over "CHOAM Company profits pouring down this rat hole [of Arrakis]" (Herbert 744).

Selling, General, and Administrative (SG&A) costs are assumed to be nearly 30% of revenue due to the Harkonnens' focus on military security costs and wasteful business practices, the latter demonstrated in banquet customs of intentionally discarding water (Herbert 206). It should also be noted that Fremen actively sabotage and destroy equipment which would result in expense write-offs for destroyed equipment (Herbert 81-82). Such costs would be recorded in EBIT (earnings before interest and taxes) which comes after the operating income line on an income statement, but given the ongoing sabotage in operations, this analysis has opted to include it in operating income. Since the extent of the Fremens' "ravages was a carefully guarded secret" (Herbert 82), and there is no good way to figure the damage numbers, it has been included under SG&A instead of as a separate line item.

Depreciation—the practice of allocating an asset's cost over its useful life—is straight-lined at 11.63% of revenue. It is important to note that the cost of equipment and depreciation are separate. This is because when equipment is purchased, items of equal value have been obtained. Depreciation occurs as those pieces of equipment deteriorate, so money is lost. The high depreciation costs in this scenario can be attributed to the desert's harsh climate and the reliance on spice-collecting vehicles called "factory crawlers" to collect spice from the top layer of sand (Herbert 189). Factory crawlers have an asset life of four years due to environmental wear and tear, excluding any Fremen sabotage.

Now that the Harkonnen operation is established, a similar chart can be created for Hawat's forecast of the Atreides's operation. The Atreides's Revenue is adjusted down to one-third of the Harkonnen's. A best attempt has been made to retread Hawat's estimate of lowered profit margins due to depreciation from replacing 75% of equipment. Further detail on depreciation calculations can be found in appendix charts 1-A, 1-B, and 1-C. Note below, the drop of 171 million in depreciation between years four and five, as many of the assets have become fully depreciated, and a more regular replacement schedule resumed.

Table: Atreides Operations Five Year Forecast

	Year One	Year Two	Year Three	Year Four	Year Five
Revenue	6,667	6,667	7,800	8,900	10,000
Cost of Goods Sold (COGS)	5,267	5,267	5,959	6,327	6,650
Salaries & Maintenance	2,000	2,000	2,005	2,010	2,215
CHOAM Lease on Prod. Facilities	1,000	1,000	1,170	1,335	1,500
Depreciation on Prod. Equipment	1,381	1,381	1,381	1,381	1,210
All Other, incl. Oper. Fuel & Utilities	886	886	1,404	1,602	1,662
Gross Profit	1,400	1,400	1,841	2,573	3,350
Selling, General, & Admin (SG&A), incl. Non-Production CHOAM Lease, Military Costs, and Non-Operations Depr.	1,000	1,000	1,170	1,575	2,063
Operating Income	400	400	671	997	1,350
Operating Profit Margin	6.00%	6.00%	8.60%	11.21%	13.50%

Between the Harkonnen operation and the Atreides operation (in year five), costs are allocated differently based on their business practice and circumstance. While the same operating profit margin is reached, House Atreides spends more on COGS, driven by depreciation on long-term equipment replacements and higher salaries. Atreides saves money in SG&A due to less wasteful business practices and savings in Fremen sabotage. Holding CHOAM payments and other expenses equal, the Harkonnen operation offers lower wages and invests more in SG&A due to higher military costs, wasteful business practices, and Fremen sabotage.

All this analysis proves that, at the very least, the numbers in *Dune* reflect a great deal of accuracy that can be rebuilt with current business practices. To better understand how this accuracy lends greater insight into character, this analysis must provide an indication whether those profit margins meet House Atreides' required return.

When there are uneven cashflows, as is shown in the five-year forecast below, Net Present Value (NPV) is often utilized by organizations to determine return. Note this chart excludes depreciation expense previously accounted for in operating income as depreciation expense is a non-cashflow item.

Atreides Incoming Cashflows, Excluding Depreciation

	Year One	Year Two	Year Three	Year Four	Year Five	Total
						in millions
Cashflows	1,811	1,811	2,081	2,408	2,590	10,764

NPV is concerned with the worth of expected future cashflows in today's terms, at a given cost of capital. This is in keeping with the concept that money today is more valuable than the same amount in five years because current funds can be used to generate further wealth in that same span. While the concept itself is ancient, Irving Fisher formulized the net present value formula in his 1907 CE work, *The Rate of Interest* (Fisher 402-405):

NPV = Sum of Present Value (PV) Cashflows – Initial Investment
Or: NPV = Cash Flow / $(1 + $ Discount Rate$)^{Time}$ – Initial Investment

The chart below shows the Atreides's return of 476 million solaris in terms of the solaris's current value by using the NPV formula with the previously calculated 6 billion solaris in new equipment purchase (who paid any transportation costs to Arrakis—the Emperor or House Atreides—is unclear,so these are thus excluded here) and an 18% discount rate to account for loan rates, political instability, and unknown Arrakis conditions. This results in a sum of cashflows for the first five years returning 476 million solaris on a six billion solaris investment, or a 7.9% return.

Net Present Value of Forecasted Atreides Solaris Inflows

	Today's Value	Year One	Year Two	Year Three	Year Four	Year Five	*in millions* Where
Incoming Cashflows	1,534	←1,811					$PV = 1,811 / (1 + 0.18)^1$
	1,300	←———— 1,811					$PV = 1,811 / (1 + 0.18)^2$
	1,267	←————————— 2,081					$PV = 2,081 / (1 + 0.18)^3$
	1,242	←————————————— 2,408					$PV = 2,408 / (1 + 0.18)^4$
	1,132	←————————————————— 2,590					$PV = 2,590 / (1 + 0.18)^5$
Initial Funds	-6,000						
NPV	476						

While a 7.9% return is solid, it is likely that House Atreides could find more lucrative short-term projects with significantly less political risk. Returns on spice profits will naturally grow post-year-five from fully functional operations. In addition, the associated CHOAM directorship that comes with House Atreides's acceptance of the project cannot be overlooked. Yet, the fact remains that for at least a five-year period, House Atreides is being asked to bear significant risk to their lives and capital for a venture with mediocre short-term returns. They also lose their seat and rice profits associated with their home planet, Caladan (Herbert 68, 829, 852).

What does this have to do with the characters of House Atreides? These numbers show a version of what they might have been confronted with: an underwhelming five-year return of 7.9% for bearing major risk to their lives and capital. The uncertainty presented here is reflected in the characters' thoughts and concerns. Much of their plan depends on the assumption of forging a positive relationship with the Fremen, as negotiated by Duncan Idaho (Herbert 72). Other political factions are moving against them through market manipulation, as previously discussed. With House Harkonnen having left them faulty equipment, they face a 1.9 billion solaris operating income deficit total in the first two years alone, which will impact CHOAM profits and therefore alienate Atreides from their allies. The CHOAM directorship they gain is mentioned as only a "subtle gain" (Herbert 67).

The Atreides are desperate, which can be seen in Leto Atreides's risky pursuit of the Emperor's sealed equipment to repair their own (Herbert 153-154). Hawat reports, "It'd be rash to move without greater knowledge" (Herbert 154-155). To the advisors' concern, Leto orders them to look into accessing the sealed equipment anyway (Herbert 154). Paul Atreides notes, "*My father is desperate*, he thought. *Things aren't going well for us at all*" and that his father looks like "*[a] caged animal*" (Herbert 156). Jessica, Paul's mother and Duke Leto's concubine, calls the alliance with the Fremen "a dangerous gamble" (Herbert 82) and has to visibly calm her anxieties. However, House Atreides believes the Fremen reduce the riskiness of the project enough to pursue the course of action; Duke Leto tells Paul, "'We have there the potential of a corps as strong and deadly as the [Emperor's] Sardaukar. [...T]he Fremen are there [...] and the spice wealth is there. You see now why we walk into Arrakis, knowing the trap is there'" (Herbert 71).

The accurate in-text numbers, when taken into full account within the context of today's financial practices, help give greater insight and bring to fullness the scope of House Atreides's desperation. The pressures they face are nearly insurmountable, and their corresponding actions demonstrate their insecurities. While House Atreides ultimately falls to the Emperor and House Harkonnen's plans, Paul Atreides will go on to wield economics in one last triumphant bid to become Emperor. Recall that spice is a scarce and crucial resource that the Imperium cannot do without (Herbert 68, 828). Once Paul Atreides unites the Fremen under his banner, he retakes Arrakis from the Harkonnens and gives the Emperor and Guild an ultimatum: "'If I hear any more nonsense from either of you,' Paul said, 'I'll give the order [to the Fremen] that'll destroy all spice production on Arrakis...forever'" (Herbert 772).

Through this analysis of *Dune*, it becomes clear how the economic elements impact setting, character, and plot. These examples show that economics give the characters tools to act within their environment. When the characters have tools and incentive, they drive the plot forward with logical choices. These choices set in motion the series of related events so that each character's choice logically leads to the next, based on their societal and economic needs. This makes *Dune* a character-driven story, which is a persuasive storytelling practice. If these economic elements were not present, the characters' decisions, the setting, and plot would lose depth.

Though some may claim that economics in *Dune* are irrelevant or less important than other considerations, especially as plot pertains to specific and accurate figures, this essay has argued that these inclusions are not only beneficial, but integral to understanding the story to its fullest. Attention to economic elements can lend benefits to writing craft in terms of worldbuilding, giving characters tools with which to act, and creating character-driven plots with logical internal consistency. Stories themselves draw from history, and from the events leading up to the Industrial Revolution, it is clear that no element exists in a vacuum but instead exists in the political, religious, social, and physical aspects of the world. Sherryl Vint writes, "SF [Science Fiction] often returns to science [studies] the full material world of people and passions and politics that is carefully excluded by its official culture" (Vint "Culture" 310). Economics can be seen to work best as a symbiotic storytelling tool. While this analysis is solely focused on *Dune*, there are greater implications for opportunities within genre fiction to incorporate economic principles and use them as a storytelling tool, so that authors can benefit their work.

This analysis has been written through the perspective of modern economic thought and U.S. writing craft, and while many of these principles are universal, it is necessarily limited in scope. There is room for further exploration of the impact of economics in genre fiction in relation to other cultural viewpoints or outlooks regarding trade between human beings or with extraterrestrials to be developed in the future as new technologies and means of communication emerge. While economics may shift in thought or practice, as the science fiction novel *Dune* predicts, economic considerations will likely continue to play a central role in the human story, long into the future.

Appendix

Data, Inferred Data, and Assumptions in Relation to *Dune*'s Spice Trade Data

Data:

- Harkonnen revenue is 10 billion solaris every 330 days (Herbert 138)
- Atreides output for the first two seasons will be down a third from the Harkonnen average (145).
- Half the equipment left to Atreides is inoperable. And, in 6 months, only a quarter will be operable (144).
- Harkonnen Operations: maintenance and salaries in relation to equipment maintenance of harvesting spice were held at 14% (assumed of revenue) (Herbert 144).
- Atreides Operation: maintenance and salaries in relation to equipment maintenance of harvesting spice will be at 30% (assumed of revenue), at first. No further data is specified (144).

- With all things accounted for, profit margin (assumed operating profit margin) will be 6-7% until equipment can be replaced. Then it will return to normal 12-15% (Herbert 144).
- CHOAM requires a percentage (of assumed operating income) (Herbert 144).

Inferred Data:

- The "profit margin" referred to in-text refers to "Operating Profit Margin" as opposed to "Gross Profit Margin" or "Net Profit Margin," as discussion includes expense items related to operating income that would exclude Gross Profit Margin (Herbert 144), but does not include mentions of tax required for Net Profit Margin.
- CHOAM company requires a percentage in terms of a cost Atreides must pay. Since no further data is given, a natural—but incorrect—conclusion could be drawn that CHOAM percentages act as a tax or dividend. Given that CHOAM is a company and not a government entity, the tax theory has been removed from consideration, as have dividends, given that Herbert refers to the "CHOAM percentage" in the context of profit margin (Herbert 144). None of the three profit margin formulas accounts for dividends, so the dividends to shareholders will also not be considered. For this analysis, consideration has been given to the early in-text stipulation that the Harkonnens were given a contract from CHOAM to mine spice on Arrakis (Herbert 5). From this, it can be assumed that CHOAM owns Arrakis spice facilities and production, and leases out these facilities. With this piece in place, it can be inferred that the "CHOAM percentage" refers to a percentage lease, as this lease type accounts for a lease paid based on income.

Assumptions Made:

- Maintenance and salaries under the COGs bracket are given as a percentage (Herbert 144). Based on the text, maintenance and salaries could be a percentage of total operating costs, revenue, or even operating income. For this analysis, a percentage of revenue is assumed.

- The Atreides operation is said to require a 30% (assumed of revenue) maintenance and salaries in relation to equipment and operation, at first. There is no specified information on where the number will settle, later. It is also stated the Harkonnen operation held salaries and maintenance at 14%. The only other info that could aid in further deducing the settled number is a reference to a "twenty per cent" raise for "spice drivers, weather scanners, dune men—any with open sand experience" in relation to some workers trying to quit (Herbert 131). And an advisor tells Leto Atreides, "'Sire, twenty per cent would hardly seem proper inducement to stay'" (Herbert 131). Given the last in-text quote, a 20% increase in wages isn't considered high, though the Duke responds, "remember that the treasury isn't bottomless. Hold it to twenty per cent whenever you can" (Herbert 131). Further adding to the confusion is that maintenance and salaries are never split into categories: the 14% is given as a whole. Without a further clue, this figure becomes murky. For this analysis, it's assumed salaries consisted of 90% of this figure (as salary is usually one of the largest expenses a business will incur) and that a total 25% wage increase (due to the in-text inference that 20% seems low) will be made from the Harkonnen operation. This places salaries at ($[14 * .90] * 1.25) = 15.75\%$, and total salary and maintenance at ($15.75 + [14 * .1]) = 17.15\%$. While not stipulated in the text, it would make sense for an additional safety margin of 5% for other increased expenses—managerial raises, hiring additional personnel to grow operations, or higher maintenance costs—over the Harkonnen operation, driven by the Atreides's less oppressive business practices. This places the total at (17.15 + 5) = 22.15%, an 8.15% additional cost over the Harkonnen operation of 14%.

- Selling, General, & Administrative (SG&A) expense assumptions will be addressed here. Military salaries are included since they act in a similar manner to security personnel. Administration, managerial salaries, and CHOAM lease payments on non-production facilities are part of this figure. Lastly, it is assumed the Atreides operation SG&A slightly more than doubles in five years. This can be attributed in part to variable costs of growing operations, but is mostly attributed to the Atreides's plan to train Fremen as security (Herbert 71).

A depreciation data figure is never provided, only a total operating profit margin. Non-operating depreciation (on office buildings and other structures) has been assumed at a fixed annual depreciation expense of 60 million solaris. For operating depreciation, it is known that 75% of the equipment will need to be replaced in the first six months (139). Below are three charts, one at a regular operation, one with 75% of assets replaced, and the last showing the effects of newly purchased items on depreciation until normal operation resumes (if all else is held constant). Straight line depreciation is used, with 60% of the assets having a four-year asset life on account of the harsh desert conditions. The rest have been allocated between assets of varying life. At normal operation, it is assumed only 80% of the assets will be actively depreciated. This is to account for fully depreciated assets that are still in operation and will not be immediately replaced. A 5% salvage value has been assumed for all assets. It is assumed assets will be rotated as needed in continued operations, even after the 75% equipment purchase. For this analysis, 8 billion in equipment is assumed.

Chart 1-A: Depreciation at Regular Operations

						in millions
Total Assets Required for Prod.	Asset Class	Avg. Asset Life (yrs)	Percentage Weight	Depr. Total with 5% Scrap Value	Straight Line Depr. / Year	Depr. / Year, discount of 20%*
8,000	Spice Equip.	4	60%	4,560	1,140	912
8,000	Factory Equip., short	8	25%	1,900	238	190
8,000	Factory Equip., long	12	10%	760	63	51
8,000	Equip. / Facilities	30	5%	380	13	10
Total			100%	7,600	1,454	1,163

*to account for operational but fully depreciated assets that will not be replaced immediately

Chart 1-B: Total Depreciation with Newly Purchased Equipment

							in millions
New Assets Purchased	Asset Class	Avg. Asset Life (yrs)	Percentage Weight	Depr. Total with 5% Scrap Value	Straight Line Depr. / Year	Depr. from "Normal" Operations*	Total Depr. / Year
6,000	Spice Equip.	4	60%	3,420	855	228.00	1,083
6,000	Factory Equip., short	8	25%	1,425	178	47.50	226
6,000	Factory Equip., long	12	10%	570	48	12.67	60
6,000	Equip. / Facilities	30	5%	285	10	2.53	12
Total			100%	5,700	1,090	291	1,381

*at a 25% weight of total depreciation at "normal," inclusive of 20% discount

Chart 1-C: Newly Purchased Equipment's Impact on Depreciation

		Annual Depreciation				
		Years				*in millions*
		1-4	5-8	9-12	13-30	31+
Asset Life	4	1,083	912	912	912	912
	8	226	226	190	190	190
	12	60	60	60	51	51
	30	12	12	12	12	10
		1,381	1,210	1,174	1,165	1,163

Works Cited

Carroll, Lewis. *Alice's Adventures in Wonderland*, Kindle ed., Puffin Books, 2015.

Chang, Ha-Joon. "Economics, Science Fiction, History and Comparative Studies." *Economic Science Fictions*, Kindle ed., edited by William Davies, Goldsmiths Press / PERC Papers, 2018, pp. 39-47.

Davies, William. Introduction. *Economic Science Fictions*, Kindle ed., edited by William Davies, Goldsmiths Press / PERC Papers, 2018, pp. 14-34.

Fisher, Mark. Forward. *Economic Science Fictions*, Kindle ed., edited by William Davies, Goldsmiths Press / PERC Papers, 2018, pp. 10-12.

Heinlein, Robert A. "Science Fiction: Its Nature, Faults and Virtues." *The Science Fiction Novel: Imagination and Social Criticism*, 3rd ed., Kindle ed., contributors Basil Davenport et al., Advent:Publishers, 2021, 1959, pp. 11-39.

Herbert, Frank. *Dune*. Kindle ed., Ace, 2003.

Herbert, Frank, and David Lynch. *DUNE A Recorded Interview*. Interview conducted by Waldentapes. *Waldentapes*, 1984, cassette tape, side two: last 3 minutes 10 seconds.

Irving, Fisher. *The Rate of Interest*. The Macmillan Company, 1907 pp. 402-405.

Locke, John. "Part 1: Whether the Price of the Hire of Money Can Be Regulated by Law." *Some Considerations of the Consequences of the Lowering of Interest and the Raising the Value of Money*, Kindle ed., WealthofNation, 2014, p. 59.

Mokyr, Joel. *A Culture of Growth of: The Origins of the Modern Economy*. Kindle ed., Princeton University Press, 2017.

Nilges, Mathias. "The Realism of Speculation: Contemporary Speculative Fiction as Immanent Critique of Finance Capitalism." *CR: The New Centennial Review*, vol. 19, no. 1, 2019, pp. 37-60. *JSTOR*, https://doi.org/10.14321/crnewcentrevi.19.1.0037. Accessed 29 May 2024.

Pearson, Joshua. "Frank Herbert's *Dune* and the Financialization of Heroic Masculinity." *CR: The New Centennial Review*, vol. 19, no. 1, 2019, pp. 155-176. *JSTOR*, https://doi.org/10.14321/crnewcentrevi.19.1.0155. Accessed 29 May 2024.

Smith, Adam. "Of Systems of Political Economy." *The Wealth of Nations*, New e. Kindle ed., Wiley-Blackwell, Hoboken, New Jersey, 2023, pp. 767–768.

Vint, Sherryl. "The Culture of Science." *The Oxford Handbook of Science Fiction*, edited by Rob Latham, Oxford University Press, 2014, pp. 305-316.

Vint, Sherryl. "Promissory Futures: Reality and Imagination in Finance and Fiction." *CR: The New Centennial Review*, vol. 19, no. 1, 2019, pp. 11-36. *JSTOR*, https://doi.org/10.14321/crnewcentrevi.19.1.0011 Accessed 29 May 2024.

Weingart, Peter, and Luz María Hernández Nieto. "From Individual to Collective Knowledge Production: A Brief Nonfiction History." *Under the Literary Microscope: Science and Society in the Contemporary Novel*, Kindle ed., edited by Sina Farzin et al., Pennsylvania State University Press, 2021, pp. 37-50.

Historical Fantasy and History

Jared van Duinen

HISTORICAL FANTASY HAS INCREASED in popularity in a variety of popular media. In television, computer games, and novels, the mix of historical context and fantasy elements has proven to be a winning combination. Nevertheless, there has been relatively little academic work to date that engages seriously with the genre of historical fantasy. What this paper purposes to do is approach the genre from the perspective of the historian in order to assess what insights historical fantasy may offer for the academic discipline of history. I begin by looking at how historical fantasy's close engagement with the received historical record has led some scholars to see in the genre a capacity for socio-cultural critique. I then examine the way in which historical fantasy's purposeful ambivalence regarding real and unreal, or fantastical or mythical, aspects of the past serves as a useful reminder of the ambiguity inherent in the historical record and historical sources. A number of examples are referred to throughout, with a longer analysis of Mary Gentle's *Ash: A Secret History* explicating this metahistorical aspect in more detail. I end by suggesting that perhaps the most valuable insight that historical fantasy holds for the historian is the propensity to take seriously, or at least lend greater credence to, past belief in the mythical and supernatural. I finish by discussing new developments in the field of history that seek to do just this.

K. L. Maund in John Clute's *Encyclopedia of Fantasy* notes that "fantasy as a genre is almost inextricably bound up with history and ideas of history" (468). This may explain why there are so many online forums and, indeed, so much academic work devoted to debating the historicity of works such as George R. R. Martin's *A Song of Ice and Fire* book series, along with the *Game of Thrones* TV adaptation, and J.R.R. Tolkien's *The Lord of the Rings*, despite these being confessedly works of fantasy fiction (Larrington; Chance and Siewers; Finander). Similarly, the desire to consume history with a large dollop of fantasy can be seen in various expressions of pop culture. Examples from television include *Outlander* (2014-), *Cursed* (2020), *Da Vinci's Demons* (2013-2015), *Penny Dreadful* (2014-2016), *Britannia* (2018-), and more recently, *The Irregulars* (2021-) and *The Nevers* (2021). This appetite for historical fantasy is mirrored in the world of video games. It is now commonplace for video game companies to employ historians as consultants, even for game series that may be most accurately filed under historical fantasy; examples include *Assassin's Creed*, *Call of Duty* in zombie mode, and the *Wolfenstein* game series (Chapman). This efflorescence of historical fantasy arguably has not been as prominent in the world of film, with a few notable exceptions—for example, *300* (2006), *Crimson Peak* (2015) and *Dracula Untold* (2014). This is possibly due to fantasy space in film being dominated by blockbuster franchises such as *The Lord of the Rings, Harry Potter* and the Marvel Universe. Historical fantasy has also made its presence felt in books: *Jonathan Strange & Mr. Norrell* by Susanna Clark, Mary Gentle's Book of Ash series, and, more recently, R. F. Kuang's *Babel: An Arcane History*. It is Gentle's novel that I explore in more detail in this essay.

First: what is historical fantasy? There have been some discussions of definitions in academic work, as well as online blogs, with a variety of views expressed, especially in the comments sections of the blogs (Walton; Finley). It must be noted that definitional clarity is not aided by the term 'historical fantasy' also being used in a loosely pejorative sense to describe what someone might consider to be wildly inaccurate history; for example, a Holocaust denier's views on history might be termed historical fantasy. While some definitions are looser than others, most agree that a fundamental requirement is a grounding in, or close connection to, received history. In 2009, Charlotte Bucher from the Williamsburg (Virginia) Regional Library offered the following:

> 'Historical fantasy' exists at the overlap of historical fiction with the fantastic, where carefully researched historical details are embellished with and altered by the addition of dragons, magic, or the otherworldly. Its fans appreciate details, the particulars that in historical fiction build authenticity and that fantasy calls 'worldbuilding'. These novels reintroduce the element of surprise to the enjoyment of history. (Bucher 228)

Ramón Saldívar puts it slightly differently in a key 2011 article when he notes that historical fantasy entails a "forcible joining of the gravitas of history with the spectral quality of fantasy" (Saldívar 585). It is this historicity, this purposeful engagement with historical realism, that gives the genre not only definitional clarity but also a certain *modus operandi*. Thus, to qualify as historical fantasy, it is not sufficient for a work of fantasy to be merely influenced by aspects of history, à la *A Song of Ice and Fire*.[1] Rather, the fantasy needs to purposely engage or interact with the received historical record in some way.[2]

For some, this lends the genre an especial facility for social, cultural or political critique. While the subversive or critical function of fantasy in general has long been recognised by scholars, it seems that historical fantasy may, in particular, offer rich scope for subverting and reconstruing dominant social, cultural and historical paradigms (Rose; Jackson). As Saldívar contends, in its historical fantasy form "fantasy loses its illicit nature and enters the ethical world at large" (Saldívar 593). An early example of this can be found in Octavia E. Butler's 1979 enslavement time-travel novel, *Kindred*. Sarah Wood observes that:

> Butler's use of fantasy is not incidental, rather it is integral to the text's impetus: fantasy becomes the means through which contemporary views on slavery can be transposed onto its reconstructed reality [...] In this sense *Kindred* is anything other than escapist fantasy. Its aim is to tackle what Butler views as the contemporary misconceptions and stereotypes that inform America's interpretation of slavery, and it does so through a revision and extension of the governing principles of the slave narrative. (Wood 86)

A more recent example of this historical-fantasy-as-socio-political-critique is R. F. Kuang's *Babel, or the Necessity of Violence: An Arcane History of the Oxford Translators' Revolution*. Set in 1830s England, the novel offers a trenchant critique of British imperialism and capitalism. The elegant magic system of the novel is based on the process of translation, and the power of the magic derives from the linguistic tension that is created when one language is translated to another. But this magic system is also the main driver of British industrialisation and imperial expansion around the world. Three of the four chief characters are representatives of countries colonised by the British. It is precisely their proficiency at translation—being fluent in both their native language and English—that makes them so valuable for working magic and, hence, driving the industrial-colonial machine. This conceit provides a motherlode of rich metaphor for the British enterprise. As one of the Oxford professors puts it, "an act of translation is necessarily always an act of betrayal" (Kuang 153), and it is the main characters' growing realisation of their complicity in this betrayal that provides much of the narrative impetus for the novel. That said, *Babel* does sometimes demonstrate a propensity towards didacticism that can be a trait of works of historical fantasy that operate in this vein of radical critique. The paradox of violent resistance is a central theme of the novel and one that could possibly have been problematized to an even greater extent. In the epilogue, one of the main characters, Victoire, articulates this point:

'Victory is not assured. Victory may be in the portents but it must be urged there by violence, by suffering, by martyrs, by blood. Victory is wrought by ingenuity, persistence, and sacrifice. Victory is a game of inches, of historical contingencies where everything goes right because they have made it go right.' (Kuang 541)

Victoire is talking here about resistance to the British colonial-capitalist enterprise but, arguably, the word "victory" could be replaced by the word "colonialism" and the passage would make just as much sense, even within the social justice purview of the novel.

The above discussion demonstrates how historical fantasy's close engagement with the received historical record gives it a potent capacity for critique of hegemonic social, cultural and political paradigms. While this is undoubtedly an important function of the genre, it would be limiting to only apply the genre to this sort of ideological project. As Dragos Manea observes, while it is true that historical fantasy:

> violate[s] the realistic conventions of historical fiction, [this] does not necessarily imply a subversive approach, neither ontologically nor ideologically [...] Whether a creator employs historical fantasy for radical or conservative purposes largely depends on the way [the genre's] conventions are framed within the narrative, as well as their own ideology. (Manea 124)

Indeed, there seems to be no intrinsic reason why a work of historical fantasy could not just as easily underscore hegemonic relations as subvert them. In fact, some might argue that until relatively recently, the overwhelming tendency of much historical fantasy has been to reinforce hegemonic gender and race relations.

Obviously, a work of historical fantasy need not contain any overt ideological bent at all, radical or otherwise. I would argue that some of the pleasure that is to be gained from reading and writing historical fantasy is due to the ambivalence or irresolution about what is supposedly real or true and what is fantasy. That is, the fun of the genre is to be found in the deliberate playfulness and ambiguity with which historical fantasy approaches the received historical account. Susanna Clark's novel *Jonathan Strange & Mr Norrell* is a good example of this, with some of the delight for the reader deriving from puzzling out what is real and what is fantasy in its Napoleonic-era setting. Clark goes so far as to support her text with sometimes very detailed apparent historical footnotes, most of which are anything but historical. This is perhaps what Bucher was getting at when she remarked that historical fantasy can "reintroduce the element of surprise to the enjoyment of history" (Bucher 228).

I believe that this lighter, more playful approach to the past could be of benefit to historians. While works of academic history are not generally known for their playfulness, Simon Schama's *Dead Certainties* perhaps stands as an early exemplar of the possibilities. In this regard, *Dead Certainties* is instructive in a couple of different ways. As a work by a historian that invents new historical characters, scenes, and sources but is also firmly grounded in the historical record, it probably bears more resemblance to *Jonathan Strange* than at first appears. Accordingly, it provides an example of what can be done when an historian approaches the past with a more creative or playful mindset. However, it is also instructive for why this kind of thing has happened infrequently within the field of history. The backlash that Schama's book received from many in the history establishment probably warned any potential creative historians away from trying anything similar for some years afterwards.[4]

Dragos Manea argues that, in its essence, historical fantasy consists of two basic elements: "the presence of magic and the existence of a story-world based on human historical reality. While it is fairly easy to observe and understand the presence of the former, the question of whether something is historical or not is much more difficult to answer" (Manea 125). I would broaden the first element to read—as per Bucher's definition earlier—"the presence of magic or the otherworldly," but the significance of Manea's comment regarding the second element is what I would like to now focus on.

As just noted, while some of the pleasure of historical fantasy can be found in the deliberate playfulness with which it approaches the historical record, this facility can also remind the historian of important implicit, or even explicit, theoretical and ontological questions about the discipline of history. Some of the more theoretically provocative examples of historical fantasy intentionally highlight the ambivalence between historical realism and fantasy, or myth or legend or fable, and, by doing so, query the nature of historical truth and the status of historical source material. In her entry on historical fantasy for *The Cambridge Companion to Fantasy Literature*, Veronica Schanoes cites four examples of historical fantasy that illustrate this, with one being Mary Gentle's *Ash: A Secret History*.[5] Schanoes describes how these novels blur the lines between history and fantasy as they interrogate what is known of history in comparison to what is imagined. By treading this hazy border between historical realism and, for want of a better term, historical unrealism, these novels implicitly point towards contingencies embedded in the received historical account. They highlight how history constantly evolves and urge one to muse on the ways in which the categories of historical fact and "fantasy" may be mutable and relative to perspective. They also pose important questions about how and why aspects of the past are included and excluded from the consensus historical record. Schanoes observes that

> historical fantasy is thus a subgenre that opens up alternative ways of understanding how history has worked, both in the sense of providing a 'secret' history, (as made explicit in the title of Mary Gentle's novel) and in the sense that they call into question the distinction between history and fantasy that underlies the legitimacy of historical discourse. (Schanoes 246)

Much historical work has been in the business of exploding myths—for example, there was no one person who can be identified as King Arthur—and explaining belief in the supernatural via cultural studies or psychology. Historical fantasy suggests that historians should not necessarily be quick to consign myth to some ahistorical realm of untruth or superstition.

I would like now to spend a bit more time looking at how the above are developed in the Gentle novel that Schanoes refers to—*Ash: A Secret History*. Gentle's protagonist, the historian Pierce Ratcliff, sets out to write the history of a fifteenth-century female warrior, Ash of Burgundy, based largely on his translation of a previously undiscovered "Fraxinus" manuscript that purports to be the memoir of Ash herself. The narrative of the novel is structured as a frame story with emails between Ratcliff and his publisher, Anna Longman, providing commentary on the unfolding life story of Ash as revealed by Ratcliff's translation. At the outset Ratcliff states that he believes the manuscript "fits, as it were, in the gaps between recorded history—and there are many such gaps" (Gentle 10). As the translation and Ash's story progress, Ash's version of history begins to diverge further and further from the received historical record, and elements of myth and legend start to appear. The cognitive dissonance this creates for Ratcliff, the historian, is the cause of much mental anguish.

There are numerous ways in which the Fraxinus manuscript diverges from, or even contradicts, the received historical account. One of the main threads of dissonance is sustained by the existence—or nonexistence—of golems: creatures that are, according to legend, themselves a hybrid product of a material substance and magic. When Ratcliff's translation claims the existence of golems in the fifteenth century, Longman responds with, "*GOLEMS*???!!! In Mediaeval Europe?! What next—zombies and the undead??!! This is fantasy!" Ratcliff explains them away as a "medieval confabulation of something undoubtedly real with something legendary" which, incidentally, could work as a neat definition of historical fantasy. Ratcliff expresses the wish to keep golems in the text although he is willing to leave them out "if too much emphasis on the 'legendary' aspect of the texts is going to weaken the historical 'evidence.'" Longman replies that it would probably be prudent to leave them out as it would not do to "confuse medieval legend with medieval fact" (Gentle 95-96).

But when an archaeological dig conducted by Ratcliff's colleague, Dr. Isobel Napier-Grant, uncovers what appears to be physical evidence of these golems, Ratcliff and Longman are forced to recant and conclude that what they'd once thought was fantasy is, in fact, real. At the same time, the inverse of this process is occurring to other sources. Suddenly—and inexplicably to Ratcliff and Longman—libraries around the world begin to reclassify the work of scholars who had previously published on the historical figure of Ash as fiction. Longman sums up their quandary when she says, "we can't publish a book that we know to be academically fraudulent [...] and we can't NOT publish one with something as mind-boggling as a fifteenth-century Carthaginian golem backing it up" (Gentle 348). But then in a further twist, carbon dating of the golems reveals that they are, as Napier-Grant puts it, "modern fakes" or, perhaps, modern fantasy. Again, Longman sums up the situation: "Ash isn't history. She's Robin Hood, Arthur, Lancelot—legend" (Gentle 545). Ratcliff is forced to agree, saying that "Ash's history was first genuine, and has now been—fading, if you like—to Romance, to a cycle of legends" (Gentle 783). Thus, the figure of Ash acts as an apposite metaphor for the blurry, indeterminate interface between history and legend, sliding, as she does, between these two categories according to shifting evidence and interpretation.

The novel goes on to encompass theoretical physics, time travel and "deep consciousness," amongst other anomalies. The contingent and mutable nature of evidence is a constant theme— archaeological evidence is contradicted by naval seabed surveys; different carbon dating tests contradict each other; Ratcliff constantly harps on about how medieval Latin translation is notoriously susceptible to interpretation. In this way, the novel implicitly critiques the status of different types of historical evidence; the provisional and unstable nature of evidence; and the interpretive conditionality of evidence. In Ratcliff's introduction, he makes a statement that ends up sounding more like a conclusion: "history is a large net, with a wide mesh, and many things slip through it into oblivion. With the new materiel I have uncovered, I hope to bring to light, once again, those facts which do not accord with our idea of the past, but which, nonetheless, *are* factual" (Gentle 10).

Works of historical fantasy, such as *Ash*, that engage critically with the received historical account bear similarities to modern historiography. Where modern historiography shows how the representation of history is often contingent and dependent on perspective, historical fantasy foregrounds these elements, deliberately playing with perspective and authority. Elmar Schenkel notes how "both modern historiography and fantasy, especially metafiction-based fantasy, stress the relational character of all 'facts'" (Schenkel 242). Schenkel quotes the fantasy theorist, William Irwin: "A fantasy is a story based on and controlled by an overt violation of what is generally accepted as possibility; it is the narrative result of transforming the condition contrary to fact [such as fantasy, myth, legend] into 'fact' itself" (Schenkel 242).[6] *Ash's* golems are an apt metaphor for this process since, as the plot progresses, they undergo ontological transformations from creatures of fantasy to carbon-dated reality and, finally, in what might be a purposeful meta twist, a modern-day hoax. Although he means it in a more literal sense than perhaps a historiographer would, Ratcliff ends up celebrating this mutability, for "if things are still changing, then this isn't 'dead history'—it isn't over" (Gentle 785).

In *Dust: The Archive and Cultural History* (2001), Carolyn Steedman ponders this close relationship between history and myth or fantasy. She avers that the grammatical tense of history is more accurately that of the syntax of the fairy tale: "Once upon a time," or "Long, long ago." Steedman goes on to say:

> We [historians] have always, then, written in the mode of magical realism. In strictly formal and stylistic terms, a text of history is very

closely connected to those novels in which a girl flies, a mountain moves, the clocks run backwards, and where (this is our peculiar contribution) the dead walk among the living. (Steedman 150)

Or, as Tolkien more succinctly put it, "history often resembles myth, because they are both ultimately of the same stuff" (Tolkien 344).[7] Instead of attempting to distance itself from, or explain away, myth or legend, historical fantasy brings the two into closer propinquity, contending that truth and meaning about the past can be found just as authentically in fantastical aspects as in more documented, empirical versions of the past. In doing so, not only can historical fantasy "reintroduce the element of surprise to the enjoyment of history" but also, more profoundly, remind historians such as myself about important questions regarding the nature of historical evidence and the close and reciprocal relationship history has with myth, legend, and fable.

I'd like to end by talking briefly about how myth and fantasy might be encompassed more satisfyingly within the field of history. Happily, there are signs within the field that there are some who are much more open to this kind of thinking. In two recent issues of *History Compass*, Clossey et al. canvass the idea of taking seriously the category of the 'Unbelieved' in history. They push back against what they call the 'dogmatic secularism' of the history discipline that has often tended to anthropologise or psychologise belief in the supernatural. They instead advocate for historians trying to understand the supernatural or spiritual events or beings that appear in the past in terms of the agency and credence people clearly possessed at the time. While these historians of the Unbelieved are mostly talking about supernatural manifestations—ghosts and witchcraft, for example—this kind of approach could easily be extended to include the fantastical and mythological more broadly.

An emergent field of history that seems well placed to do this is that of Creative Histories. As William G. Pooley states, "creative histories bring creative practices into conversation with historical research to provoke new methods, develop alternative generic conventions, and suggest new questions" ("Three Definitions" np). Historians in this field not only acknowledge the uncertain and speculative nature of history but positively lean into it. In a methodological sense, Pooley has called for new, hybrid forms of writing that explicitly blend historical research and creative writing or practice. Following Christine de Matos, Pooley suggests, perhaps half-seriously, that those working in this mode could be called "fictorians" and their work styled as "faction" (Pooley, "Show Your Workings" 75). Creative Histories thus seems an apt place for the further development of historical fantasy from within the discipline of history. By this I mean two things: 1) work by historians that engages or collaborates with fantasy writers, artists, and filmmakers; and 2) historical work that takes seriously mythological or fantastical aspects of the past in a speculative, yet credulous and historically grounded, way. This approach could, in fact, herald a new way of thinking and talking about historical fantasy, this time from within the discipline of history.

Notes

1. Martin has mentioned many times the influence that history has on his writing. See, for example, his interview with Channel 4 News.
2. In this way it has some overlap with adjacent genres such as magic realism and alternate history and, as with all matters of generic definition, there are examples that sit somewhere between these various genres and share characteristics of each or either. See, for example, Junot Diaz's *The Brief Wondrous Life of Oscar Wao*. It is commonly categorised as magic realism, but Saldívar contends it is more accurately a work of historical fantasy or what he sometimes refers to as 'speculative

realism', using the terms interchangeably in his article ("Historical Fantasy," 574-599).

3. A review in the New York Times titled "A Historian Enters Fiction's Shadowy Domain" describes how Schama had "intentionally crossed a frontier into the promising but, for a historian, always shadowy domain of invention, fictionalisation, imagination" (Bernstein, para. 4). Schama responds, in a preface to the new edition in 2013, by expressing his surprise that "a modest, playful piece of self-evident fiction would be regarded by the sentinels of the academy as a betrayal of History; an outrage against the profession and its code of conduct; a manifesto of ultra-relativism; the Enemy against whom a Stand Had to be Taken" (p. xi). Indeed, Schama's preface and afterword in *Dead Certainties* present a thoughtful and erudite contemplation of the fraught state of the relationship between history and fiction at this time.

5. Barbara Hambly's *Those Who Hunt the Night* (1988), Susanna Clarke's *Jonathan Strange & Mr Norrell* (2004), Mary Gentle's *Ash: A Secret History* (2001), and Elizabeth Hand's *Mortal Love* (2004).

6. Schenkel is quoting William Irwin in *The Game of the Impossible: A Rhetoric of Fantasy* (1976), x.

7. This blurring of myth and history is the de facto setting for "Arthurian fantasy," as delineated in Philippa Semper, "'My Other World': Historical Reflections and Refractions in Modern Arthurian Fantasy" in Ashton, Gail & Kline, Daniel T. (eds.) *Medieval Afterlives in Popular Culture*, 2012, 173-186.

Works Cited

Bucher, Charlotte, et al. "Core Collections in Genre Fantasy: Fantasy Fiction 101." *Reference & User Services Quarterly*, 48 (2009), pp. 226-231.

Chance, Jane, and Alfred K. Siewers. *Tolkien's Middle Ages*. Palgrave Macmillan, 2005.

Channel 4 News. "George R.R. Martin: Game of Thrones to have 'a bittersweet ending.'" *Youtube*, August 15, 2014. https://www.youtube.com/watch?v=HaFViB8mZ9I.

Chapman, Adam. "Playing the Historical Fantastic: Zombies, Mech-Nazis, and Making Meaning about the Past through Metaphor." *War Games: Memory, Militarism and the Subject of Play*, edited by Holger Pèotzsch and Phil Hammond, Bloomsbury, 2019, pp. 91-110.

Clarke, Susanna. *Jonathan Strange & Mr Norrell*. Bloomsbury, 2005.

Clossey, Luke, et al. "The Unbelieved and Historians, Parts I: A Challenge." *History Compass*, vol. 14, no. 12, 2016, pp. 594-602.

Clossey, Luke, et al. "The Unbelieved and Historians, Parts II: Proposals and Solutions." *History Compass*, vol. 15, no. 1, 2017, e12370. https://doi.org/10.1111/hic3.12370 Accessed 21 May 2022.

De Matos, Christine. "Fictorians: Historians Who 'Lie' About the Past and Like It." *Fictional Histories and Historical Fictions: Writing History in the Twenty-First Century*, special issue of *TEXT: Journal of Writing and Writing Courses*, April 2015. https://doi.org/10.52086/001c.27293 Accessed 15 April 2022.

Elliot, Michael A. "Strangely Interested: The Work of Historical Fantasy." *American Literature*, vol. 87, 2015, pp. 137-157.

Finander, Caroline. *Fantasy, Imagination and History: A Historiographical Study of J.R.R. Tolkien's* The Lord of the Rings *and Gene Wolf's* The Book of the New Sun. 2010. University of Western Australia, unpublished honours thesis.

Finley, Joseph. "The Fine Line Between History and Fantasy". *Authorjosephfinley*, 2011. https://authorjosephfinley.com/2011/08/the-fine-line-between-history-and-fantasy/. Accessed 12 June 2021.

Gentle, Mary. *Ash: A Secret History*. Gollancz, 2001.

Irwin, W.R. *The Game of the Impossible: A Rhetoric of Fantasy*. University of Illinois Press, 1976.

Jackson, Rosemary. *Fantasy: Literature of Subversion*. Routledge, 2003.

Kuang, R. F. *Babel, or the Necessity of Violence: An Arcane History of Oxford Translators' Revolution*. HarperCollins, 2022.

LaFaye, Alexandria R. T. *In the Garden of the Soul*. 2015. University of Louisiana, Lafayette, unpublished doctoral dissertation.

Larrington, Carolyne. *Winter is Coming: The Medieval World of Game of Thrones*. I.B. Taurus, 2016.

Manea, Dragoş. "Evil Nuns and Useless Priests: On the Representation of Christianity in Contemporary Historical Fantasy Television Series." *Religious Narratives in Contemporary Culture: Between Cultural Memory and Transmediality*, edited by Maria-Sabina Draga Alexandru and Dragoş Manea, Brill, 2021, pp. 117-138.

Maund, K. L. "History in Fantasy." *The Encyclopedia of Fantasy*, edited by John Clute and John Grant, St Martin's Press, 1997, pp. 468-469.

Pooley, William G. "Three Definitions of Creative Histories." *Creative Histories of Witchcraft: France, 1790-1940*, https://creativewitchcraft.wordpress.com/2019/12/19/three-definitions-of-creative-history/. Accessed 15 April 2022.

---. "Show Your Workings: Towards a Creative Historical Toolkit." *Speculative Biography: Experiments, Opportunities and Provocations*, edited by Donna Lee Brien and Kiera Lindsey, Routledge, 2022, pp. 75-94.

Rose, Jacqueline. *States of Fantasy*. Clarendon Press, 1996.

Saldívar, Ramón. "Historical Fantasy, Speculative Realism, and Postrace Aesthetics in Contemporary American Fiction." *American Literary History*, vol. 23, no. 3, 2011, pp. 574-599.

Schama, Simon. *Dead Certainties: Unwarranted Speculations*. Granta, 1992.

Schanoes, Veronica. "Historical Fantasy." *The Cambridge Companion to Fantasy Literature*, edited by Edward James and Farah Mendlesohn, Cambridge University Press, 2012, pp. 236-247.

Schenkel, Elmar. "Dreaming History: Fantasy and Historiography in Ursula K. Le Guin's *The Lathe of Heaven*." *Historiographic Metafiction in Modern American and Canadian Literature*, edited by Bernd Engler and Kurt Müller, Ferdinand Schöningh, 1994, pp. 241-251.

Semper, Philippa. "'My Other World': Historical Reflections and Refractions in Modern Arthurian Fantasy." *Medieval Afterlives in Popular Culture*, edited by Gail Ashton and Daniel T. Kline, Palgrave MacMillan, 2012, pp. 173-186.

Steedman, Carolyn. *Dust: The Archive and Cultural History*. Rutgers University Press, 2001.

Tolkien, J.R.R. *Tales from the Perilous Realm*. Houghton Mifflin Harcourt, 2012.

Walton, Jo. (2009). *What is Historical Fantasy?* TOR.com. https://www.tor.com/2009/07/31/what-is-historical-fantasy-anyway/. Accessed 13 Oct. 2021

Wood, Sarah. "Exorcising the Past: The Slave Narrative as Historical Fantasy." *Feminist Review*, vol. 85, 2007, pp. 83-96.

Faith, Dogma and Vision in *Mr. Pye*: A Quest for Synthesis

Ruchira Mandal

PUBLISHED IN 1953, Mervyn Peake's comic novel, *Mr. Pye*, is about an odd but affable evangelical who arrives at the island of Sark to convert its population to his creed of love. The novel not only reflects the author's ambivalent attitude toward Christianity but also becomes a discourse on art and artistic vision and the wholeness of the human experience. This essay examines the theme of shared human experience via the fantastic through the lens of a Jungian reading.

Mr. Pye arrives at Sark on a boat, and despite his eccentric, presumptuous interference in the lives and relationships of the island's inhabitants, especially that of Miss Dredger and Miss George, manages to charm the general population and develop a cult-like following. Pye plans to solidify this coup with a grand spectacle: having the mobility-impaired Miss George descend from the mountain in her armchair as an example of the power of the spiritual to defeat the physical. However, Pye's planned miracle is ruined by the sudden appearance of a dead whale in the harbour, driving everyone away with its terrible stink. Soon after this disappointment, Mr. Pye discovers that he has wings growing out of his shoulder blades. Horrified, Pye engages in what he considers to be evil activities in order to lessen his apparently angelic blessings. Pye's resistance is successful: his wings recede, and he soon has horns growing out of his forehead, instead. Pye spends the rest of the novel trying to balance these two opposing aspects within himself. At the novel's end, Pye flies away after being chased by the islanders, knowing his evangelical mission has been a failure.

Peake's distaste for any kind of absolutist religious doctrine is evident in his other works. In 1939, Peake wrote a poem titled "No Creed Shall Bind Me to a Sapless Bole" in which he argues,

> No creed shall bind me to a sapless bole–
> Dig I for the dark roots beneath the soil.
> No foliaged candle and no areole
> Shall lure me from my toil
> And snare my soul
> When I stand fighting the Cathedral [. . .] (Peake *Collected Poems* 61)

In a poem written in 1937 titled "How Foreign to the Spirit's Early Beauty," Peake speaks about the unkindness of "tired creeds" which he finds to be antithetical "to the amoral integrity of the mind" (Peake *Collected Poems* 39). The oxymoronic quality of the second phrase suggests that Peake believes in an ethical belief system that is beyond the binaries of conventional morality. Etymologically, the term integrity also evokes the quality of wholeness, as opposed to the presumably fragmented existence imposed by the rigidity of "tired creeds".

Such tired creeds may be observed in the iron laws of Gormenghast castle in the Titus Groan novels. While Gormenghast does not have religion, it exacts absolute obedience and conformity to its repetitive rituals from all its inhabitants. Despite the loss of their symbolic meaning, the rituals attain a religious quality by virtue of the reverence accorded to them. The exhausting demands of these rituals eventually leads Titus to seek escape and meaning outside the castle walls. In the novella *Boy in Darkness*, Peake subverts the Christian image of the Lamb by creating a blind tyrant who converts people into humanoid animals to fit its vision of perfection. However, this conversion inadvertently drains their life forces in the process, leading to their early deaths with "the brain running away too sharply from the body, or the body leaping like a frog in search of the brain" (Peake *Boy in Darkness and Other Stories* 69). The characters in Peake's Groan trilogy and in *Boy in Darkness* are thus repressed, having lost touch with half of their own consciousness. The Earl of Gormenghast regresses to imagining himself as an owl, the Countess sleepwalks through everyday life except during times of crisis, and the twins, Cora and Clarice, are physically paralyzed along one side of their bodies, a narrative prosthesis that Peake seems to use as a deliberate metaphor for their hampered mental state (Peake *The Gormenghast Novels* 90).

It is in this anti-religious light that the reader should examine the wings and horns of Mr. Pye. For while it is possible to trace the trajectory of a tragic over-reacher in the rise and fall of the island's missionary, Mr. Pye's downfall is caused not so much by his hubristic pride as by his struggle to keep his spiritual balance in the "ding-dong battle between the warring forces of good and evil" (Peake *Mr. Pye* 208). Mr. Pye thus becomes, as it were, an unwitting site for psychomachia. Pierre Francois argues in *"Mr. Pye*: An Ovidian Curse for a Dichotomized Evangelist," that "the reasons for his metamorphosis into angel and/or goat should not be sought in hubris (which is a symptom, not a cause), but in fragmentation, indeed in Peake's deep mistrust of the Christian division of body and soul" (François 40). Indeed, the epigraph to *Titus Groan*, taken from John Bunyan's *Pilgrim's Progress*, reflects the author's preoccupation with this rupture between the material and spiritual planes:

> Dost thou love picking meat? Or woulds't thou see
> A man in the clouds, and have him speak to thee? (Peake *The Gormenghast Novels* 10)

The fact that Mr. Pye's moment of spiritual triumph is marred by the malodourous decomposing flesh of the dead whale is indicative of this rupture. As Jungian psychology postulates, what the consciousness fails to acknowledge nevertheless surfaces negatively in the form of the Shadow. Mr. Pye's rejection of the physical thus results in its manifesting first in the corrupt and disruptive shape of the dead whale, which literally rises to the surface from the depths of the sea as a potent symbol of the unconscious, and then in his own physical body, in the form of wings. Analyzing brutal, violent deaths in fairy tales as resulting symbols of unresolved shadow, Marie-Louise von Franz argues that in refusing to accept one's shadow, one may, "in modern times, become a pilot and crash, or go to the mountains and fall" (von Franz *Shadow and Evil in Fairy Tales* 14). In the case of Mr. Pye, he does not quite fall, although an earlier draft of the novel does end with his death (Maslen "Mervyn Peake on Sark" np). However, Pye's mission fails to recover from the impact of the manifestation of his shadow, and he is ultimately forced into exile.

G. Peter Winnington notes that the missions of Mr. Pye and the Lamb are the same: "Like the Lamb of *Boy in Darkness*, Mr. Pye wants to re-form the stone island of Sark and its inhabitants" (Winnington *The Voice of the Heart* 361). However, while the Lamb focuses on the bestiality believed according to Christian dogma to be inherent in every human being at the cost of the soul, the missionary stresses instead a rather sanctified version of Christian goodness, failing to make allowances for the presumed universal propensity for both the divine and the animalistic, thereby leading to a schism within himself. *Boy in Darkness* may make for a darker reading than the comic tone of *Mr. Pye*; the latter's portly eponymous hero may not appear on the surface to be as sinister as the Lamb. However, if the reader observes Pye's actions, he comes across as consciously, meaning deliberately, manipulative and absolutely convinced of the rightness of his evangelical cause, which he uses to justify overstepping.

Upon arriving at Sark, Pye overrides Miss Dredger's decision regarding the carriage despite her being the person who actually hired it, assuming moral authority over the incident by declaring that, "I would have offered you a sweet [...] but [....] You are not worthy of the gesture in your present mood [....] I will speak to you both later. You have distressed me" (Peake *Mr. Pye* 22-3). Despite Miss Dredger's fierce initial resistance to his overstepping, Pye manages to take over the running of her house and make her "like clay on the wheel of his love" (Peake *Mr. Pye* 43). Pye convinces Miss George to leave her house, which he proposes to sell for her, thereby setting her "free from earthly ties" and settling her in a room at Miss Dredger's (Peake *Mr. Pye* 81), all to set up an example of amity for the other residents of the island. In other words, Pye invades these women's spaces and forces them to alter their lives in order to use them as tools for his evangelical mission. Pye's methods become the direct cause for the ensuing humiliation and trauma that Miss George suffers when Mr. Pye's grand miracle is interrupted by the dead whale. This failed spectacle pushes Miss George to anger and hatred, which Mr. Pye later exacerbates by provoking her and stealing her hat in his quest of "lengthening his sin-list" (Peake *Mr. Pye* 162). She chases him in response, which results in a heart attack and a fall down the stairs (Peake *Mr. Pye* 163) of a house where she only was in the first place because of Pye's insistence. In this way, Mr. Pye becomes the indirect cause of Miss George's eventual death.

The justification Pye gives himself for his unwarranted meddling sounds surprisingly close to what Rudyard Kipling calls "the White Man's burden" (Kipling 82): "for they must learn that it was to their ultimate good that he should hold a spiritual mandate over their wasp-waisted rock" (Peake *Mr. Pye* 49). Winnington notes that the nonsense poem written by Pye, "O'er seas that have no beaches" (Peake *Mr. Pye* 230) is a parody of the hymn, "From Greenland's Icy Mountains" (Winnington, *The Voice of the Heart* 242), that calls upon enlightened souls to deliver heathen lands "from error's chain" (Heber). Historically, John Allen Chau, the American evangelist who was killed by the Sentinelese, a protected traditional nation in the Indian Union Territory of Andaman and Nicobar Islands in November 2018, may have held similar beliefs about these supposedly uncivilized islanders whom he had tried to convert (Sohn np). As Robert Maslen points out regarding Pye,

> The wings and the horns mark him out as different; but this physical difference can also be seen as a demonstration of his underlying links to the local community. He is not simply an angelic missionary, but also that benevolent being's devilish equivalent, the colonial invader. He is, in fact, a human being, and the principal strangeness about him is his ability to demonstrate his human tendency to contradiction and paradox in a strikingly physical way. (Maslen "Mervyn Peake and the Queering of Sark" np)

While Mr. Pye's mission is not overtly political—although one of his admitted aims is to replace the "Chief Pleas" or the "Island Parliament" as the first arbitrator of all island disputes (Peake *Mr. Pye* 78)—there is certainly an element of at least geographical conquest in the way Pye explores the island, in his intellectual, arguably masculinized desire to master or dominate the femininized island and uncover the secrets hidden in its dark, primordial caves and nooks. Throughout the first half of the novel, repeated emphasis is made on Pye's "intellect" and on the "vitality" of his brain which is likened to "modern machinery" (Peake *Mr. Pye* 120). Thus, as with most colonizing conquests, Mr. Pye's "Kingdom of Love" (Peake *Mr. Pye* 43) does not brook dissent or debate. And although he claims to preach a creed that encompasses "the fullness of life" (Peake *Mr. Pye* 100), Pye repeatedly avoids unpleasant or uncomfortable discussions. In this way, Pye overrides all of Miss Dredger's objections to hosting Miss George in her house, refuses to address Major Havershot's concerns about a possible Russian invasion, and dismisses Miss George's legitimate concerns about her descent down the cliff, saying, "'There's no need to see. Vision needs no spectacles'" (Peake *Mr. Pye* 112). His assertion that one must look inward and heal Sark before turning to Russia (Peake *Mr. Pye* 101) has a seed of truth in it. As Maslen notes, "The West needs to examine *itself* before turning its gaze on others; only then can the process of healing be effective" (Maslen, "Mervyn Peake on Sark" np). The irony however is that Pye has failed to turn that inward gaze upon himself, making him a microcosmic representation of the fragmented colonial civilization of the mid-twentieth century.

Despite Mr. Pye's cheerful affability, he is, objectively, a disruptive influence in the life of Sark. As François states, "what epitomizes Mr. Pye is his unshakable faith in the righteousness of his cause. In a different literary context, he would be a religious fundamentalist, unaware that the capitalization of 'truth' in human societies is tantamount to a denial of otherness" (François *Mr. Pye*: An Ovidian Curse for a Dichotomized Evangelist 40). Pye's veneer of cheerful equanimity is thus broken by Thorpe, the artist who refuses to play into Pye's condescending appropriation of his artistic endeavours as "the reflection of our Pal" (Peake *Mr. Pye* 87)—Pye's idiosyncratic pet name for God—and who constantly debates with and questions the missionary, until the text's very end.

Thorpe, however, is an exception, as is Tintagieu, the island's very voluptuous divine feminine figure, whom Peake draws as an Aphrodite rising naked from the sea with seaweed dripping from her shoulder (Peake *Mr. Pye* 123). What makes the figure of the evangelical Mr. Pye somewhat sinister, despite his obvious belief in what he preaches—harmony and love—is his inexplicable ability to manipulate and charm and to provoke the absolutely devoted loyalty that he inspires in Miss Dredger, in particular, and in the island population, in general. That Pye is able to override both Miss Dredger's and Miss George's reservations with such ease, so much so that Miss Dredger answers his beckoning "like a somnambulist" (Peake *Mr. Pye* 31), suggests that Pye has the hypnotic power of a cult leader. It is important to note in this respect that both of these old women are psychologically starved. Miss George, for instance, has no appreciation for artistic beauty (Peake *Mr. Pye* 40), and Miss Dredger has, over the years, cultivated a "code of tough virginity [... a] detestation of all that was 'feeble'" (Peake *Mr. Pye* 33), including "Art, Religion and [...] Love" (Peake *Mr. Pye* 20). Thus, when Mr. Pye offers a spiritual outlet, it is as if he had "unlatched a window and flung it open," giving them something that they had unknowingly "yearned for" all their lives (Peake *Mr. Pye* 61). Despite Mr. Pye's faith in what he preaches and his supposedly benevolent ends, his ability to manipulate these women's vulnerabilities makes him comparable to Gormenghast's villainous Steerpike, who similarly manipulates women in his climb to power, as well as the Lamb who physically reshapes people to fit his personal vision.

Jung explains this phenomenon as collectively falling for the cult of personality: **"in order to compensate for its chaotic formlessness, a mass always produces a 'Leader,' who almost infallibly becomes the victim of his own inflated ego-consciousness, as numerous examples in history show"** (Jung *The Undiscovered Self* 130). Yet another Peakeian motif, that features in *Titus Groan* and *Titus Alone* and is very subtly hinted at in *Pye*, is the author's horror of absolute homogeneous conformity, which is the result of cult-consciousness. The Grey Scrubbers in the kitchens of Gormenghast are so identified with their social function that their faces, without "the faintest sign of animation," are indistinguishable from the slabs they scrub (Peake *The Gormenghast Novels* 19), while the scientist in *Titus Alone*, through his life-annihilating experiments, creates compliant workers who all have the same face (Peake *The Gormenghast Novels* 973), provoking revulsion in both Titus and Cheeta. *Mr. Pye*, an arguably lighter work, portrays Mr. Rice, "with so flat a face that it seemed to have been created by some sculptor who [...] was inquisitive to know quite how low a relief could go without disappearing altogether" (Peake *Mr. Pye* 97). While the effect here is primarily comic, the patterns are familiar to readers of Peake. More serious is the implication of Miss Dredger moving across her room, one foot following another not "as an affair of character, but an automatic operation drained of purpose" (Peake *Mr. Pye* 30). All these serve as reminders that despite Mr. Pye's affable vitality, his mission is not vastly different from that of the Lamb or the Scientist who both seek to transform people into something less than their individuated selves. Peake appears to write in agreement with von Franz that, "The achievement of psychological maturity is an individual task—and so is increasingly difficult today when man's individuality is threatened by widespread conformity" (Franz "The Process of Individuation" 238).

As the Lamb separates soul from body, his successor, the Scientist, separates free will from people, whereas Steerpike and Mr. Pye both charm people into believing in them. But despite their differing abilities, these manipulators are all doomed to fail one way or the other because, like their congregations, they have an incomplete understanding of life. Von Franz, in *Individuation in Fairy Tales*, refers to a story by Anatole France in which another missionary arrives to convert the inhabitants of an island but, due to his literal short-sightedness, ends up converting a colony of penguins (Franz "The Process of Individuation" 25). While the Lamb in *Boy in Darkness* is physically blind, Mr. Pye suffers from a symbolic lack of vision.

Although Pye speaks of balance, his view of good and evil is extreme, sanctified, and makes a judgment on even petty squabbles and hostilities, such as that between Miss George and Miss Dredger, propelled by a belief that absolutely everyone in the island must live in complete harmony and love one another. While Pye appears to achieve this goal for a short time, so much so that even the tourists notice a change in the islanders (Peake *Mr. Pye* 79), this lack of conflict obviously cannot last. Pye forces upon the people of the island an unnatural harmony which does not truly resolve their fear or discontent or malice, but only acts as a temporary veneer over those feelings. The grand "Kingdom of Our Pal" (Peake, *Mr. Pye* 99) is thus broken long before Pye suffers his personal crisis of wings and horns following the arrival of the dead whale: "It seemed they had already forgotten all that Mr. Pye had taught them about love" (Peake *Mr. Pye* 130). Pye is also limited by his Christianized understanding of the body-soul/good-evil dichotomies. François observes that Pye is described almost as a "sexless" man of intellect (François 41), his "athletic brain" complemented by "almost transparent features" (Peake *Mr. Pye* 76). In his brief sermon to the islanders during the midnight picnic at Derrible, Pye speaks of the need to feed the hunger of the mind and soul (Peake *Mr. Pye* 103). Tintagieu, who does not live by a Christian moral code, provokes in Pye a need to bring her into his fold, into his evangelical mission, or, as he calls it, "to gather the outcasts to our hearts" (Peake *Mr. Pye* 128). Ironically, Tintagieu, whose name, Winnington notes, "derives from an immense rock off the coast of Sark, "[is] a mini-island in herself" (Winnington *The Voice of the Heart* 260), and in her more-animal-than-human laughter (Peake *Mr. Pye* 158), is more attuned to the island's subterranean life than he is.

Incidentally, Tintagieu is the first to note the darkness in Pye, even before he actively engages in his devil-worshipping ritual. Having involved herself in the affairs of the missionary as a joke, she finds herself in the midst of "something more satanic. The neat little missionary had another side" (Peake *Mr. Pye* 166). It is Pye's initial lack of self-awareness that causes his fragmentation. Alice Mills notes the oddity of an evangelist who is apparently "overflowing with love for his fellow human beings" but does nothing to aid characters who keep falling around him, fatally or otherwise (Mills 29). Excess characterizes everyone who comes in contact with Mr. Pye, with people constantly falling and slipping around him, starting with the boatman who falls and breaks his leg during Pye's first trip to Sark and ending with Miss George's fatal fall down the banisters. These falls ultimately exemplify Mr. Pye's own excessively intellectual understanding of faith, which results in something utterly irrational happening to him. Carl Jung recalls a theologian telling him that

> Ezekiel's visions were nothing more than morbid symptoms, and that, when Moses and other prophets heard "voices" speaking to them, they were suffering from hallucinations [....] We are so accustomed to the apparently rational nature of our world that we can scarcely imagine anything happening that cannot be explained by common sense. (Jung *Man and His Symbols* 31)

And so, Mr. Pye tries to rationalize his predicament. If he has sprouted wings, it must be because of too much piety, and thus seemingly angelic wings must be countered by doing evil.

Ironically, although Karen Armstrong argues that "myths about flight and ascent in different cultures express a universal desire for transcendence and liberation from the constraints of the human condition" (Armstrong 12), Mr. Pye's wings instead become a constraint that threatens to expose him to ridicule as a freak. Thus, although Pye arranges the flight of Miss George as a miracle to guide the islanders' transcendence from the confines of the flesh, when he is offered his own miracle, he panics: "It was one thing to be an angel in Paradise, but quite another to be an angel in Sark" (Peake *Mr. Pye* 136).

In his unpublished play, *Cave or Anima Mundi*, Peake dramatizes the conflict between faith and reason, good and evil, tracing humanity's psychic journey from the Paleolithic to the modern age. In Act Two of his play, set in the medieval period, Mary, the divine feminine or the Anima Mundi who is being hunted as a witch due to her iconoclastic beliefs, defends a gargoyle sculpted by the artist that is deemed satanic by his more militant father and brother: "God who created the camel, the toad, the scorpion or the owl; God who created the goat—He would enjoy it" (Peake *The Cave* 15). When Pye's response to wings is to indulge in supposed satanic worship, he is still thinking in terms of dichotomy and failing to see the fullness of the divine vision, as Jung explains:

> Primitive man was much more governed by his instincts than are his 'rational' modern descendants, who have learned to 'control' themselves. In this civilizing process, we have increasingly divided our consciousness from the deeper instinctive strata of the human psyche [. . .] (Jung *Man and His Symbols* 36)

For Peake, the divine vision representing the wholeness of the psyche is conflated with the truth of artistic vision. In a radio talk published as *The Artist's World*, Peake says that, "We only see what we understand; and we are thus very nearly blind. But total blindness is reserved for those whose vision is functional" (Peake *Artist's World* 5). Peake is of course talking not of actual physical blindness, but using it as a metaphor for insensitivity. It takes artistic vision to see the beauty of a yellow chair against a blue wall, as van Gogh does, while functional vision is an animal ability to which it is argued that no beauty or truth is revealed (Peake *Artist's World* 5). It should be noted here that Mr. Pye has no appreciation of art and thus denies Thorpe his agency as an artist, calling him "only a medium" (Peake, *Mr. Pye* 88) and advising him to "leave the actual process of painting to the Deity" (Peake *Mr. Pye* 88). Later on, he flippantly describes the process of painting as "slap[ping] the colours on, one! two! three!" (Peake *Mr. Pye* 184). This prompts a passionate outburst from Thorpe that emphasizes the visionary role of the artist in depicting truth: "Colour, Mr. Pye, is a process of elimination. It is the d-distillation of an attitude. It is a credo" (Peake *Mr. Pye* 186).

Much of *Mr. Pye* proves to be a discourse on artistic truth. Early in the novel, an example of functional vision is offered when Miss George recalls a sea storm painting by her late brother-in-law. In fact, Miss George's prolonged observation of the sea storm at the harbour and the repeated assertion that she has never seen "a storm at sea, or anywhere else" that resembles her late brother-in-law's painting (Peake *Mr. Pye* 40) might remind the reader of the most famous of the English seascape painters with a propensity for depicting storms and sea storms: the Romantic painter J.M.W Turner, criticized for the lack of form in his colorful fusions of spray and mist. Selby Whittingham says, "Turner was a synthetic rather than an analytic painter. His sketchbooks show someone with a magpie mind and observant eye combining visual data into artistic wholes as he looked rather than dissecting appearances" (Whittingham 315). This is something that Thorpe, the island's resident artist, wants to attempt: "It's a kind of synthesis I'm after, and it seems to me that there'll be such a staggering lot of d-data down there tonight" (Peake *Mr. Pye* 88). Nor is Thorpe the only artist in the novel. Pye seeks to realize a certain synthetic artistic vision through his evangelical mission in Sark, "where, upon a small canvas, he hoped to complete a picture to its last brush stroke" (Peake *Mr. Pye* 198) by unifying the island in his creed of love. The author of the novel was a visual artist, himself. Robert Maslen says of Peake that his art "exposes disturbing parallels between his lifelong creative impulses and the impulse to dominate or wreck the world, as manifested first in the career of Adolf Hitler and later in the threat of global nuclear war" (Maslen "Mervyn Peake, *Boy in Darkness* (1956), and the Nightmare of Complicity" np).

The difference between Pye and Thorpe is that while the former rearranges stones in order to achieve symmetry and the notion of perfect evangelical beauty (Peake *Mr. Pye* 45), the latter paints a rock only to discover that it has a little face (Peake, *Mr. Pye* 72). While Thorpe struggles to discover the truth through artistic vision, to find "the heart of bone" (Peake *Mr. Pye* 93), Pye brings his vision to Sark and treats the island as his canvass that he can reshape according to his predefined truth. Its people, according to Pye, are "like clay on the wheel of his love" (Peake *Mr. Pye* 43). Mr. Pye is assured of his own righteousness whereas Thorpe constantly suspects that he himself is a fake (Peake *Mr. Pye* 69), "which is no doubt why he stammers, in contrast to Mr. Pye's skill with words" (Winnington *The Voice of the Heart* 253). Taken together, Thorpe and Pye are foils to one another. Although Thorpe starts out as a Romantic, speaking of capturing light and atmosphere, he ends up as a Cubist, splitting up his imagined canvas into overlapping rectangles of a "leper whiteness" from which he erases the moon (Peake, *Mr. Pye* 93), which in Peake's fiction and poetry is often the neglected, unconscious part of the psyche. In a 1932 essay on Picasso, Jung describes the Cubist as a "schizoid" artist (Jung *The Spirit* 137 n.3) who, instead of seeking meaning, seems to be more concerned with fragmentation or the so-called "lines of fracture" (Jung, *The Spirit* 137) in paintings that reveal an "alienation from feeling" (Jung *The Spirit* 137). In the light of the violence of the Second World War, artistic wholeness might be difficult to comprehend, and a fragmented reality may be all that is possible. Thorpe thus moves from a quest for synthesis to a fractured dream, failing repeatedly to execute his vision, and calling himself a "stillborn" painter (Peake *Mr. Pye* 215). In a poem titled "Shapes" that depicts the horrors of war, Peake refers to "Guernica," conflating past and present civilizations:

> The rubble that is rotting in the rain
> Exhales the death of Warsaw and Pompeii,
> Guernica, Troy and Coventry. (Peake *Collected Poems* 84)

As the novel draws towards a close, Peake alludes to darker artists such as Bosch, known for his "compelling visualisations of human sinfulness" (Heal np) and Goya whose *Witches' Sabbath* would offer a close parallel to Pye's Satanic worship in Dixcart Valley. Thorpe, on seeing Miss George's corpse in Miss Dredger's home, describes the scene as "pure Goya" (Peake *Mr. Pye* 165), and immediately complains of feeling "sick and dizzy" (Peake *Mr. Pye* 165). This suggests a resistance to the darker aspects of human experience within the artist, and possibly the reason for his repeated failures at artistic expressions. Interestingly, before his exit from Sark, Pye drinks to Thorpe "in the name of Bosch" (Peake *Mr. Pye* 230), promising that Thorpe will one day prove his artistic mettle "in amazing pigment" (Peake *Mr. Pye* 230). Pye's parting advice to Thorpe is "Ars longa, vita brevis" (Peake *Mr. Pye* 250), perhaps a belated realization that the truth of art is not realized through the imposing of external truth, as Pye has done, or by the constant struggle to find a style, as Thorpe does, but in the living of life, which is brief, in all its multifaceted variety.

Mr. Pye's struggle with wings and horns suggests not only his personal schism but a split in the collective psyche of Sark itself, of which Pye becomes emblematic: a metaphor that he might eventually fit into by achieving wholeness. Like Steerpike, Pye becomes the scapegoat of the whole island and must therefore go into exile: "leaving the island "suddenly empty [...] nothing but a long wasp-waisted rock," bereft of visions, and even of an artist capable of doing Stevensonian justice to its beauties" (Maslen, *Mervyn Peake on Sark* np). Just as Titus must leave Gormenghast in search of wholeness, so must Mr. Pye leave to unlearn his dichotomies and "face the goat within instead of demonizing it" and to channel its "life-force into creative works and into more compassionate relationships" (François 46). Thorpe remains on Sark to continue his artistic quest. Perhaps one day he might face his own inner darkness and achieve his desired synthesis on a canvas. Pye escapes on his journey into the unknown as he learns to balance his wings and horns, so that "one day [he may] fit the thing [that he is] metaphorizing" (Peake *Mr. Pye* 229). As he flies away from Sark, his horns dwindling as his wings push forth, he finds himself for the first time with "a foot in either camp" (Peake *Mr. Pye* 241), a metaphor for synthesis. To unify the kingdom of love, one must first find synthesis within oneself.

Acknowledgements

I am grateful to Mr. G. Peter Winngington for sharing his digital copy of the manuscript *The Cave*, Peake's unpublished play.

Works Cited

Armstrong, Karen. *A Short History of Myth.* Canongate Books, 2008.

Aymès, Sophie. "'A Quality of Flux': The Formal Logic of Mervyn Peake's Illustrations and Texts." *Peake Studies*, vol. 8, no. 1, 2002, pp. 6-34. *JSTOR*, http://www.jstor.org/stable/24776597. Accessed 14 June 2023.

Coursen, H.R. *The Compensatory Psyche: A Jungian Approach to Shakespeare*. University Press of America, 1986.

François, Pierre. "*Mr. Pye*: An Ovidian Curse for a Dichotomized Evangelist." *Peake Studies*, vol. 6, no. 2, 1999, pp. 39–47. *JSTOR*, http://www.jstor.org/stable/24776069. Accessed 2 August 2020.

Franz, Marie-Louise von. *Individuation in Fairy Tales*. Shambhala, 1990.

—. "The Process of Individuation." *Man and His Symbols*. Edited by C. G. Jung, Dell, 1968.

—. *Shadow and Evil in Fairy Tales*. Shambhala, 1995.

Heal, Bridget. "The Devil Is Always Lurking: On Hieronymous Bosch." *The Art Newspaper*, 10 Mar. 2017, https://www.theartnewspaper.com/2017/03/10/the-devil-is-always-lurking-on-hieronymous-bosch. Accessed 28 June 2023.

Heber, Reginald. "From Greenland's Icy Mountains>" The Victorian Web, 28 May 2011, victorianweb.org/religion/religion/hymns/heber1.html. Accessed 9 March 2025.

Jung, Carl Gustav, et al. *Man and His Symbols*. Edited by C. G. Jung, Dell, 1968.

—. *The Spirit in Man, Art, and Literature*. Princeton, 1975.

—. *The Undiscovered Self*. Routledge, 2002.

Kipling, Rudyard. *Selected Poems*. Penguin, 1993.

Maslen, Robert. "Mervyn Peake, *Boy in Darkness* (1956), and the Nightmare of Complicity." *The City of Lost Books*, University of Glasgow, 22 June 2023, https://thecityoflostbooks.glasgow.ac.uk/mervyn-peake-boy-in-darkness-1956-and-the-nightmare-of-complicity/. Accessed 22 June 2023.

—. "Mervyn Peake and the Queering of Sark." *The City of Lost Books*, University of Glasgow, 26 Jan. 2023, https://thecityoflostbooks.glasgow.ac.uk/mervyn-peake-and-the-queering-of-sark/. Accessed 28 Jan. 2023.

—. "Mervyn Peake on Sark." *The City of Lost Books*, University of Glasgow, 22 Dec. 2022,

https://thecityoflostbooks.glasgow.ac.uk/mervyn-peake-on-sark/.
  Accessed 5 Jan. 2023.

Mills, Alice. "Literalized Metaphors and the Comedy of Excess in 'Mr.
  Pye.'" *Peake Studies*, vol. 6, no. 3, 1999, pp. 25–39. *JSTOR*,
  http://www.jstor.org/stable/24776155. Accessed 11 November 2018.

Peake, Mervyn. "The Artist's World." *Peake Studies*, vol. 12, no. 2, 2011,
  pp. 5–9. *JSTOR*, http://www.jstor.org/stable/24776563. Accessed 15
  February 2019.

—. *Boy in Darkness and Other Stories*. Edited by Sebastian Peake, Peter
  Owen, 2007.

—. "The Cave or Anima Mundi" (Unpublished manuscript courtesy of Mr.
  G. Peter Winnington, June 25, 2018), PDF.

—. *Collected Poems*. Edited by R. W. Maslen, Fyfield Books/Carcanet,
  2008.

—. *The Gormenghast Novels*. Centenary ed., Overlook, 1995.

—. "In Search of Mr. Pye." Peake Studies, vol. 10, no. 3, 2007, pp. 3–4.
  JSTOR, http://www.jstor.org/stable/24776394. Accessed 9 June
  2023.

—. *Mr. Pye*. Vintage, 1999.

Shayer, David. "The Great Stone Island: Gormenghast Castle and Sark."
  Peake Studies, vol. 4, no. 3, 1995, pp. 29–36. *JSTOR*,
  http://www.jstor.org/stable/24776003. Accessed 19 July 2020.

Sohn, Tim. "Inside the Story of John Allen Chau's Ill-Fated Trip to a
  Remote Island." *Smithsonian*, 7 Dec. 2018,
  https://www.smithsonianmag.com/history/inside-story-john-allen-
  chaus-ill-fated-trip-remote-island-180970971/. Accessed 16
  February 2023.

Whittingham, Selby. *Albion: A Quarterly Journal Concerned with
  British Studies*, vol. 31, no. 2, 1999, pp. 314–
  16. *JSTOR*, https://doi.org/10.2307/4052775. Accessed 26 June
  2023.

Winnington, G. Peter. *The Voice of the Heart: the Working of Mervyn
  Peake's Imagination*. Liverpool University Press, 2006.

"I'm Dead, I'm Dead, It's Good to Be Dead!": The Uncanny Epiphanies of Ray Bradbury's "Jack-in-the-Box" and H. P. Lovecraft's "The Outsider"

Misty L. Jameson

R AY BRADBURY IS AN AUTHOR of vast range and skill; while arguably most celebrated for his works of science fiction such as *The Martian Chronicles* or *Fahrenheit 451*, he began his career as a writer of the weird tale. H. P. Lovecraft famously outlined the weird tale as having "something more than secret murder, bloody bones, or a sheeted form clanking chains according to rule. A certain atmosphere of breathless and unexplainable dread of outer, unknown forces must be present; and there must be a hint" of a "malign and particular suspension or defeat of those fixed laws of Nature" that sustain the sense of the rational (Lovecraft "Supernatural" 84). This definition, found in Lovecraft's essay "Supernatural Horror in Literature," is an important one in the history of the American Gothic tradition, which "develops a brooding atmosphere of gloom and terror, represents events that are uncanny or macabre or melodramatically violent, and often deals with aberrant psychological states" (Abrams 111). The American Gothic tradition originated with Lovecraft's and Bradbury's influences such as Cotton Mather, Charles Brockden Brown, Nathanial Hawthorne, Robert W. Chambers, and—most importantly—Edgar Allan Poe

(Goho 21-33). From this tradition, the weird tale, as an offshoot of the American Gothic, developed its focus on the uncanny, the unknown, the macabre, and what Lovecraft terms "cosmic horror," which can be understood as the fear, shock, or awe experienced when humans confront the unexplainable, particularly that which suggests the indifference of the universe to human affairs (Lovecraft "Supernatural" 88). Breaking away from the old-fashioned European gothic tale, American Gothic is no longer necessarily confined to the ancestral castle and its excessive ornamentation; instead, these works often center on the traditional family and their unadorned home. To sustain an atmosphere of gloom, these gothic presentations of family and home allow both the reader and the main characters to "discover the terror that lurks in the heart of the familiar, the evil in the mundane and the banal" (Waller 5). In the weird tale, this process of defamiliarization, of making the familiar or everyday unfamiliar, is part of "the pursuit of some indefinable and perhaps maddeningly unreachable understanding of the world beyond the mundane" (VanderMeer and VanderMeer np). It is this search for understanding, "even when something cannot be understood," that usually leads to a "dark reverie or epiphany" (VanderMeer and VanderMeer np). This epiphany is another marker of the weird tale, as it brings the horror of knowledge both to the reader and to the main characters.

In his examination of Lovecraft within the American Gothic tradition, James Goho claims that "the greatest haunted house story is Poe's 'The Fall of the House of Usher.' Lovecraft's 'The Outsider' may be a sequel to it. Lovecraft confessed that 'Poe affected me most of all horror-writers'" (Goho 26). Ray Bradbury also freely admitted that Poe was a primary influence upon him as a writer; in an interview, Bradbury explains that "I read 'The Fall of the House of Usher,' and Poe completely enchanted me. I was ten years old, and for the next two years, I read Poe every day of my life" (Cantalupo 133). Bradbury also claims that his story "Usher II," included as part of *The Martian Chronicles*, "was the sequel to 'The Fall of the House of Usher'" (Bradbury *Martian* 134). In "Usher II," Bradbury lists Poe "and Lovecraft and Hawthorne and Ambrose Bierce" as part of the tradition of great writers in America, those whose works were banned and burned in the dystopic world of "Usher II" (Bradbury *Martian* 105). However, "Usher II" is more of an homage to Poe and the other writers Bradbury wished to honor; Lovecraft's "The Outsider" with its moldering house and familial mysteries is much more akin to the atmosphere of Poe's original story. Lovecraft, who, later in his career, was not particularly satisfied with "The Outsider," claimed that the story "represents my literal though unconscious imitation of Poe at its very height" (qtd. in Joshi *Subtler* 86).

Thus, if "The Outsider" can be seen as Lovecraft's sequel, and "Usher II" as Bradbury's homage, to *The Fall of the House of Usher*, then I would argue that "Jack-in-the Box"—published in Bradbury's first short story collection, *Dark Carnival*, released by Arkham House—is Bradbury's sequel to, or even rewriting of, "The Outsider." Both stories involve the same basic plot structure and similarly naïve protagonists, and both exploit unusual variations on the traditional gothic house setting. An epiphany marks the ending of each narrative, and these epiphanies are reached only after a celebration, a party, forces them to confront the abject—a confrontation that will unsettle, even reverse, the protagonists' worlds. While "Jack-in-the-Box" is not particularly well known among Bradbury's works, there is a natural progression from "The Fall of the House of Usher" to "The Outsider" to "Jack-in-the-Box." The tropes of the uncanny, the defamiliarized home, issues of family and familial relations, various states of psychological distress, and a dark epiphany mark all three stories; however, Lovecraft focuses more on "cosmic horror" in his tale, as he considered "the touch of cosmic outsideness—of dim, shadowy non-terrestrial hints—to be the characteristic feature of [his] writing" (Lovecraft "Letters" 14), while Bradbury moves the weird tale into the world of childhood. "Jack-in-the-Box" is not Bradbury's first story to feature a child as the protagonist, but Bradbury's sustained use of children and childhood in his narratives moves the weird tale away from the primarily exclusive world of adults, allowing him to blend a nostalgia for childhood with a "dark vision" of American life and love (Fiedler 28). It is a subtle shift that helps to open up the weird tale to further narrative possibilities.

Ray Bradbury wrote "Jack-in-the-Box" early in his writing career, during the time when he would select a single item—such as a jar, a lake, a coffin, a crowd, the wind, or a cistern—as the inspiration for a short story. In *Ray Bradbury*, David Mogen sees "Each of the stories creat[ing] an eerie context in which the central object evokes a haunting atmosphere and theme" (Mogen 47). In this case, the child's toy becomes symbolic, primarily for the almost impossibly large country house in which the thirteen-year-old protagonist, Edwin, has been raised and, ultimately, imprisoned by his mother. Each floor of this house—named the lowlands, two middle countries, and highlands—constitutes "the Universe. Father (or God, as Mother often called him) had raised its mountains of wallpapered plaster long ago. This was Father-God's creation, in which stars blazed at the flick of a switch. And the sun was Mother, and Mother was the sun, about which all the Worlds swung, turning" (Bradbury "Jack" 414). This is, indeed, "a vast house designed as a substitute for the natural world" as Lahna Diskin, in "Bradbury on Children," claims (Diskin 150). It is also a symbol "of the compulsively ordered fantasy world of [Edwin's] mother" (Johnson 45). In gothic terms, the house symbolizes "the crumbling shell of paternal authority" for the dead father where, underneath, "lies the maternal blackness," which is ultimately both a physical and mental "prison" of the mother's making

(Fiedler 132). The story opens with Edwin staring out the "cold morning windows" in hopes of finding "another World beyond" this one, his attempts thwarted by "the trees surround[ing] the house which surrounded Edwin" (Bradbury "Jack" 412-13). Thus, the reader is introduced to his predicament: Edwin loves his mother, yet he desires to know what lies beyond the confines of her solar system, the stultifying atmosphere of this house and the tree-filled environs encompassing it. Even though Edwin has been raised with the idea that someday he must "grow into a Presence, he must fit the odors and the trumpet voice of God. He must some day stand tall [. . .] he must be God himself! Nothing must prevent it. Not the sky or the trees or the Things beyond the trees," he has also been taught to fear the Monsters that lurk outside his home (Bradbury, "Jack" 416-17). His mother has described these "Beasts" as things that "run down paths and crush people like strawberries"; she also reminds Edwin that his father "was killed, struck down by one of those Terrors on the road" (Bradbury, "Jack" 413). While it is plain to the reader that the mother has turned the cars and trucks on the road outside their home into something monstrous, manipulating Edwin through her tales of horror, Edwin, young and inexperienced, believes his mother's stories—but still wants to "see the Beasts, horrible as they are," for himself (Bradbury "Jack" 413). Like any child, particularly one in a Ray Bradbury story, his curiosity about the outside world is piqued, not quelled, by her warnings.

As inventor of these tales and this circumscribed world, Mother is herself a complex character, to be pitied on one hand and reviled on the other. She either provides Bradbury's readers with "one of the best parental abuse stories ever written" (Cannon and Zaleski 52) or "one of Bradbury's more serious stories of madness" (Johnson 44)—or perhaps both. Wayne Johnson goes on to say that the Mother is "apparently deranged since the death of her husband some years before" and that she is not simply impersonating Teacher but suffers from "split personalities" (Johnson 44). In either case, the Mother certainly seems to have "internalized concerns about her own security" and Edwin's to the point that she is "unable to leave behind the obsessive desire for perfection that led to the erasure of her life beyond the walls of the home" (Krafft 37). Assisting his mother in fashioning both their unusual universe and this neurotic young boy is Teacher, who lives in the Highlands where the schoolroom is located. It is her job to educate Edwin, but that education comes from books "from which pages had been razored, and clipped, certain lines erased, certain pictures torn, the leather jaws of some books glued tight" (Bradbury "Jack" 418). Anything that might distract Edwin from the world of their home or might encourage his imagination has been excised; in fact, Edwin is so unimaginative that he ignores all the obvious evidence and simply *cannot* realize that his mother and Teacher are the same person. Like his toy jack-in-the-box, which is stuck inside its container, young Edwin is "crushed under the lid, in [his] jail" where he "stay[s] crammed tight" (Bradbury "Jack" 412).

Edwin's home, then, is immediately established by Bradbury as an uncanny or "unhomely" place—one that should be comfortingly familiar but is, instead, defamiliarized by the potential menace suggested by Edwin's longing for the forbidden knowledge of the outside world and his childish attempts to explore the secret areas of his family home.[1] This defamiliarization continues as Bradbury describes the mother as being "the pale woman that no one but the birds saw in old country houses in fourth-floor cupola windows [. . .] there she would be, in her tower, silent and white, high and alone and quiet" (Bradbury "Jack" 413); she is like the "last wild white blossom" in a "deserted greenhouse" or like a ghost restlessly haunting her home while Edwin himself "had a haunted look," the look of a nervous, even "feverish" child (Bradbury "Jack" 413). This family dynamic—

godlike deceased father, ghostly mother, and haunted child—seems akin to that found in traditional gothic melodramas, uncanny narratives of family and home in which traumas are often repressed, only to return in an unpredictable fashion.

The unhomeliness of Edwin's childhood universe links Bradbury's story to Lovecraft's "The Outsider," for the unnamed first-person narrator begins his story by announcing, "Unhappy is he to whom the memories of childhood bring only fear and sadness" (Lovecraft "Outsider" 97).[2] The narrator then goes on to describe the "vast and dismal chambers" of his family manor with its "twilight groves of grotesque, gigantic, and vine-encumbered trees" comparable to those lurking outside Edwin's family home (Lovecraft "Outsider" 97). Unlike Edwin, however, Lovecraft's narrator claims to learn all he knows, not from any teacher, but from "the mouldy books" he finds, and he only thinks of himself as young because he "remembered so little" (Lovecraft, "Outsider" 98. Indeed, the Outsider does not remember his family at all; as he says, "Beings must have cared for my needs, yet I cannot recall any person except myself; or anything alive but the noiseless rats and bats and spiders" (Lovecraft "Outsider" 98). Similarly, Edwin sees his house as containing a kind of enchantment that provides for his needs—to him, meals appear magically on the table at meal times, and fires appear merely on command. Because he is so naïve and sheltered, he does not understand how the basic household works, that his mother is responsible for providing for him.

However, while Edwin describes his home—maternal prison though it may be—as being filled with sunlight, the narrator of "The Outsider" lives where "[i]t was never light" and he has no access to the sun (Lovecraft "Outsider" 98). In both stories, the light—or lack thereof—becomes part of the impetus for each character to seek new worlds, new spaces. Edwin goes through a sunlight-filled "forbidden door" and follows the spiral stair, leaping "around and around and up until his knees ached and his breath fountained in and out and his head banged like a bell and at last he reached the terrible summit of the climb and stood in an open, sundrenched tower" where he can finally see that there is another world beyond the trees and realizes that it is not simply the "nightmare nothingness" his mother has trained him to believe (Bradbury "Jack" 415-16). Edwin is terrified, screaming with horror and becoming sick when he learns of the vastness of the world beyond his house, ultimately fearing that he will go blind in seeing this forbidden territory. Like Edwin, the Outsider decides to scale to the top of the "single black ruined tower" reaching above the forest that surrounds him because he feels that "it were better to glimpse the sky and perish, than to live without ever beholding day" (Lovecraft "Outsider" 99). He climbs "worn and aged stone stairs" until he reaches "the level where they ceased, and thereafter [clings] perilously to small footholds leading upward" until he finally opens a trap-door at what he thinks is "a prodigious height, far above the accursed branches of the wood" only to discover, not the sun, but the full moon (Lovecraft "Outsider" 99). He also realizes that, instead of being at a great height and seeing the "dizzying prospect of treetops seen from a lofty eminence, there stretched [. . .] nothing less than *the solid ground*" (Lovecraft "Outsider" 100). The Outsider feels the "most daemoniacal of all shocks" at the revelation that he has traveled ever upward in the tower only seemingly to reach the earth's surface—his mind is "stunned and chaotic" but still "frantic[ally] craving for light" (Lovecraft "Outsider" 100). Both characters, then, embark on a journey, climbing ever upward, to test the limits of their worlds, and both find the world to be confusingly, unexpectedly immense.

Each story is structured at least partly around this journey, but this journey, which can be seen as a traditional movement from unconscious ignorance to conscious understanding, only marks the beginning of these characters' discoveries. The desire for light, and for enlightenment, that both these characters share drives their plots forward to their final epiphanies. After arriving in the schoolroom late, Edwin confesses his travels to the top of the tower to Teacher, and after this revelation, his mother announces that the following day is Edwin's birthday, even though, according to Edwin, "it's only been ten months" since they last celebrated his birthday. To placate his uncertainty, Mother reminds him that he is allowed to "open another secret room" on each birthday until his twenty-first, when he will be "Man of the House, Father, God, Ruler of the Universe" (Bradbury "Jack" 419). Edwin is initially excited by this prospect until he is alone in bed that night and thinks that "things had gotten [. . .] Nervous [. . .] things had begun to shimmer by day as well as by night" (Bradbury "Jack" 419). As naïve as Edwin seems, the fact that he is aware of his mother's anxiety reveals the severity of the strain she feels in maintaining their household charade, a strain exacerbated by his recent curiosity.

Edwin's birthday party is a raucous affair for two: they eat, drink, sing, and then whirl "away to more strawberries, more wines, more laughter that shook chandeliers into trembling rain" (Bradbury 420-21), but beneath this joy and frivolity, Mother cannot contain her increasing nervousness. As she and Edwin lounge in the garden, she "jump[s] twice when she hear[s] Monsters roar beyond the forest," looking in fear at the trees separating them from the road and its terrible "chaos," and she eventually leads Edwin to run, ducking for cover, back into the house when an airplane flies overhead. That night, as the "birthday burnt away to cellophane nothingness," Edwin returns to his room, thinking of his father, asking himself, "What was killed? What was Death? Was Death a feeling? Did God enjoy it so much he never came back? Was Death a journey then?" (Bradbury 422). To Edwin, whose only journeys have been to different, sometimes previously secret, parts of their house, death becomes as simple as opening the door to a new room—albeit a room of no return.

The next morning, when he finds his mother "collapsed on the floor in her shiny green-gold party dress, a champagne goblet in one hand, the carpet littered with broken glass," Edwin assumes that she is asleep—as does the reader (Bradbury 422). However, it does not take long for readers to realize that she is, in fact, dead. With no Mother, no Teacher, no food, and no fire, Edwin does not know what to do until he decides that, if Teacher is missing, she must be lost, that "she had wandered, by error, into the Outlands," and that he must find her so that she can help him wake up his mother (Bradbury 424). Edwin bravely makes the journey past the garden and the trees to the road, all while his mother's words echo in his mind: "If I run beyond the trees I'll die [. . .] for that's what Mother said. You'll die, you'll die" (Bradbury 424). Anita Sullivan, in "Ray Bradbury and Fantasy," even claims that Edwin's leaving the house is "an act which for him amounts to committing suicide" (Sullivan 1311). Stumbling, "laughing and crying, crying and laughing," he runs to the end of his Universe, past a policeman on the sidewalk who sees Edwin "jumping up and down and touching things. Things like lampposts, the telephone poles, fire hydrants, dogs, people." While Edwin is savoring the newness of the world around him, he yells, "I'm dead, I'm dead, I'm glad I'm dead, I'm dead, I'm dead, I'm glad I'm dead, I'm dead, I'm dead, it's *good* to be dead!" (Bradbury "Jack" 425).

This ending, while insuring Edwin's freedom from the confines of his possessive mother's manipulations, is not simply a happy one and is, instead, fraught with complications—even though critics such as Hazel Pierce or Lahna Diskin read this ending as purely a joyful one, focusing solely on the final moments of Edwin's freedom and not considering the ramifications of this freedom too closely. However, Diskin does take a particularly dismal view of Edwin's previous home life: "Edwin is an innocent incarcerated by adult neuroses, subjugated by the delusions and defenses erected as compensation by adults in retreat from life" (Diskin 150). Regardless of how one might view Edwin's life with his mother, Edwin's new life without her will bring with it new challenges, which his past life as an outsider has sadly done little to prepare him for.

While Edwin does finally free himself both from his literal imprisonment in their house and from "his mother's disordered view of the world" (Johnson 45), it is in a manner similar to that of the Jack-in-the-box. When he cannot pry the toy out, Edwin thinks, "I'll get you out [. . .]. Just wait, just wait. It may hurt, but there's only one way." He then decides to "[fling] the box out" of the window, to break it in order to allow the doll's escape (Bradbury, "Jack" 420). In his own escape through the garden, Edwin finds the doll "sprawled with its arms overhead in an eternal gesture of freedom" (Bradbury, "Jack" 424). Like the doll, Edwin, too, is free of his "box," and while this may be the only practical way out, it will also *hurt*—his mother is dead, Edwin has no idea what this outside world is like, and he does not even fully grasp the differences between life and death. Therefore, his joyous discovery at the end of the story is tinged with desperation, his shouting not merely a childish "game" as the policeman thinks, but the manic cries of someone who truly is lost and alone in his brave new world (Bradbury, "Jack" 425). This ending is the culmination of the narrative tension running throughout Bradbury's story between the protagonist's naïve understanding of his situation and the reader's ability to see through Edwin's childish impressions; with this closing, readers are presented with a kind of "monstrous joy," wondering what lies next for young Edwin (Chopin 224).

The narrative tension between the protagonist's and the reader's interpretation of events is also key to Lovecraft's "The Outsider." This narrative strategy, which involves a "judicious parceling out of information" ultimately "adds a wider ambiguity and creates a stronger story" than if the Outsider were equipped with the same faculties as Lovecraft's reader (Norris 210). For example, while the reader easily understands that the narrator, after his long journey upward, is in a cemetery, the Outsider simply describes the ground as "decked and diversified by marble slabs and columns, and overshadowed by an ancient stone church," seemingly unaware of the implications of his locale (Lovecraft, "Outsider" 100). When he, "determined to gaze on brilliance and gaiety at any cost" (Lovecraft "Outsider" 101), begins his next journey outside the tower, the reader's sense of the uncanny has been heightened by this discovery, an awareness the narrator apparently does not share. Instead, he confesses that he seems to know even less than he did before and can no longer remember anything about himself: "I knew not who I was or what I was [. . .] though as I continued to stumble along I became conscious of a kind of fearsome latent memory that made my progress not wholly fortuitous" (Lovecraft 101). He is driven by his desire, seemingly for "brilliance and gaiety," but actually it is his need for knowledge that presses him forward. As S. T. Joshi has pointed out, "knowledge itself is a very complicated issue in Lovecraft" (Joshi *Subtler* 262). On one hand, Lovecraft speaks of the "joy in pursuing truth" but also acknowledges that "the truth," once found, "may cause suicidal or nearly suicidal depression" (qtd. in Joshi *Subtler* 262). This paradox often puts Lovecraftian protagonists in a double-bind—scientific truths, individual or family truths, and even cosmic truths are all worthy of pursuit, but the result of such knowledge, in the end, may be personally destructive for the seeker. The Outsider finds himself in this same double-bind, with twin cravings for enlightenment and literal light instinctually impelling him forward on his quest.

When he reaches his goal, "a venerable ivied castle," the Outsider senses that it is "maddeningly familiar, yet full of perplexing strangeness" because of the modifications made to the moat and some of the towers since his own time living there; thus, while the reader understands that this used to be his home, the Outsider is still grappling with its significance (Lovecraft "Outsider" 101). As the narrator looks through an open window, his description of the people and interiors of the castle is one of uninhibited admiration. He sees that a party is taking place—the windows are "gorgeously ablaze," the sounds are "of the gayest revelry," and the company are all "speaking brightly" to one another (Lovecraft 101). He seems to have finally found the light he has been seeking, but this moment of blissful observation shifts rapidly from his "single bright moment of hope to [his] blackest convulsion of despair and realisation" when, as he steps into the room, the guests suddenly scream with "hideous intensity" and flee in panic (Lovecraft 101). While already knowing that the Outsider is the cause of their extreme reactions, the reader can only wait as he reports searching the rooms and finding "the inconceivable, indescribable, and unmentionable monstrosity which had by its simple appearance changed a merry company to a herd of delirious fugitives," a being which he goes on to describe as "a compound of all that is unclean, uncanny, unwelcome, abnormal, and detestable" (Lovecraft 102).

Although the reader has grasped the Outsider's position as a ghoul-like Lovecraftian creature returning to his former home, the final line of the narrative when he reveals that, in touching the "*rotting outstretched paw of the monster*" (Lovecraft 103), he actually touches the "*cold and unyielding surface*" of a mirror (Lovecraft 104), maintains its uncanny power because it suggests the cold horror of the grave entwined with the warmth of home while also mixing the living with the dead.[3] As Jesse Stommel claims, "His response [to his reflection in the mirror] is a quintessentially abject one, almost as though [Julia] Kristeva was channeling Lovecraft in theorizing the term" (Stommel 341).[4]

Stommel goes on to say, "Lovecraft's monster sees an image (in the mirror) that simultaneously captivates and repels, beseeches and frustrates, exactly because it doesn't and won't ever make rational sense. That he can't know further propels his desire to know" (Stommel 342). The Outsider's quest has led him to this moment; in his anguished epiphany, the Outsider must face himself as the abject horror which defies boundaries and "defies categorization, because he is both human and not human" (Stommel 342). Like Edwin in Bradbury's "Jack-in-the-Box," the Outsider must face the trauma of knowledge specifically reached through an encounter with abjection—a dead mother in one case and an undead self in the other—but where Bradbury's story focuses on the uncertainty and innocence of a child, Lovecraft's tale deals with the "unknown forces" of cosmic terror (Lovecraft, "Supernatural" 84), which are presented as "gaps in our understanding both due to the narrator's limited knowledge in some aspects and by what he chooses to withhold from the reader" (Norris 210).

Most critics have viewed the ending of "The Outsider" as rather bleak, with S.T. Joshi seeing the protagonist as "emotionally crippled" after facing "the horrors of *self-knowledge*" (Joshi *Subtler* 263); R. Boerem claiming that, after all his searching, the Outsider only "discovers a type of hopelessness" (Boerem 221); and T. S. Miller viewing the narrative as drawing "a far more sinister and far more fundamental connection between humanity and monstrosity" when the narrator "discovers that he is the cosmic horror" of the tale (Miller 139).[5] However, while it is true that the narrator's epiphany happens in "a single and fleeting avalanche of soul-annihilating memory" (Lovecraft "Outsider" 103), this moment is mercifully brief, and with it comes knowledge but, more importantly, freedom. As the narrator states, "in the cosmos, there is balm as well as bitterness, and that balm is nepenthe"; he tells us that he is able to forget "what had horrified me" (Lovecraft 104). Nevertheless, something of this experience must still linger for him to narrate this tale; as Carl Buchanan claims, this statement by the narrator "is literally untrue, since of course he has not 'forgotten' what horrified him, his image; he has just related it, so we know it is present in his memory. Yet he is not horrified *now* by what spooked him then" (Buchanan 13). Thus, in no longer remembering the abject horror of the moment, the Outsider can now face the truth of his existence. Realizing that he cannot return to his churchyard home, he proclaims, "I had hated the antique castle and the trees. Now I ride with the mocking and friendly ghouls on the night-wind and play by day amongst the catacombs of Nephren-Ka [. . .]. I know that light is not for me, save that of the moon" (Lovecraft "Outsider" 104).

Instead of simply being overshadowed by "the horrors of self-knowledge," this ending is, like that of "Jack-in-the-Box," more ambiguous, a kind of "monstrous liberty" for one who had been trapped below a world that was no longer his yet who instinctively desired to return. While he may still be "a stranger in this century and among those who are still men," his painful moment of epiphany allows him to find his true place with the "friendly ghouls" and to no longer feel the desire for light, for what he can no longer be (Lovecraft 104). Hence, his naïve yearnings are replaced by a bitter, but better, truth. Like Bradbury's Edwin, who can only gain his freedom through "hurt" (Bradbury "Jack" 420), the Outsider, too, can only gain freedom first through the pain of discovery and then, finally, through what Buchanan calls the "mature acceptance of his lot" (Buchanan 13). While the Outsider can lay claim to this acceptance at the end of his narrative, young Edwin has only begun to experience the freedom beyond the lies that Mother and Teacher have used to construct his childhood thus far. As Ann and Jeff VanderMeer explain, through narrative epiphanies, the "Weird can be transformative—sometimes literally—and it entertains monsters while not always seeing them as monstrous" (VanderMeer and VanderMeer np); these monsters may be the inhuman monsters of Lovecraft's cosmic terror or the very human, overprotectively cruel monster of motherhood in Bradbury's story.

With the uncanny, that which should be familiar, even comforting, becomes defamiliarized—often because something hidden or repressed has come to light. The protagonists of "Jack-in-the-Box" and "The Outsider" find themselves literally unhomed at the end of their narratives because, after their discoveries about the nature of life and death and about the boundaries of the self and the world, neither can return to the home he once inhabited. These places have been rendered uncanny—*unheimlich*—by each character's epiphany, the sudden knowledge they have obtained because of carnivalesque celebrations as well as confrontations with abjection—transgressive moments that reveal horrible yet freeing truths. These ambiguous narratives and their unreliable protagonists were created by two exemplary practitioners of the weird tale who, despite their similarities, are not often studied together or considered comparable writers.[6] However, by examining both "Jack-in-the-Box" and "The Outsider" for parallels in plot, setting, characterization, and theme, my goal has been to reveal the literary continuity from Lovecraft to Bradbury while simultaneously showing how Lovecraft's emphasis on cosmic terror in the weird tale was transformed by Bradbury to an emphasis on the uncertainties and fragility of childhood. Both of these types of the weird tale have influenced countless numbers of horror writers today—Stephen King being the primary, most influential author who successfully blends both. Overall, Lovecraft and Bradbury, along with Stephen King, are integral parts of the "dark carnival," to borrow Bradbury's phrase, of American literature, "a literature of darkness and the grotesque in a land of light and affirmation," as Leslie Fiedler has famously argued (Fiedler 29).

Notes

1. The German word for uncanny, *unheimlich*, literally translates as "unhomely" in English. Thus, my use of "unhomely" or "unhomeliness" comes from notions of the uncanny, taken from this literal translation. Part one of Freud's "The Uncanny" discusses the meaning of this term and presents examples of the uncanny both from other languages and from German. Defamiliarization is a term that originates with the Russian Formalists in the early twentieth century; in literature, it can most easily be defined as presenting everyday objects in an unfamiliar, even strange, way, in order to induce new ideas, new perspectives, in the reader or audience.

2. Dirk W. Mosig, in "The Four Faces of the Outsider," describes H. P. Lovecraft as "deprived of a paternal figure at the age of three [and] controlled by an overprotective mother," which makes Lovecraft sound very much like Bradbury's protagonist (Mosig 18). Of course, many critics and readers have made biographic connections between the Outsider and Lovecraft himself.

3. Ghouls, as George Wetzel reminds the reader, "inhabited the nameless regions below the graveyards" in Lovecraft's fiction (Wetzel 57). However, Duncan Norris tells the reader that "What is certain is that the titular Outsider is fundamentally the classic *revenant*, the returned who was once dead and carries with it the decay and detestation of the grave as it returns to a place no longer its own" (Norris 209; emphasis added). See Norris's "*Zeitgeist* and *Untoten*: Lovecraft and the Walking Dead" for more information about the various types of undead used by Lovecraft in his fiction.

4. Julia Kristeva's notions of abjection in "Approaching Abjection" have to do with the idea of ambiguity—particularly objects that figure ambiguously in terms of categorical oppositions (me/not me; inside/outside; living/dead) and limits. She describes abjection thus:

> This massive and abrupt irruption of a strangeness which, if it was familiar to me in an opaque and forgotten life, now importunes me as

radically separated and repugnant. Not me. Not that. But not nothing either. A "something" that I do not recognise as a thing. A whole lot of nonsense which has nothing insignificant and which crushes me. At the border of inexistence and hallucination, of a reality which, if I recognize it, annihilates me. (Kristeva 126)

While Stommel claims Kristeva seems to have been "channeling" Lovecraft in her examination of the abject, Noel Carroll, in *The Philosophy of Horror*, directly uses "The Outsider" as an example of "indescribability," one of the ways horror fiction provokes an emotional, if not physical, response in its audience, a response that is similar to Kristeva's discussion of abjection (Carroll 20). For a thorough examination of Lovecraft's own notion of "outsideness" and his "dialectics between self and other," see "Self, Other, and the Evolution of Lovecraft's Treatment of Outsideness" by Massimo Berruti (Berruti 112).

5. Of course, many other interpretations and readings of "The Outsider" have been posited; as Leslie S. Klinger states in his introduction to this story in his *The New Annotated H. P. Lovecraft: Beyond Arkham*, "The Outsider" is "perhaps the single most analyzed story of any of Lovecraft's considerable output. It has been considered from biographical psychoanalytic angles, as an antireligion polemic, an expression of philosophy a criticism of progress, and a depiction of 'homosexual panic'" (Klinger 97).

6. Aside from their previously discussed shared affinity to Edgar Allan Poe, both Lovecraft and Bradbury established their careers as writers in *Weird Tales* magazine. In 1923, Lovecraft's story "Dagon" was published in *Weird Tales*, the magazine that would publish more of his short fiction than any other periodical, and in 1942, at the age of 22, Ray Bradbury published his first short story, "The Candle," in *Weird Tales*; he would then publish stories in every single edition of *Weird Tales* for 1944 (Thomas np). The similarities in the two men's careers would only continue, as both men later joined circles of writers in the same vein as themselves and even fostered the careers of younger, up-and-coming authors. After Lovecraft's death in 1937, Arkham House was founded in 1939 by August Derleth and Donald Wandrei to publish quality editions of Lovecraft's fiction; *The Outsider and Others* was their first volume.

Coincidentally, Ray Bradbury's first short story collection, *Dark Carnival*, was published by Arkham House in 1947.

Works Cited

Abrams, M. H. "Gothic Novel." *A Glossary of Literary Terms*. 7th ed., Harcourt, 1999, pp. 110-12.

Berruti, Massimo. "Self, Other, and the Evolution of Lovecraft's Treatment of Outsideness." *Lovecraft Annual*, no. 3, 2009, pp. 109–46. *JSTOR*, https://www.jstor.org/stable/26868393. Accessed 23 June 2025.

Boerem, R. "A Lovecraftian Nightmare." *H. P. Lovecraft: Four Decades of Criticism*, edited by S. T. Joshi, Ohio University Press, 1980, pp. 217-21.

Bradbury, Ray. "Jack-in-the-Box." *The Stories of Ray Bradbury*. Knopf, 1980, pp. 412-25.

---. *The Martian Chronicles*. 1950. Bantam, 1979.

Buchanan, Carl. "'The Outsider' as an Homage to Poe." *Lovecraft Studies*, vol. 31, 1994, pp. 12-14.

Cannon, Peter, and Jeff Zaleski. "*Dark Carnival* (Book Review)." *Publishers Weekly*, vol. 248, no. 47, Nov. 2001, p. 52. *EBSCOhost*, https://search.ebscohost.com/login.aspx?direct=true&AuthType=ip,shib&db=a9h&AN=5566106&site=ehost-live&custid=s9007104. Accessed 3 Feb. 2023.

Carroll, Noel. *The Philosophy of Horror or Paradoxes of the Heart*. Routledge, 1990.

Cantalupo, Barbara, and Ray Bradbury. "Interview with Ray Bradbury: March 22, 2010." *The Edgar Allan Poe Review*, vol. 10, no. 3, 2009, pp. 133–36. *JSTOR*, http://www.jstor.org/stable/41506376. Accessed 23 June 2025.

Chopin, Kate. "The Story of an Hour." *Literature: Reading, Reacting, Writing*, edited by Laurie G. Kirszner and Stephen R. Mandell, 8th ed., Wadsworth, 2013, pp. 223-24.

Diskin, Lahna. "Bradbury on Children." *Ray Bradbury*, edited by Martin Greenberg and Joseph D. Olander, Taplinger, 1980, pp. 127-55.

Fiedler, Leslie. *Love and Death in the American Novel*. 1960. Anchor, 1992.

Goho, James. "The Shape of Darkness: Origins for H. P. Lovecraft within the American Gothic Tradition." *Lovecraft and Influence: His Predecessors and Successors*, edited by Robert H. Waugh, Scarecrow Press, 2013, pp. 21-33. *ProQuest Ebook Central*, https://ebookcentral.proquest.com/lib/lander/detail.action?docID= 1375706. Accessed 13 June 2025.

Johnson, Wayne L. *Ray Bradbury*. Frederick Unger, 1980.

Joshi, S. T. "Lovecraft Criticism: A Study." *H. P. Lovecraft: Four Decades of Criticism*, edited by S. T. Joshi, Ohio University Press, 1980, pp. 20-26.

---. *A Subtler Magick: The Writings and Philosophy of H. P. Lovecraft*. Wildside Press, 1999.

Klinger, Leslie S. *The New Annotated H. P. Lovecraft: Beyond Arkham*, edited by Leslie S. Klinger, Liveright, 2019, p. 97.

Krafft, Andrea. "Housewives and Witches: Finding Feminism in Ray Bradbury's Fiction." *Critical Insights: Ray Bradbury*, edited by Rafeeq O. McGiveron, Grey House, 2017, pp. 34-45.

Kristeva, Julia, and John Lechte. "Approaching Abjection." *Oxford Literary Review*, vol. 5, no. 1/2, 1982, pp. 125–149. *JSTOR*, http://www.jstor.org/stable/43973647. Accessed 26 June 2025.

Lovecraft, H. P. "The Outsider." *The New Annotated H. P. Lovecraft: Beyond Arkham*, edited by Leslie S. Klinger, Liveright, 2019, pp. 97-105.

---. "Supernatural Horror in Literature." *Collected Essays Volume 2: Literary Criticism*, edited by S. T. Joshi, Hippocampus Press, 2004, pp. 82-135.

Lovecraft, H. P., et al. "Letters to Farnsworth Wright." *Lovecraft Annual*, no. 8, 2014, pp. 5–59. *JSTOR*, https://www.jstor.org/stable/26868482. Accessed 23 June 2025.

Miller, T. S. "From Bodily Fear to Cosmic Horror (and Back Again): The Tentacle Monster from Primordial Chaos to Hello Cthulhu." *Lovecraft Annual*, no. 5, 2011, pp. 121–154. *JSTOR*, https://www.jstor.org/stable/26868434. Accessed 23 June 2025.

Mogen, David. *Ray Bradbury*. Twayne, 1986.

Mosig, Dirk W. "The Four Faces of the Outsider." *Discovering H. P. Lovecraft*, edited by Darrell Schweitzer, Wildside Press, 2001, pp. 17-34.

Norris, Duncan. "*Zeitgeist* and *Untoten*: Lovecraft and the Walking Dead." *Lovecraft Annual*, no. 14, 2020, pp. 189–240. *JSTOR*, https://www.jstor.org/stable/26939817. Accessed 30 June 2025.

Pierce, Hazel. "Ray Bradbury and the Gothic Tradition." *Ray Bradbury*, edited by Martin Harry Greenberg and Joseph D. Olander, Taplinger, 1980, pp. 165-85.

Stommel, Jesse. "The Loveliness of Decay: Rotting Flesh, Literary Matter, and Dead Media." *Journal of the Fantastic in the Arts*, vol. 25, no. 2/3 (91), 2014, pp. 332–46. *JSTOR*, http://www.jstor.org/stable/24353032. Accessed 23 June 2025.

Sullivan, Anita T. "Ray Bradbury and Fantasy." *The English Journal*, vol. 61, no. 9, 1972, pp. 1309–14. *JSTOR*, https://doi.org/10.2307/813228. Accessed 3 Feb. 2023.

Thomas, G. W. "Ray Bradbury in *Weird Tales*." *Darkworlds Quarterly: The Culture of Science Fiction, Fantasy, and Horror*, 22 Sept. 2020, gwthomas.org/ray-bradbury-in-weird-tales/. Accessed 3 Feb. 2023.

VanderMeer, Ann, and Jeff VanderMeer. "The Weird: An Introduction." *Weird Fiction Review*, 6 May 2012, weirdfictionreview.com/2012/05/the-weird-an-introduction/. Accessed 30 June 2025.

Waller, Gregory A. Introduction. *American Horrors: Essays on the Modern American Horror Film*, edited by Gregory A. Waller, University of Illinois Press, 1987, pp. 1-13.

Wetzel, George. "Genesis of the Cthulhu Mythos." *Discovering H. P. Lovecraft*, edited by Darrell Schweitzer, Wildside Press, 2001, pp. 54-62.

Creative Think Piece: What One Can Become on the Verge of Global Unity

Tracy Ross

I
T IS THE TIME OF ANXIETY. People have become a species that is physically in a perpetual hot zone of fear, immunological catastrophe, and outright panic over ecological collapse. Rightly so.

At the moment, I'm sick at home with a cold, and I am thinking about aliens. Yes. Aliens. Extraterrestrials from Mars. I'm feeling miserable, feeling as if doctors should just by-pass the round of antibiotics and penicillin, dig a hole in the ground for me, and call it a day. In fact, people might just be too late to protect themselves from the mayhem ... of invasion, of course ...

According to leading ufologists, they're here; they've cut up cattle, left crop circles in corn fields, touched people's private parts, and then promptly flown away. People probably made them sick in hindsight. They gave people tiny implants in the back of their shins, but people gave them germs.

I'm pondering alien life forms, but not in the way that anyone would expect. With nothing to do but get over a cold, I've been subjecting myself to myriad television programs, all of which are self-help-inspired, punditry spins on current news stories in chaos, or afternoon talk shows featuring the new wave of Hollywood up-and-comers. I'm reflecting on how in the movie *The War of the Worlds (1953)*, all it took was the common cold virus to bring down an entire alien invasion and save planet Earth from hostile, body-snatching forces of the science fiction apocalypse.

There I was, grounded at home with a cold, wishing for the olden days of alien nostalgic flights of fancy to resolve many of the problems of political, social, and generational conflict. Instead of dealing with reality on the level of practicality, Americans used to have the metaphor-curtain of alien invasion and hostile one-eyed monsters from Venus/Mars to take the place of the deepest fears of the unknown and threatening. Everything could be solved with the right invented weapon to kill the green little bastards, once scientists eventually found out what they were not immune to, and had a soft spot for.

In the movie *War of the Worlds*, all it took was for the people of the good old American small town to get together in survivalist mode—young, old, and stranger alike—and find out what could not only save the town of Linda Rosa, California, but the entire planet of Earth. Sometimes it was spectacular, the weapon of choice to protect humanity. More often than not, though, it was something that was common and overlooked that turned out to be harmful for alien life forms—like normal table salt, water, or electricity.

Ah yes, those were the good old days. It was a relief when the average American kitchen table condiment could unite everyone to save Earth, instead of violence, war, pestilence, and extraterrestrial no-exit strategies involving Pentagon-funded Star Wars. I long for the simpler, more quaint days when Morton salt, used with the right finesse and town unity, could destroy not only hostile beings wanting to eat people or blow up two-car garages in the suburbs, but keep the growing blob of impending doom and future apocalypse at bay for another generation.

The reality of the situation is that the common cold will eventually destroy everyone ... and this is the sad truth. The world won't go out with a big bang but with a slow, snuffly whimper. The other sad truth is that alien invasions were a metaphor to openly express the most deep-seated and deeply seeded fears of the nation, and to be able to resolve the problem by the end of the film with an all-American rounding up of people united in the one cause that really mattered—peace on Earth. If this seems a little Utopian and idealistic, well ... it was, and this was the charm of the science fiction films of the 1940s, 50s and 60s.

But what happened? What happened to the alien nostalgia of yesteryear? What happened to the freedom to create fantasy for the benefit of giving a face to not only deep-seated fears and conflicting mores but to creatures not of this world, without it being cliché to the point of flopping at the box office?

When Ridley Scott's *Alien* (1979) came out, it changed the threat of the metaphorical bug-eyed creature into something that was more personal in nature, a predator who had its sights on one's innards as an incubator for a new life form. There was no metaphor here, just pure survivalist fear and panic about having one's head torn off. Where did the poetry go? Yes, later on one does learn in the film *Alien* that there is an evil corporation leading the mission to retrieve the alien life form as a tool to use in war weaponry. However, this is weak and late in coming to the continual bloodshed and carnage of the film's suspenseful momentum. The audience is drawn in by the alien's total barbarism and ugliness, its arbitrary violence and animal drive, not by its ability to stand in as a metaphor. The audience wants to vomit its guts out by the end of the film, not save the world in united empowerment.

What I am trying to say is, I miss old Hollywood bug-eyed alien films that took chances on personifying the enemy as a larger-than-life threat. They had courage, way back when, to not only suggest that the human species didn't have ultimate dominion over the universe or fate, but also to put a face to the enemy without fear of offending anyone politically or socially. The enemy usually had four or more eyeballs and a penchant for human brains for breakfast, so it was a force the audience could hate in unison without any reservations. I am homesick for not only alien nostalgia but good old jingoistic reasons to destroy all monsters in the name of peace on Earth and good will toward men. Is that so wrong?

I think about this for a minute .... Wait! There is something wrong with this. Ultimately, why can't humanity unite not in the face of an enemy but for the good of the species ... just for the hell of it ...? Does there always have to be a them and an us? I sit and think about my argument to bring back the old days of 1950s sci-fi and nostalgic old-world paranoia. Then I realize: it is the paranoia of the 20th century that is holding everyone back. The 20th century established the American consciousness in a stronghold of uniting in convention to beat the masked enemy. Yet, what if, in 21st century politics, globalization, communication, and one-world economics, there is no enemy? What does the human race unite for, if not for beating the bad guys? If the villain isn't as clear-cut good or bad as it used to be, or even definable in this new age of technology and invention?

I sit here with a cold and realize I must not only move forward in my old-world sensibilities but also evolve for the betterment of all creatures great and small, the Eco-sphere, and the very human species, itself. The 21st century is an uncharted frontier, on the verge of global unity in culture, language, and political governing economics. Who is the enemy now?

I would have to say the human psyche's ignorance has replaced the green-eyed monster of yesteryear as the greatest enemy of man/woman, and ultimately his/her greatest threat. People now, in 2025 and beyond, are being threatened by extinction, not due to green body-snatching pods growing in basements, but because of thinning oxygen, and the proliferation of plastics, pollution, and synthetics causing disease.

It is now that I realize that the sentimentality that I carry around with me for 1950s alien films is an indirect desire to rekindle a past civilization that wasn't to blame for its own implosion and extinction. I miss the lack of accountability that I could afford during the 1950s, 60s and 70s, when I wasn't my own worst enemy due to lack of recycling, vaccination, and eating farmed meat and genetically modified wheat and corn.

Yes...I am the green bug-eyed monster of tomorrow. Welcome to the brave new world of human self-actualization and new world enlightenment. What a sad tale it is; but oh, pay no attention to that man behind the curtain, because the world is indeed a heavy burden for Atlas to carry. After all, sublimation and denial can go a long way, and as long as there is finger-pointing going on, one can still get coffee during the morning rush at the Starbucks and pretend to be getting things done in the name of humanity and progress. Pass the caramel swirl, would you? I think this café mocha is helping me get over my cold. Despite an inept awareness at the Starbucks counter, could it possibly be that the art of film can present viewers with the benefits of pushing the outside of the envelop of potentials, where fear can be conquered and transcended?

... And, anyway, I love film.

I like the people I become after I see a film, and am different afterwards because of seeing a film. I like them so much because they are, in effect, a journey through the mind of man/womankind's identity. One can even say that the best movies stand the test of repeated viewing and change one a little bit each time one sees them. This is why one goes on the ride—suspending disbelief to bend perceptions permanently, to alter who one is for the better, leaving behind convention and expired belief for something new.

Two films that have stood the test of time and sustained repeated viewing for me have been Stanley Kubrick's *2001: A Space Odyssey* (1968) and Peter Weir and Andrew Niccol's *The Truman Show* (1998). These two examples have survived to become timeless capsules that embody the altering spirit of film, its ability to change minds, perceptions of time and space, and ultimately change one's vision of the world over and over again.

I saw *2001* when I was 11 years old, in 1980, after its original release date of 1968, and I was fortunate enough to see *The Truman Show* when it came out on DVD shortly after it was released, in 1998. It happens to be that Truman Burbank, the hero in *The Truman Show*, is the same age as the years separating the release of these two films—thirty. The audience is introduced to Truman Burbank just 48 days before his thirtieth birthday, just like the film *2001* quietly highlights the fact that it is Dr. Frank Poole's birthday on Hal's ship, the spacecraft Discovery One. Birthdays are important in both these films, specifically because they are the foundation of the characters' origins and represent a celebration of the acknowledgment of identity.

I have often surmised that Peter Weir and Andrew Niccol, the writer and director of *The Truman Show*, were paying homage to Stanley Kubrick's masterpiece by creating analogies that are in perfect alignment with each other in both meaning and ideology. For example, when I saw *2001* at the age of 11, I realized that, despite my young hubris, after viewing the ending scene of the movie, I knew nothing about the world around me. It was revelatory to the point of affecting my perception in the real world. It's the same with *The Truman Show*. Truman Burbank is cleverly named after the true man and Burbank, California, where most films are made that need studios for illusion. After I saw the last scene of *The Truman Show*, I had the same experience of a shift in my own outer reality, which the movie successfully changed for the better. Both films had a ta-dah moment that I couldn't shake, and this is what makes both films very similar in my mind.

Weir/Niccol and Kubrick dare to ask the question: what is reality, and can one relinquish the control necessary to move beyond reality and not sacrifice identity? Will I remain the same, in awareness and personhood, if I leave the props and technology of appearance and sentient proof—ultimately dislodge myself from the rational and controlled, and break through to the other side of the unknown? Is it worth it? In the unknown, do I exist as Truman or Dr. David Bowman? *The Truman Show* poses this question with a higher power embodied in the character of Christof (played by Ed Harris), who controls reality, and *2001* asks the same question—with HAL at the helm, who eventually must have his memory banks removed in order for Bowman to be free of lethal, controlling technology.

Both reigning forces in the films, Christof and HAL are powers that are in control, surveying human free will, and directing the actions of their respective movie's hero—Truman or Bowman. At the beginning of *The Truman Show*, the light fixture that falls out of the sky and wakes Truman to a different reality is named Sirius (Canis Major), also the name of the brightest star in the sky. Yet, it falls to Earth, waking Truman to his new fate. Dr. David Bowman is falling through space toward Jupiter, eventually to be witness to Kubrick's vision of a star baby as large as a planet. Each film asks the viewer to abandon what is known for what is unknown, to give up what one once was for what one can become.

Each man, Truman and Bowman, must go through altered states, facing fear to break through to the other side of awareness, whether it be a world without Christof and the eagle eye of TV or a world where, beyond the Jupiter Mission and HAL's disconnection, there resides a very different reality, where Bowman sees himself dying and then being reborn as a star baby.

The question arises again: What is reality, and can one relinquish the control necessary to move beyond reality and not sacrifice identity? Should one even attempt to answer this question, if it is an existential problem that has no one answer? It is, in effect, a paradox, because when one totally relinquishes what is known in exchange for the unknown, they are not themselves anymore. Hence, I am left in *The Truman Show* to ponder what is beyond the dark door of Christof's studio, and in *A Space Odyssey* what or who is the star baby, and what is it doing in the middle of space, the size of a planet? Where did Truman go? Where did Bowman go? Where is everyone, and why am I in this handbasket?

This is the answer—there is no answer that can be shared with the audience because it is every man for himself. In other words, each person must go through their own epiphanies and their own battle with the powers that be, the confines of reality, and the next step of the unknown. When Christof says, "Cue the sun..." or when HAL won't open the pod bay doors, the audience realizes it is at the mercy of the conditions of life, whether they be technological or artificial. People are at the mercy of the Pavlovian conditions of existence, and this is why both *The Truman Show* and *2001: A Space Odyssey* draw the audience in, in real time, begging viewers to experience the film in real time, to awake to the epiphany of the ending scenes again and again. Hence, repeated viewing succeeds in its transcendental purpose.

Each film holds up its story as a timeless metaphor for the human condition that can be shared in the dark with popcorn, soda, and wide-eyed wonder, forever preserving its form and function in conjunction with the audience's own personal vision. What is reality, and can one relinquish the control necessary to move beyond reality and not sacrifice identity? The answer is different for each person. I may not know the nature of reality, but what I do know is that in 103 minutes and 139 minutes, Peter

Weir, Andrew Niccol, and Kubrick came pretty damn close.

END

Reviews

Gil'Adí, Maia. *Doom Patterns: Latinx Speculations and the Aesthetics of Violence*. Duke University Press, 2025. 265 pages. ISBN: 9781478031208. $27.95.

Prominent examples of Latinx speculative fiction, such as Sabrina Vervoulias's novel *Ink* and Alex Rivera's film *Sleep Dealer*, feature an abundance of violent scenes and depictions. Any scholars studying the genre and seeking a better understanding of the patterns of violence therein would be well served to apply a theory such as that developed by Maia Gil'Adí in her monograph *Doom Patterns: Latinx Speculations and the Aesthetics of Violence*. Gil'Adí does not use those two specific stories as primary sources, but she presents a compelling theory for other scholars to apply to works beyond the ones she assesses. Gil'Adí's theory builds upon and responds to the interdisciplinary theoretical foundations of several fields. Her concept of doom patterns and reading protocols for Latinx speculative fiction builds upon Samuel Delaney's essay "Generic Protocols," as well as Jeremy Rosen and Lauren Berlant's definitions of "genre" (Gil'Adí 8-9). For her concept of form and the aesthetics of violence, Gil'Adí builds on Ramón Saldívar's neo-formalist approach to Latinx fiction, "in dialogue with postmodern literary aesthetics" (11). Gil'Adí also builds on Linda Hutcheon's concept of "historiographic metafiction." The texts explored in *Doom Patterns* merge metafictional techniques and historical elements in such a way that Gil'Adí was required to construct her theory, at least in part, out of conversations between postmodern theorists such as Hutcheon, Uri McMillan, and Anne Anlin Cheng, to name a few (12). With the question of violence and representations of violence, among many others, Gil'Adí cites Elaine Scarry's work as a major inspiration (13). Last but not least, she adds to the field of Latinx speculative fiction studies in two powerful ways. In suggesting that the same "reading protocols" applied to speculative works should also be applied to texts from neighboring genres such as historical fiction and magical realism, Gil'Adí adds to the mission of the editors of *Altermundos*, Cathryn Josefina Merla-Watson and B.V. Olguin, most clearly through her selection of primary sources (24-25). Several of her sources affirm the existence of the Latinx speculative fiction genre, while other sources work to broaden those genre parameters. Gil'Adí explains early on that some of her sources, such as *Dreaming in Cuban* and *The Brief and Wondrous Life of Oscar Wao*, are not "typically classified as speculative fiction"; however, she shows "how they exhibit the otherworldly, fantastical, and horrific through their representations of historical violence" (5). She also considers sources by both African-American and Asian-American authors to demonstrate her theory's broader applicability beyond only Latinx speculative fiction. Her broad sampling of sources reminds readers that the Latinx subgenre is not a topic for a separate conversation, but very much an essential piece of the broader speculative fiction conversation. Those concerned as to why the field seems to return time and time again to fantasy and science fiction about extreme violence and atrocity would do well to read this monograph as a starting point in their research.

In *Doom Patterns,* Gil'Adí asks the question, "How can the history of violence in the Americas be rendered in language? And how can these depictions of historical violence be paradoxically pleasurable as well" (3-4)? In answer, she proposes her theory of doom patterns. She defines these patterns as "textual forms and narrative strategies such as thematic repetition, non-linear narration, character fragmentation, unresolved plots, tropes, and archetypes that, in these literatures, consistently return readers to instances of destruction" (Gil'Adí 4). Not only does she choose to analyze a multitude of works exemplifying these forms and strategies, some of which are not traditionally associated with Latinx speculative fiction, but she also aims to distance her doom patterns analyses from any that seek to assess simply the cathartic, reparative, or healing nature of violence in fiction. Gil'Adí is far more interested in the aesthetics of violence and enjoyable experiences of both reproducing and enjoying violence in the written word (Gil'Adí 180).

Gil'Adí divides her book into five chapters, all of which serve to explore different authors and texts to challenge and test her theory. In Chapter One, she explores the fiction of Junot Díaz and the postapocalyptic nature of the Caribbean as depicted in his novel *The Brief Wonderous Life of Oscar Wao*. In Chapter Two, Gil'Adí shifts her focus to the brutality of the sugar industry, and the irony of how production and consumption of such a sweet substance can rely on patterns of violence, as evidenced by Christina Garcia's novel *Dreaming in Cuban* as well as Colson Whitehead's novel *Zone One*. In Chapter Three, she explores the US-Mexico border and doom patterns of sexual assault in that setting in Roberto Bolano's novel *2666*. For Chapter Four, Gil'Adí turns to time travel and the cyclical repetition of violence in Sesshu Foster's *Atomik Aztex*. Finally, for Chapter Five, Gil'Adí analyzes doom patterns present throughout the collected short fiction of Carmen Maria Machado, reemphasizing one of her book's secondary focuses on women's bodies as an important site at which these patterns of violence perpetuate.

Chapter to chapter, Gil'Adí consistently holds her audience's attention by quickly familiarizing them with the texts and writers specific to each section. By the time she narrows her focus to a closer reading of a text, she has already provided enough context and theory so that readers can play along and deduce the connections between her specific analysis of each case study and her broader doom patterns theory. For example, in Chapter One, "Doom Patterning the Post-Colony and the New Caribbean

Mythology," Gil'Adí's analysis of Junot Díaz's fiction functions as an exploration of "Fuku" and the repetitions of violence inherent in the postcolonial curse. She is specifically concerned with how Díaz explores these violent repetitions in *The Brief Wonderous Life of Oscar Wao* (6). Gil'Adí provides plenty of context for readers unfamiliar with Díaz's novel to follow along. She reads the lives of Oscar and the narrator, Yunior, as a microcosm of the "Fuku" or repetitive "Doom of the New World" experienced on a larger scale over the course of the last few centuries in the Caribbean (Gil'Adí 39). She explains how Yunior narrates Oscar's life in the late twentieth century while simultaneously narrating the history of the post-Columbian "New World." This comparison invites Díaz's and Gil'Adí's readers alike to look for ways in which doom patterns can operate across wildly different time scales and spaces. Gil'Adí explains that Yunior spends much of his time describing violence in the Dominican Republic under the reign of the dictator, Rafael Trujillo, from 1930 to 1961 (38). One might expect her analysis to eventually circle back to this figure, finding a representative individual with whom to compare Trujillo. Gil'Adí fulfills this expectation but in the most compelling and thought-provoking manner, as she does not compare Trujillo to any characters of Díaz's novel but rather to Díaz himself.

Near the end of Chapter One, Gil'Adí delicately and poignantly addresses Junot Díaz's sexual misconduct, as well as his essay "The Silence," in which he describes his own experience as a victim of sexual assault. Gil'Adí writes, "Like Trujillo, Díaz is both Fuku's servant and its master—his experience of sexual abuse is Fuku's aftermath, and his victimization of others its inevitable repercussion" (59). This comparison and blending of the themes in fiction to the themes of the real world is a perfect example of how Gil'Adí's theory can be applied on a metatextual level. Her use of such creative and compelling techniques, in turn, makes for an enjoyable experience for her audience. Gil'Adí explains that the texts she analyzes "are representative case studies for how violence happens concomitantly with the humorous, with expert writing or beautiful prose, or with an entertaining plot" (22). Her own book fulfills this same function, both reproducing numerous accounts of fictional and real violence but simultaneously being so expertly written as to be aesthetically enjoyable.

There is a slight tension in the book's unbalanced structure. Roughly half of the book—the introduction, chapters One, Four, and the Coda—functions as space for Gil'Adí to further develop her theory and to emphasize examples of the repetitive and cyclical nature of doom and violence in postcolonial America. Meanwhile, chapters Two, Three, and Five all feature a stronger and more specific focus on not only patterns of violence against women but violence against monstrous women's bodies. While all chapters do build upon each other clearly, and while the structure is never so strange as to confuse readers, those same readers might be left wondering if this should have been two books instead of one. If that had been the case, Chapter Two, for example, could have been divided in half, and both Christina Garcia's *Dreaming in Cuban* and Colson Whitehead's *Zone One* could have received more thorough and critical attention in their own chapters. That said, as evidenced by the above assessment of Chapter One, Gil'Adí does successfully connect and allude to a number of consistent themes throughout every chapter, so that it is never too jarring a transition between subtopics.

With *Doom Patterns,* Gil'Adí has thoroughly and compellingly applied her doom patterns theory to various Latinx speculative works. By expanding her methodology and analysis to include works outside of the typical Latinx speculative fiction canon, Gil'Adí is able to more rigorously test her theory and method than if she had only examined those works typically associated with the field. For this reason, Gil'Adí's book and theory would serve as a great resource for those studying the aesthetics of violence. Gil'Adí has provided scholars of multiple disciplines with her clear and well-developed theory, building out of an analysis of Latinx speculative fiction but more widely applicable across a variety of genres and fields. This book serves as a great addition to the bibliographies of any scholars studying the prevalence and patterns of violence broadly encountered in science fiction and fantasy literature. Specifically, Gil'Adí has successfully built upon conversations central to the field of Latinx speculative fiction: apocalypse, women's bodies, immigration, and generational trauma, to name a few. Her major contribution to the field is her new and refreshing lens of the theory of doom patterns.

Works Cited

Bolaño, Roberto. *2666: A Novel*. Translated by Natasha Wimmer. Picador, 2009.

Delany, Samuel R. "Generic Protocols: Science Fiction and Mundane." In *The Technological Imagination: Theories and Fictions*, edited by Teresa de Lauretis, Andreas Huyssen, and Kathleen M. Woodward, 175-93. Madison, WI: Coda, 1980.

Díaz, Junot. *The Brief Wondrous Life of Oscar Wao*. Riverhead Books, 2008.

Díaz, Junot. "The Silence: The Legacy of Childhood Trauma." *New Yorker*, April 16, 2018, 24-28.

Foster, Sesshu. *Atomik Aztex*. City Lights Publishers, 2005.

García, Christina. *Dreaming in Cuban*. Ballantine Books, 1993.

Gil'Adí, Maia. *Doom Patterns: Latinx Speculations and the Aesthetics of Violence*. Duke University Press, 2025.

Merla-Watson, Cathryn Josefina, B. V. Olguin, editors. *Altermundos: Latin@ Speculative Literature, Film, and Popular Cultures*. UCLA Chicano Studies Research Center Press, 2017.

Rivera, Alex, director. *Sleep Dealer*. Performances by Luis Fernando Peña, Leonor Varela, and Jacob Vargas. Produced by Anthony Bregman, 2008.

Vourvoulias, Sabrina. *Ink*. Rosarium Publishing, 2018.

Whitehead, Colson. *Zone One*. Doubleday, 2011.

ALEXANDER BANKS is a student in the Comparative Studies PhD program at Florida Atlantic University. In this program, he is studying representations of genocide in fantasy and science fiction literature. His research pulls from the fields of history and literary studies. His academic background includes a BA in history from Truman State University and an MA in history from the University of Missouri-Kansas City, with emphases in both public history and genocide studies. Mr. Banks has been a member of the IAFA for nearly three years, and he has attended and presented twice at the international conference in Orlando.

Charles L. Crow, *California Gothic: The Dark Side of the Dream*.
Anthem Press, 2024. 96 pages. £20.99 / $24.95 ISBN 978-1-
83998-379-5

The concept of the American Gothic and its association with
darkness and the uncanny in literature and film is often linked to
settings in the Eastern United States such as Massachusetts.
However, as telefantasy series such as *Charmed* set in San
Francisco and *Buffy the Vampire Slayer* set in the fictional town
of Sunnydale, California have shown, the Gothic is no stranger to
the western part of the country. While Charles Crow's book does
not address these specific works, he offers a detailed examination
of how the Gothic has populated narratives in literature and film
from the nineteenth century to the early 2000s. Crow's study
includes a particularly insightful literary and historical analysis of
the California dream in relation to Asian, Indigenous and women's
experiences that he argues return as "uncanny nightmares" (xi) in
these narratives. Photos and images, including the artwork of
Thomas Cole of *The Course of Empire* Series, are addressed at
various points in the book, forming part of this study as well,
enhancing the discussion of various authors and the expression of
the California Gothic in literature and film.

Crow's book is divided into a preface, six chapters and an
afterword, with the first five chapters following a broader
historical trajectory as various ideas are explored in relation to the
Gothic and the California dream. In the preface, he addresses the
image of California as a "land of perpetual sunshine" that might
appear as "the least Gothic of American regions" (xi). Despite the
optimism one might associate with the California Dream in
general, or what Crow describes as "a variation on the American
Dream" (xi), he contends that the California Dream has

underpinned Gothic narratives, but in an ironic or disaster-focused fashion. Key historical researchers such as John Muir—described by Crow as the "last great American romantic writer" (6)—and Ishi, an "Indigenous Californian" (xii) who was the last of the Yahi Nation, are mentioned in connection with loss and longing that contribute to the Gothic atmosphere. Crow also acknowledges that he "shares an approach and many attitudes about California" (xiv) with Bernice M. Murphy who has published a book about *The California Gothic in Fiction and Film*. However, it is important to note that Crow addresses many works in his study that are not included in Murphy's and offers a native Californian perspective, which undoubtedly allows him to consider the realities of California life, such as fires and state policies.

Chapter 1, "The Magic Island," examines the history of exploration, colonization. The name California, Crow writes, derives from the explorer Cortéz's belief that the area was an island, thus encouraging the connection to a Spanish island romance novel that featured an Amazon queen, Califia (1). Crow notes that this island association, with a map from the period included, contributed to the remoteness surrounding California and links the California wilderness and the frontier experience to the dichotomy of "reason and madness" (3). The inclusion of the terrifying w*ndigo figure in Alma Katsu's retelling of the Donner tragedy and acts of cannibalism in *The Hunger* (2018) evokes not only an Indigenous connection but also highlights the greed of squatters associated with the Gold Rush. Crow also discusses how the repression of Indigenous people, sometimes represented by Ishi, the last of the Yahi Nation, has found its way into Gothic literature. The end of the chapter consists of a brief discussion of the 2018 burning of the town of Paradise and an area known as Ishi Trail. This historical destruction of the landscape demonstrates the effects of the repression of the Indigenous experience, including traditional burning practices that were suppressed by "federal and state fire-fighting agencies" (9) in the mistaken belief that this would improve fire prevention.

Chapter 2, "Ambrose Bierce and San Francisco's Gothic Frontier," speaks to another form of cultural exclusion in California. Ambrose Bierce's "The Haunted Valley" (1871) is analyzed as an example of California Gothic, reflecting the writer's use of California as a setting in his fiction as well as his representation of the erasure of Chinese identity in America, thus anticipating "the suppression of this community" (14) during the Chinese Exclusion Act of 1882. Crow ends this chapter with an analysis of Emma Francis Dawson's writing that foregrounds a feminist sensibility and attention to the Chinese in California's San Francisco area, while incorporating Gothic ghosts and doubles.

In Chapter 3, "Lost Coasts," the depiction of artists, "bohemians, beats, or hippies" (19) and various Indigenous communities in California literature suggests the search for California dreams and the Gothic shattering of those dreams. In Mary Austin's novel *Outland*, a group of "forest dwellers" (22) interacts with characters resembling historical members of the bohemian Carmel artist colony. Thomas Pynchon's *Vineland* is analyzed for its Gothic content and reference to an Indigenous "Yurok hell" (29). Kem Nunn's *The Dogs of Winter* is included as a novel in which surf culture is infused with a Gothic darkness. Nunn's California Gothic is certainly a far cry from the carefree surfing world constructed in the songs of The Beach Boys that many might associate with California's ocean paradise.

An even darker aspect of the California Gothic is examined in Chapter 4, "Disease, Pandemics, and the Monstrous," which explores plagues, syphilis, AIDS, vampires, and zombies in literature and film. The crime focus of Chapter 5, "The Shadow Line: Noir and California Gothic," adds even more films to the mix, including Hollywood representations of the femme fatale in noir films such as Raymond Chandler's *The Lady of the Lake*,

Alfred Hitchcock's set-in-San Francisco *Vertigo*, and David Lynch's *Mulholland Drive*, among others. Dark and disturbing images and actions create the worlds of the California Gothic in works such as James Elroy's noir novel *The Black Dahlia*, which incorporates the Black Dahlia theme, an image based on the murder of Elizabeth Short and her Goth-like appearance, and Thomas Pynchon's detective novel *Inherent Vice*, which mentions the Manson Family murders of Sharon Tate and others. As Crow points out, the Great Depression and local sex scandals (46) serve as historical background or trauma for these creative works. Here, as in other chapters of Crow's study, the California Gothic and aura of mystery negate or destroy the California dream, and more specifically, the Hollywood dream of some of the female characters and actresses in the narratives.

The final chapter, "California Ecogothic: What's Buried in the Basement," considers the end of the "natural environment" (xiii), including the animal world and California's image as an island of romance, as mentioned in Chapter 1. Octavia E. Butler's novel *Parable of the Sower* (199) and its near future setting, along with Lydia Millet's trilogy—*How the Dead Dream* (2008), *Ghost Lights* (2011), and *Magnificence* (2012)—set in a "recent past, the 1990s" (61), are highlighted in this section. As readers of Gothic literature will know, subterranean passages in earlier Gothic writing—or basements in the depiction of modern California buildings in more recent narratives—are pervasive features of the Gothic genre. Crow's chapter title is fitting since basements are the lowest habitable point in a building and often house forgotten family relics or hidden histories; in the case of Millet's novel *Magnificence*, the final novel in the trilogy, basements house secrets linked to an Indigenous past and exhibits of extinct animals (66).

While there are other studies of the American Gothic that address the representation of a specific cultural context such as

Maisha L. Wester's *African American Gothic: Screams from Shadowed Places*, and theoretical studies of Gothic texts such as essays in Robert K. Martin's and Eric Savoy's edited collection, *New Interventions in a National Narrative*, *California Gothic: The Dark Side of the Dream* will undoubtedly surprise both American and international readers with the range of texts mentioned that include California Gothic content, specifically. Sections of Crow's book that provide a more fulsome analysis are stronger than sections with a more general overview of specific works. Readers with an interest in a more substantial study of the Gothic may want to delve into Crow's earlier book, *History of the Gothic: American Gothic* which includes a short analysis of *Buffy the Vampire Slayer*; however, even the sections of *California Gothic* that offer a less sustained analysis will still serve as an instrumental point of departure for future studies on the California Gothic. Such studies might address how the California Gothic in literature and other media has developed even further in relation to the realities of "ecological disaster and global pandemics" (xi) or examine how an analysis of Asia to the west of California (Afterword, 72) might facilitate Gothic intersections for comparative research.

DR. KARIN BEELER is Professor Emerita in the Department of English at the University of Northern British Columbia in Canada. Her research and teaching interests include film studies, television studies, Comparative literary studies, and representations of animals in film. She has published work on a variety of fantastic narratives including *Supernatural, Smallville, Angel,* and *Charmed.* Her books include *Tattoos, Desire and Violence: Marks of Resistance in Literature, Film and Television* and *Seers, Witches and Psychics on Screen.* She has also co-edited *Animals in Narrative Film and Television: Strange and Familiar*

Creatures and *Investigating Charmed: The Magic Power of TV* with Stan Beeler.

Wosk, Julie. Artificial Women: Sex Dolls, Robot Caregivers, and More Facsimile Females. Indiana: Indiana University Press, 2024. 220 pp. IBSN: 9780253069252. $30.00.

During the 1980s, feminist science and technology studies emerged as a theoretical subfield of science and technology studies, exploring the co-constructed relationship between gender and technology. Quintessential works such as Donna J. Haraway's "Cyborg Manifesto" and Ruth Schwartz Cowan's *More Work for Mother* respectively deconstructed the binaries between man/woman and organism/machine and examined how technology has been used to discipline human bodies into specific gendered roles. Feminist science fiction writers and scholars have subsequently probed the posthuman in its multitudinous iterations, as exhibited in the writings of N. Katherine Hayles, Anne Balsamo, Rosi Braidotti, Patricia Melzer, Sherryl Vint, and more (Wosk 4). Placing speculative fiction in conversation with the history of robotics, scholars such as Sherryl Vint, Jennifer Rhee, Despina Kakoudaki, Ruha Benjamin, and Gregory Hampton have illuminated how the design of robots and AI is "deeply entrenched in racialized and gendered assumptions" (Vint 6). It is through this feminist lens that Julie Wosk's *Artificial Women: Sex Dolls, Robot Caregivers, and More Facsimile Females* interrogates not only real-life artificial females, but those portrayed in popular culture, film, television, literature, art, and drama.

Wosk examines the ways in which artificial females mirror cultural conceptions around women and gender roles, shifting as our ideas about gender, sexuality, and female identity evolve. She argues that the artificial women presented by writers, artists, and roboticists—from talking sex dolls and AI assistants to robot prostitutes and compassionate caregivers—are "wide-ranging": they are obedient servants and fearsome Medusas, alluring companions and outlaws, and maternal figures and murderers (Wosk 13). Fictional representations, Wosk displays, reflect specific cultural anxieties and fascination with new technologies as well as how dominant notions about sexual difference, methods of understanding consciousness, and the meaning of the human are constantly fluctuating and being redefined (161).

In Chapter One, Wosk delves into sex robots and sex dolls, describing how these artificial females in both real-life and fiction often resemble long-standing conceptions of the "perfect woman" and embody contemporary gender attitudes and cultural values (25). Noting how men are the primary purchasers of these dolls, she details how desired features for women include unwavering obedience, compassion, passivity, and sexiness. Wosk compares the customizable, never confrontational, and lifelike talking sex dolls (e.g., Abyss Creations' RealDolls) to simulated females in television, novels, films, and plays, with the latter presenting an increasingly wider range of possibility. Unlike current real-life sex dolls and robots, the fictional artificial women of *Blade Runner 2049* (2017), *Westworld* (2016-2022), and *Ex Machina* (2014), for example, have agency and control; pleasurable, lethal, comforting, and dangerous, they may resort to violence for self-protection, revenge, or to gain their own freedom and autonomy.

In Chapter Two, Wosk critically analyzes the films *Under the Skin* (2013), *Ex Machina* (2014), and *Ghost in the Shell* (2017), as well as the television series *Westworld*, adaptations which explore what lies under the beautiful synthetic skin of female androids, or the fabricated femme fatale. She asserts that the simulated female's unpeeling of her skin to reveal her synthetic nature is an act of agency (Wosk 84), linking the android's performative act of masking their skin to human women's altering of their bodies with cosmetics to conform to changing cultural norms and standards of beauty. Such endeavors, Wosk contends, can be perceived as both an empowering form of self-expression and a submission to conventional gender norms. In Chapter Three, Wosk probes the representation of female robot caregivers, doubles, and companions in film, television, literature, and robotics labs, unpacking their potential to enhance our lives by providing health care and companionship to the elderly, disabled, and terminally ill, while acknowledging the current development of robotic replicas of deceased family members.

Chapter Four discusses prevalent concerns around automated female servants as the boundaries between the artificial and the human grow ever more blurry in the 21st century. Whereas the out-of-control mechanized maid in 19th century texts reflected anxieties about emerging technologies and the "New Woman" (Wosk 121), shows such as *Humans* (2015-2018) embody fears that female androids, endowed with consciousness, will replace humans in relationships. In Chapter Five, Wosk examines talking dolls such as Mattel's Hello Barbie and disembodied female voices in aircraft warning systems, GPS systems, and virtual personal assistants such as Amazon's Alexa and Apple's Siri, connecting them to the ideals of the "perfect woman" who is always nice, helpful, and compliant (150-151). She further addresses how productions such as *The Big Bang Theory* (2007-2019), *Her* (2013), and *Barbie* (2023) have satirized this sexualization, and argues one way to diminish servant and consent issues is by reprogramming digital assistants to teach users socially appropriate behavior and promote men's engagement in "wifework" (Wosk 151). The book's final chapter, "Coda," spotlights women artists and fiction writers who have reframed the narrative about artificial women in striking ways—from Julie Weitz's female golems fighting white supremacy and wildfires to Samantha Hunt's seductive sex doll operating as both sex symbol and explosive device ("bombshell") in her short story "Love Machine" (171).

Wosk's commitment to balancing divergent perspectives on artificial technologies with close reading of numerous texts throughout history substantiates her claims. *Artificial Women* is an insightful package of feminist theory, science fiction, film, television, and real-life technologies, interwoven with immersive photographs and artwork, including a provocative cover photograph of a mannequin captured by Wosk herself. She expertly organizes the chapters of her book in a concise manner that foregrounds her central arguments, while enabling her to closely analyze each literary, artistic, and media text and compare it to previous examples and existent artificial technologies. By contextualizing the history and patriarchal values affiliated with simulated females, Wosk uniquely emphasizes the tension between prevailing expectations of specific cultures that female-coded creations be submissive and the narratives presented by artists, filmmakers, and writers in which such robots, dolls, androids, and cyborgs resist their subjugation and assert their autonomy. As such, she contributes a compelling way of conceptualizing how gender, like technology, is culturally manufactured and reflected across various mediums of the fantastic. Quite impressive, too, is Wosk's use of accessible language: devoid of jargon or abstract terminologies, her work can be enjoyed by a wide audience, including those potentially outside academia.

Notably, due to Wosk's primary focus on artificial women, the majority of the texts she examines are popular Eurowestern and Japanese science fiction films, shows, and writings intended for adults. Consequently, *Artificial Women* only scratches the surface in covering the diverse range of female robot/cyborg/android characters represented in children's literature and media and the messages these works impart specifically to young adult audiences. Unexplored YA texts such as David Bowles' graphic novel *Clockwork Curandera, Vol. 1: The Witch Owl Parliament* (2021), Marissa Meyer's retelling of Cinderella in *Cinder* (2012), and Akira Toriyama's shōnen manga (and anime) *Dr. Slump* (1980-1984) and *Dragon Ball* (1984-1995), for instance, portray artificial women and girls as superpowered heroines with their own families, dreams, and desires. Nevertheless, Wosk raises vital questions about the role speculative fiction can play in presenting alternative visions of artificial women and girls defying not only the social stereotypes traditionally associated with them, but long-standing literary precedents in certain cultures.

As an innovative overview of artificial women in real-life, literature, and some popular cultures, this extensively researched, interdisciplinary book appeals to academics interested in science fiction, and, more specifically, in the scholarly niches of feminist science and technology studies and posthumanism. Undeniably, *Artificial Women* makes an excellent addition to existing scholarship in science fiction, media studies, and gender/sexuality studies. Its timely relevance and interdisciplinary approach are paramount for the digital age, as real simulated females increasingly resemble the artificial women of speculative fiction.

Works Cited

Balsamo, Anne. *Technologies of the Gendered Body: Reading Cyborg Women*. Duke University Press. 1995.

Benjamin, Ruha. *Race After Technology: Abolitionist Tools for the New Jim Code*. Polity Press. 2019.

Hampton, Gregory Jerome. *Imagining Slaves and Robots in Literature, Film, and Popular Culture: Reinventing Yesterday's Slave with Tomorrow's Robot*. Rowman & Littlefield. 2015.

Haraway, Donna Jeanne. "A Cyborg Manifesto: Science, Technology, and Socialist-Feminism in the Late Twentieth Century." Haraway, Donna

Jeanne. *Simians, Cyborgs and Women: The Reinvention of Nature*. Routledge. 1991

Haraway, Donna J. "A Manifesto for Cyborgs: Science, Technology, and Socialist Feminism in the 1980s." (AKA "Cyborg Manifesto"). *Socialist Review*. 1985

Kakoudaki, Despina. *Anatomy of a Robot: Literature, Cinema, and the Cultural Work of Artificial People*. Rutgers University Press. 2014.

Melzer, Patricia. *Alien Constructions: Science Fiction and Feminist Thought*. University of Texas Press. 2010.

Rhee, Jennifer. *The Robotic Imaginary: The Human and the Price of Dehumanized Labor*. University of Minnesota Press. 2018.

Schwartz Cowan, Ruth. *More Work for Mother: The Ironies Of Household Technology From The Open Hearth To The Microwave*. Basic Books. 1983

Vint, Sherryl. "Introduction: Sociotechnical Design and the Future of Gender." Vint, Sherryl and Sümeyra Buran, Editors. *Technologies of Feminist Speculative Fiction: Gender, Artificial Life, and the Politics of Reproduction*. Palgrave Macmillan. 2022. pp. 1-17.

Wosk, Julie. *Artificial Women: Sex Dolls, Robot Caregivers, and More Facsimile Females*. Indiana University Press. 2024.

ASHLEY PERRY is a graduate teaching assistant and Arts and Letters Fellow at Florida Atlantic University (FAU), pursuing her M.A. in English with a concentration in science fiction and fantasy. She graduated summa cum laude from FAU's Harriet L. Wilkes Honors College with a B.A. in English Literature and a minor in Women's Studies. Her research draws on intersectional feminist theory to analyze representations of girlhood and girl power in science fiction and fantasy literature, popular culture, and film, with especial interest in young adult fantasy. She received the Isabel Sparks President's Award (2024) for her critical essay presentation on *Barbie* (2023) at the 2024 Sigma Tau Delta Convention and has also presented at the International Conference for the Fantastic in the Arts, the Wilkes Honors College Symposium, and the Florida Collegiate Honors Council

Conference. Ashley's work can be found in the *Sigma Tau Delta Review*, *RCA Proceedings*, and *Cliché Literary and Arts Magazine*.

www.ingramcontent.com/pod-product-compliance
Lightning Source LLC
Chambersburg PA
CBHW011459170626
46814CB00008B/2962